CU00736285

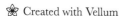 Created with Vellum

MR NICE GUY

Suits & Sevens

Book 3

ISLA OLSEN

Chronology

The *Suits & Sevens* series is set in my *Love & Luck* universe (aka the Kellyverse) and there is some cross-over between the books. It's not necessary to have read the earlier books, but if you'd like to read the books from this world in chronological order you should start with *Fake it 'til You Make Out (Love & Luck #1)*

Chronology:

More information about all these books and other stories by Isla Olsen can be found at islaolsen.com

Real Good Looking Boys

(AKA Spencer's rugby team)

Spencer Cox [Fly Half] 34, *dating Will (Book 1: Mr. Big Shot)*

Charlie Campbell [Scrum Half] 38

Cole MacCaffrey [Wing] 34

Sullivan Stapleton [Prop] 34, *engaged (in theory) to Drew (Book 2: Mr Right Now*

Deacon Stapleton [Hooker] 27, *dating Tanner (Book 3: Mr Nice Guy)*
THIS IS HIS BOOK

Aaron Wells [Prop] 35, *married to Kylie, father of Brandon and Daisy*

Bryce Kennedy [Center] 31, *dating Emme*

Jackson Downey [Reserve Forward] 27

Skyler Mason [Reserve Back] 27

Pax Greenwood [Occasional Practice Ringer] 46, *father of Kaley*

As of final chapter of main book

Trigger Warning

General Anxiety Disorder: This book focuses heavily on living with and managing anxiety.

Special Needs Children: This book features a child with Down's syndrome

Deacon

"He's here again," my colleague Julia tells me in a conspiratorial whisper as she sidles up to me.

"Who is?" I ask a little distractedly. It's pick-up time so I'm a bit preoccupied with all the five-year-olds whizzing around me with all that end-of-the-day energy their parents will have the pleasure of dealing with now.

"Duh. Mr Sexy McSexypants." She bobs her head toward the door, displaying no discretion whatsoever as she hungrily drinks in the man currently helping his daughter with her backpack.

"If you could stop drooling, that'd be great," I say dryly. Not that I can really blame her. The guy is gorgeous. Actually, I'd go so far as to call him beautiful. It's not a word I use all that often, but it definitely fits here. He's a fair bit older than both Julia and me—around fifty, I'd guess—but that just makes him even more attractive. With neatly styled silver hair, strong facial features, and piercing blue eyes, not to mention the tall, fit body wrapped in a designer suit that fits him like a glove, it's easy to see how

Julia came up with her nickname for him, as ridiculous as it might be.

"I can't help it," she practically whines. "Is there anything hotter than a gorgeous guy who's also a good father? My ovaries are exploding over here."

"Okay, I think it's time for you to go back to your own classroom." I give her a gentle nudge toward the door that connects my room to hers. "You'll get all the gawking opportunities you can imagine next year when Isobel moves up to the first grade."

"That's almost a year away," she says with a pout, but returns to her room anyway.

Once she's gone, I make my way over to Mr Sexy—I mean, Mr Grimsay—so I can provide him with an update about his daughter.

I know teachers shouldn't have favorites, but let's face it, we all do. And Izzy is definitely one of mine. She's such a beautiful little girl, and while she's definitely capable of the odd temper tantrum, for the most part she's so happy and warm, it's just impossible not to adore her.

She's the first child with Down's syndrome I've ever taught, so I'll admit that before she started I was nervous as hell, but fortunately I was able to connect with her therapists and doctors to work out the best plan for her this year, and her family are very involved which makes things so much easier.

Frankly, the most difficult aspect of having Izzy in my class is the effort it takes not to spring a boner whenever I catch sight of her dad's ass. Which basically makes me the biggest creep on the planet.

I push those thoughts as far out of my head as I can get them as I approach the pair where they're standing by Izzy's hook.

"Hey Mr. Grimsay," I say with a smile.

"Deacon, please, how many times have I told you to call me Tanner?" He offers a bright grin that almost makes me swoon.

"Right. Tanner." I give a nod and manage to shake myself from my daze before I go all weird on him. "Izzy, did you tell your dad about the painting we did today?"

A bright smile flashes across her little face and she holds up both hands to Tanner, scrunching them open and closed. "My fingers."

Tanner's eyes widen with amazement. "Wow, finger-painting! That must have been fun. Did you use lots of colors?"

Izzy nods and then takes Tanner's hand, leading him over to where the kids' finger painting masterpieces are all drying on a wire that stretches across the room in front of the window. She points out her own, which is actually one of the better ones. Most of the kids just went crazy with smearing every color paint imaginable over every inch of the paper's surface, but Izzy took her time, carefully matching colors together. There was a moment of great frustration for her when she kept unintentionally mixing the colors together, but once she learned how to rinse her fingers before selecting each new one she was on a roll.

"Wow, that's beautiful, baby girl," Tanner gushes as he bends down to collect Izzy and hoist her into his arms. "What do you say—you want to take this home and put it on the fridge so Jazz and Piper can see it?"

Izzy grins and nods eagerly, so I step toward the wire and carefully unpin the painting.

"It might still be a little wet," I warn Tanner as I hand it over.

"I'm sure it'll be fine." He carefully rolls up the paper, and without any concern over getting paint on his designer

3

suit, tucks it into his inside pocket. "Alright, we'd better get going. Don't want to be late for Dr. Mandy, do we?"

Izzy shakes her head in agreement. "Can Dr. Mandy see my painting?"

"I'm sure she'd love to see it," Tanner says, voice full of affection. "Okay, say 'bye' to Deacon."

"Bye, Deacon," she says, offering me a wave.

I smile at her, waving back. "Bye Izzy. See you tomorrow."

As Tanner and Isobel leave, I can't help recalling Julia's words from just before. And, yeah, I have to agree—there's nothing hotter than a sexy guy who's also a great dad.

***

"WHAT'S WITH YOU?" my best friend, Skyler, asks me as I slip into the booth seat opposite him at, Doyle's, one of our favorite bars.

"What do you mean?"

He reaches across the table to run a finger over the space between my eyebrows. "I'm talking about this. Your brow is furrowed. Deacon Stapleton does not have a furrowed brow. Should I call an exorcist?"

I bat his hand away, rolling my eyes. "Shut up, asshole. I'm allowed to frown once in a while. I don't always have to be the happy, shiny, nice guy."

"Ah, but you are," Skyler says wryly. "Like, basically all the time. It's very annoying."

I give an exasperated shake of my head and flag down a server so I can order a beer.

"So what is it that's got you all twisted up?" he presses.

Figuring he's not going to stop pestering me until he

gets an answer, I relent. "I think I have a crush on a parent."

"Well this just got juicy." His eyes widen in excitement and he leans forward across the table, as though not wanting to miss a morsel of this story.

I roll my eyes. "Calm down. There's nothing juicy about it. Nothing's happened, and nothing will."

"Why not?"

"Well, because he's a parent, for one. And also I'm pretty sure he's straight."

"What makes you say that?"

I shrug. "I don't know. He just doesn't give off those 'I want to have sex with men' vibes."

"Not everyone gives off those vibes," Skyler points out. "I mean, look at Spence—closeted for years, and then bam! Happily banging his male assistant."

"Um, I don't know how happy he is considering they broke up," I point out.

Skyler gives a dismissive wave. "They'll work it out. Besides, my point is that none of us thought Spencer was into guys until recently, so who's to say that's not the case for your crush?"

He has a point, although I think he might be clutching at straws. One important fact remains, however. "Even if by some fluke chance you're right, he's still a parent."

The server brings my beer and I take a generous swig.

"What's he like?" Skyler asks, sounding like a little kid asking about a magical fairy creature. "Paint me a word picture."

I let out a sigh and take another sip of my beer. Damn it, I *so* should not be arming him with this information, but what the hell. "I can do one better. Google Tanner Grimsay."

His eyes widen with excitement and he grabs his phone

from his pocket, completing the search in record speed. "*Holy fucking shit balls!* I mean, he's not exactly my type, but...*damn.*"

I sigh in defeat. "You can see my dilemma."

"Deac, you have *got* to go for this guy," Sky insists.

I almost choke on my beer. "Are you insane? He's a parent. And he's probably straight. And he could be in a relationship for all I know." He doesn't wear a ring, and I've never seen any sign of Izzy's mother in the months since she's been in my class, but that doesn't mean Tanner's single.

"Let me do some digging—"

I snatch the phone from his hand, my eyes narrowed at him in a hard glare. "No. No, no, no. Do *not* do any digging. Just forget I told you any of this. Got it?"

After a long beat of hesitation, he sighs, visibly deflating. "*Fine.* The most interesting thing to happen to you in ages, but whatever. I'll respect your wishes because that's what buddies do."

I quirk an eyebrow at him. "Yeah, why *are* we buddies again?"

"Because you were the only guy in our frat who didn't want to suck my cock," he reminds me, one shoulder lifting in a casual shrug.

I let out a snort of laughter. "Ironic considering I was also the only guy in our frat, apart from you, who identified as gay."

Skyler just smirks at me. "You might not realize this, but you just proved my point."

2

Tanner

I let out a grunt of annoyance when my phone goes off during Izzy's occupational therapy session. I always make sure to turn it off during all of her appointments, because I don't want to get distracted and miss things, but clearly I forgot about it this afternoon. I retrieve it from my inside breast pocket and am about to ignore the call and turn it off when I see the name on the screen. It's one of my lawyers, and generally speaking if a lawyer is calling it's not news I want to wait to hear.

"Sorry, I'll just be a second," I tell Edie, Izzy's OT, as I rise from my chair. She gives a tight smile and returns her attention to Izzy's word recognition exercises.

I quickly stride from the room and answer Leona's call before it goes to voicemail. "What's up?"

"I've spent the past two days being pestered by Sullivan Stapleton because apparently you've been ignoring his requests for a meeting?"

I groan and run a hand over my face. I should have just ignored the fucking call. "I've already given him a meeting and told him I'm not selling. Nothing's changed in the past four weeks."

"Apparently it has," she says. "They've got a new offer for you."

"The answer's still no."

"Just hear them out, Tanner," she says with a tired sigh. "I do not need Charlie Campbell crowing about how I can't get his buddy a simple sit-down."

I give an exasperated shake of my head. Honestly, sometimes it seems as though the partners in some of the top tier law firms are competing against each other in blood sports rather than practicing law. "Fine," I finally relent. "But don't start counting your billables from the sale. It's not happening."

She lets out a cackle of laughter. "Well, damn, there goes the new kitchen."

"Bye, Leona," I say wearily.

"Monday morning okay for the meeting?"

I let out a heavy breath. "Yeah, okay. Fine. You don't need to be there, though. I can tell them to fuck off just fine on my own."

She laughs again. "Alright, I'll set it up. Bye, Tanner."

I end the call and return to the OT room to see Izzy has moved onto some physical exercises. Fortunately, she's doing some balance ones that I'm already familiar with, so it doesn't look like I've missed anything new.

"Well done, Izzy," Edie says with an encouraging smile. "You've been practicing, haven't you?"

For a long moment I don't think she's going to answer; she often has trouble putting words together when she's busy concentrating on something else, and at the moment all her attention seems to be focused on keeping her balance as she walks slowly along the low, narrow platform, turning carefully when it zigzags. But then she says one word that makes me smile. "Lots."

And it's true, she does practice *a lot*. Between myself, my two older kids—who are both in their early twenties—and Izzy's nanny, Kit, we've got every day of the week well and truly covered. We all know how important all the different types of therapy are to make sure Izzy can live as happy, and healthy, and long a life as possible.

I continue to watch with pride as my little girl moves through the rest of her exercises. I'm especially proud of her when she doesn't even bat an eye at Edie correcting her movements, which is something that will often result in either an all-out tantrum, or at the very least a fierce scowl and a declaration of "I know how!" My girl has a stubborn streak, that's for sure, and she doesn't particularly like it when things are done differently than the way she's used to. Either we've just been lucky today, or Edie's found a better way of explaining to Izzy why she needs to be corrected.

Once the session is over, Izzy waves goodbye to Edie and takes my hand as we exit the room. "I was good today."

"You were very good," I agree, smiling down at her.

"Can Jazz do swings?"

I let out a breath of amusement. My son Jasper—Jazz—is probably Izzy's favorite person in the world, and vice versa. I'm sure she can't wait to tell him about her OT triumph when he comes over later today, and I have no doubt he'll be happy to oblige her with a trip to the park. "I'm sure he'd love that. As long as it's not raining."

It's early October and, like it often is in New York in the fall, the weather has been pretty amazing lately. We did have some showers yesterday afternoon, however, so you never know.

"Sunny, Daddy," she says when we get outside, her arm lifting to point at the sky in case I've missed the glaring light up there.

"But weather can change, baby girl. Hopefully it stays like this and you and Jazz can go to the park. We'll just have to wait and see."

She nods and we walk the short distance to where my driver, Gary, has pulled up to the curb and is holding the door of my black SUV open for us. I help Izzy up and into her car seat, fastening the restraints and making sure she's properly secured before closing the door. As usual, the second I turn around, I find Gary standing there with the front passenger door held open for me.

I know I should probably act like a proper rich guy with a chauffeur and sit in the back seat, but this just became habit back when Jazz and Piper were younger and it was beyond ridiculous for all three of us to squeeze into the back. Besides, I like being able to see what's going on out on the road.

I'm not entirely surprised to find that Izzy has nodded off by the time we get home. It's been a big week for her with five full days of kindergarten, a specialist appointment on Thursday evening and now occupational therapy today. She's doing really well to keep up with everything as far as I can tell, and her specialist seems to have the same opinion.

Fortunately, her teacher has been very cooperative and willing to work around her needs. I'll admit, when I learned how young he is I had some serious doubts, but it's been over a month now since school actually started and close to two months since we met Deacon and started figuring out a plan, and in that time I've been nothing but impressed. It's clear he's never taught a kid like Izzy before, and for someone else that would be an indisputable black mark against them. But Deacon has somehow turned it into a good thing, because it's made him completely open and flexible, without any biases formed from past experience.

I manage to get Izzy out of her car seat without waking her up. She'll be even more worn out after Jazz's visit this afternoon, so an extra half hour or so now will be helpful.

"Oh, did OT wear her out?" Kit asks me in a soft voice as I carry Izzy past the downstairs living room, where my godsend of a nanny is currently folding clean laundry.

"I think the whole week wore her out," I murmur back. "First week without any half-days."

I make my way to the stairs and take them slowly, making sure not to jostle my sleeping daughter.

"Ah, fuck," I murmur, as I get to the top step and almost go flying over the baby gate. I don't usually have it closed during the day but I must have forgotten to prop it open this morning. With Izzy's bedroom the first one off the landing, I get incredibly anxious about the possibility of her getting up in the middle of the night for some reason and tumbling down the stairs after making a wrong turn. Hence the gate. Admittedly, the risk is low considering she's not night trained yet, but I still prefer to be careful.

Adjusting my hold of her, I manage to unfasten the gate and push it open, letting us onto the landing. Then I walk the short distance to her room and carefully set her on her bed. She fusses a little when I remove her shoes, but doesn't wake.

***

. . .

"YOU LOOK TIRED," I observe as Jazz takes a seat on one of the stools at the island counter. He bears a striking resemblance to myself in my youth, with raven-dark hair, strong features, and a lean frame. His eyes are his mother's, however, and I can never get enough of the sight of them.

Jazz rolls his shoulders and stretches his arms up above his head, his mouth forming a wide yawn. "Yeah, it was a late one. The guy I hooked up with was so fucking needy. Not in a submissive way, just really eager for cock," he explains, making me regret asking the question. "Don't get me wrong, I love topping, but it really takes it out of you. I'm not sure if it's really worth it unless the guy's up for being totally dominated."

I give an exasperated shake of my head and turn my attention back to the salad I was making. "Jazz, we've talked about this. I really don't need to hear the details of your sex life."

It's not as though I haven't known for a while that my son is…rather active. But I certainly don't need it shoved right in my face. And yes, I would feel the same way if he were straight. He's my son, I taught him what his penis was when he was a toddler; I sure as hell don't need to know what he does with it now.

"Right…prude alert," he says in a sardonic tone.

"*Normal person* alert," I shoot back.

"Where's Izzy, anyway?"

"He asks *after* regaling his father with every detail of last night's conquest."

Jazz scoffs. "That was hardly *every* detail. I didn't even mention the—"

"She's in the playroom with Kit," I say, cutting him off before he can scar my brain any further. "She wants you to take her to the park after lunch."

He nods. "Yeah, I can do that. We'll go on the swings."

I smile to myself as I finish up with the salad. Jazz definitely knows the way to his sister's heart.

I set the salad aside and check on the chicken I have baking in the oven. It all looks good, so I grab a couple beers from the fridge and snap their caps off before sliding one across the island to Jazz. I feel a lot less irresponsible sharing a beer with him since he turned twenty-one earlier in the year, but considering he's technically owned a bar since he was twelve the ship probably sailed a while ago.

Jazz's phone goes off and he tugs it from his pocket, scowling at the screen.

"Something wrong?"

"Star wants me to go out to LA and meet with these record label guys she knows," he grumbles, his expression making him look as though he's been asked to undergo surgery without anesthesia.

"And you don't want to go?" I probe gently, aware that an outburst is likely forthcoming. Jazz has never been one to hold back. Whether it be his opinions, his emotions, or his thoughts; everything is just full steam ahead.

"Of course I don't want to go," he cries, throwing up his hands. "Now she's saying just come for a visit and forget about the label meetings. But you know once I'm out there she'll find some way to rope me into it."

For most musicians with Jazz's level of talent, getting a sit-down with a single label exec, let alone several, would be a dream come true. But Jazz only ever had one dream of playing professionally and it was shattered when he broke his hand in the car accident that killed his mother and completely broke our world. He went from dreaming of being a classical pianist to not even wanting to touch a piano. It wasn't until Izzy was born and he learned about musical therapy that he finally sat down at one again.

But his main focus now is the guitar and song-writing,

and he's just as gifted in that area as with the piano. I have a fair bit of fatherly bias, of course, but I'm certainly not the only one who thinks he could become a superstar if he wanted to.

But he doesn't want to. And while I admit I probably expected more from him than managing the bar he inherited and singing nineties covers, if that's where he finds his happiness I'm not going to complain. It sure beats blowing through his trust fund on endless partying.

"Why don't you just say no?" I ask reasonably.

"Because it's *Star*," he says, as though it should have been obvious. I guess it should. Star Bryant was Jazz's best friend in high school, and she was a really sweet girl...then. But she moved to LA a few years ago and I get the impression—mainly from my daughter Piper—that she's changed quite a bit in that time.

I shrug. "Then go."

Jazz lets out a loud groan of frustration. "You are no help whatsoever. Why do I even tell you things?"

"I'm constantly asking myself the same question," I say dryly.

The oven timer goes off and I check to see that the chicken is ready before pulling the steaming tray from the oven.

"Can you go get Izzy and Kit?" I ask Jazz. "I'll have everything ready when you get back."

He dutifully slides from his stool and heads for the stairs, while I dish up the chicken and set the table.

Deacon

"Told you they'd work things out," Skyler says with a satisfied smirk.

"Huh?"

He nods at the cluster of guys who have already gathered in the park for Saturday afternoon rugby practice. I check my watch and see we're a couple minutes late. Fuck —with the mood Spencer's been in lately, this definitely wasn't the day to be late.

"Spencer and Will," Skyler clarifies. "They're obviously back together."

"What? How do you know that?"

"Look at him." Skyler gestures to our teammates. "That's not the face of a heartbroken man. That's the face of a man who got his dick sucked about fifteen minutes ago."

"Well, if anyone knows that face, it's going to be you," I say wryly. But looking closer at Spencer, I can tell Sky might be onto something. Our captain definitely looks a hell of a lot happier than he has over the past week.

"Please, as if you don't love swallowing cock just as

much as I do," Skyler drawls. "You might be all sweet and fuzzy and prefer when there's "feelings" involved," he continues, holding his fingers up to form air quotes, as if the concept of having feelings for a guy is something ludicrous that I've invented on my own. "But that doesn't mean you don't still get off on sucking dick, Mr I Love It When They Fuck My Throat So Hard I'm Practically Choking."

I let out a groan of exasperation. "I am never telling you anything ever again."

I hear someone jogging up behind us, and then another of my teammates, Jackson Downey, is there, looking like he's just sprinted about five blocks.

"Fuck, I thought I was going to be late."

"We are," I tell him. "But it looks like Spence is in a good mood so I think we're off the hook."

I've known Jackson for as long as I've known Skyler, because the pair of them are pretty much inseparable. I remember my early days rooming with Skyler at college I actually thought Jackson was his boyfriend back home. Not an unreasonable assumption to make considering all the texting and the long phone calls and the Skyping and the way Skyler seemed to be pining for him.

When Jax visited for the weekend about a month after school started, I was definitely surprised to find he was a tatted-up car mechanic taking classes at their home town's local community college, but the way they interacted with each other did absolutely nothing to alter my initial assumptions. Until I saw Skyler hooking up with another guy right in front of Jackson...and Jax not even batting an eye.

And that's when I discovered Jax is straight as an arrow and the two of them are just friends. Or maybe brothers is more accurate. Although their relationship is a hell of a lot more intense than the one I have with my own brother, Sullivan, that's for sure. Of course, that could just be because Sully's seven years older than me and we've got three sisters between us.

Jax seems to have made looking out for Skyler his number one priority in life, and while Sky always projects an air of casual confidence, he only ever truly relaxes when Jackson's around. I'm sure the word co-dependency would come to mind for most people, but to me it's just how they are.

"What's going on?" Jax asks curiously.

"We were talking about how much Deacon loves sucking dick," Skyler announces, loud enough for the entire team to hear now that we're almost upon them.

"That's *not* what we were talking about," I grate out, sending him a frustrated glare.

"Do I need to hire a court reporter to read the conversation back to you?" he asks, one eyebrow raised. "Don't try to gaslight me, man."

I roll my eyes and walk over to my brother, grabbing the rugby ball he's holding out of his hands, merely for something to do. It's not as though I'm an overly self-conscious guy, but I really don't need all my brother's friends thinking about me giving blow jobs. They're way too interested in my dating life as it is.

"He's *your* friend," Sullivan says with a twitch of his lips.

"Shut up," I grumble.

Fortunately, Skyler has a knack for being easily diverted, so just as Spencer is about to call us together to lay out the plan for practice, Sky butts in and takes the opportunity to test his theory. "Hey, congrats Spence. Glad to see you and Will have made up."

Fucking hell. If he's wrong about this Spencer's going to

explode. I mean, it's not as though Spence has anger issues or anything, but breaking up with the love of your life because you think he's screwed you over by outing you to the press is bound to shorten anyone's fuse. Let's not even go into how the actual culprit was my brother's asshole ex.

Fortunately, Spencer doesn't explode. He just stares at Skyler, completely slack-jawed. "What...how...I haven't even told these guys yet..." he finally manages to stammer out, sounding very much unlike his usual calm, composed billionaire CEO self.

Skyler rolls his eyes. "If you were hoping to keep it under wraps you shouldn't have worn one of your boyfriend's t-shirts."

I eye the dark blue t-shirt Spencer's wearing. At first I don't understand how Skyler could know it's one of Will's —we've only met him a couple of times and I definitely don't remember seeing him in this shirt. But then I look closer at the white print on the front and realize it's an artsy image of a dalek from *Doctor Who*, one of Will's obsessions. *Well spotted, Skyler.*

"Also you have this whole orgasmic glow about you," Sky adds. He scans critical eyes up and down Spencer's body, tilting his head this way and that the way Jackson does when he's inspecting the damage on the outside of a car. "Are you sure you're up for practice today? Looks like Will went pretty hard on you last night. You sure you don't want to rest up and take a soak in a nice warm bath?"

Spencer yanks the ball from my grip and tosses it to Skyler—or, more accurately, *at* Skyler—hitting him in the chest with enough force to prompt Sky to let out a grunt. "Shut the fuck up and get into position. We need to make the most of today and next week seeing as these two have decided to ditch practice the week before the tournament."

"It's our sister's wedding," I say defensively, unable to

stop myself from cowering back a little under Spencer's disapproving glare. It's not as though Sully and I are choosing to miss Saturday practice in a deliberate attempt to screw over the team. And this is an amateur comp anyway, not the fucking World Championship. The only person who takes it as seriously as if his life were on the line is Spence.

"Her wedding's on the Sunday," Spencer shoots back.

"How about we get on with practice?" Charlie Campbell, my brother's best friend and Skyler's future boss, suggests.

Everyone murmurs agreement, looking relieved to be actually getting on with what we all came here for. And I don't blame them. Giving up a large chunk of a Saturday afternoon is a lot to ask, especially for guys who don't get a whole lot of free time. But the annual New York rugby sevens tournament is only a few weeks away and we all want to win—even if it is just an amateur comp.

To be honest, I can't even really remember how I got into playing rugby. I was a football guy in high school, but college ball had a completely different vibe and after a year I knew it wasn't for me. I guess the whole rugby thing just started as a bit of fun with my frat brothers, and then once I'd graduated Sullivan recruited me for this team and I dragged Skyler and Jax along with me.

The difference in age and paychecks was a little intimidating at first—my brother and his friends are some of the wealthiest guys in the country, after all—but that sorted itself out pretty quickly once I saw just how normal they all were.

"Deacon, have you been working out?" Bryce Kennedy asks me from his spot in the back row of the scrum. "Your ass looks very toned today."

"I think it's the shorts," Jackson comments. "They accentuate his natural curves."

"Stop staring at my brother's ass," Sully says from next to me.

"What? I can't compliment a buddy?" Bryce asks. "Your butt looks great too, Sully."

"You realize how gay you sound right now, don't you?" Sullivan says, and I can hear the eye roll in his voice.

"Well it's not like I'm saying I want to fuck it," Bryce shoots back.

I give a wry shake of my head. Okay—*almost* normal.

"Crouch," Spencer calls, prompting us to stop pissing around and tighten up our formation. "Bind…"

***

AFTER PRACTICE, Skyler and Jackson come back to my place to chill out for a bit. I'm keen to watch the Notre Dame game, but Skyler's done with sports for the day and wants a reality binge. And because Jackson can never resist giving Skyler whatever he wants, we end up settling on a *Drag Race UK* marathon.

"Just remember you did this to yourself, man," I say to Jackson, giving a wry shake of my head.

"You sure you don't want *Next Top Model?*" he suggests again, a little more insistent this time. I have no doubt that he's been thinking if he's going to be stuck watching reality TV, at least we could watch something with a bunch of hot women.

"We're all caught up on *Next Top Model,*" Skyler points out. "We haven't seen the latest season of UK *Drag Race.*"

"We're not caught up on *Next Top Model* Australia,"

Jackson says. "We only got up to, like, season six on that one."

Skyler sighs and hits me with a questioning look. "I guess it's your choice then, Deac."

The fact that Skyler's willing to leave it up to me instead of stamping his foot and demanding he gets his own way means that he'd be happy with either option, and I know that's the only reason Jackson's pushing so hard.

Considering my choice has been taken off the table, I also don't mind what we watch now. I'm not a particular fan of either program, or reality TV in general, really—I only really watch it when I can't convince Sky to watch sports or a movie. Despite this, my choice is a pretty easy one. If Jax is just going to blindly indulge Skyler on every single whim, he'll have to reap some consequences.

I stretch out casually in my armchair, reaching my arms up to rest my head back on my joined palms. "I'm thinking *Drag Race,*" say, hitting Jackson with a smirk.

He glares right back, knowing I've based my decision around ensuring he doesn't get what he wants.

I shrug. "Like I said, man. You brought this on yourself."

He mutters something under his breath that I'm sure is about me and likely not very flattering. But then he glances at Skyler, the dark expression leaving his face the moment he clocks the bright grin on Skyler's.

Fuck, now I feel bad. I might give Jax a lot of shit, but I'm honestly not sure I've ever met anyone so selfless.

I point the remote at the TV and scan through all the options before getting to the one we need. Then I hit play and set down the remote.

"You guys want a beer or something?" I ask, getting to my feet, feeling a little sore and stiff now that I've been sitting down for a bit. A couple hours of being thrown into the ground and throwing other guys into the ground will do that to you.

Jackson nods. "Yeah, thanks.".

"I'm good," Skyler says through a yawn.

I head to the kitchen, which is attached to the living room, separated only by a small breakfast bar.

"Fuck, I'm beat," Skyler says, giving another giant yawn. Then he shifts around on the sofa, stretching his long legs over one end and laying his head on Jackson's lap.

"Did you consider maybe other people might want to sit on the sofa?" Jackson asks wryly, even as he lifts his hand to gently stroke Skyler's hair.

"And where are these other people?"

As if on cue, the front door of my apartment swings open and my roommate, Drew, strides in. He takes one look at Skyler and Jackson, blinks a few times, and then shakes his head and glances away. He's pretty used to this behavior by now, having witnessed it on many occasions in the past. Like me, Drew's known these two for quite a while, even though we've only been living together for three years. He's been friends with Jackson for over a decade, ever since they worked part time at an auto-shop together. Now they co-own an auto repairs business that specializes in luxury cars. They're doing really well, and have even managed to expand to include a retail storefront, selling a whole bunch of shit I have no idea how to describe, let alone how to use.

Drew strips off his leather jacket and hangs it on the rack by the door, the gray t-shirt he's wearing revealing curls of black and green ink at his collar and upper arm. Based off of these two, anyone would think ink and piercings were mandatory for mechanics. Although it's always amusing to see them side by side because it makes Drew look practically clean cut compared to Jackson's tattoo sleeves, facial piercings, thick black beard, and shaved head. I'm not sure many people would want to meet him in a dark alley, even though the worst thing he'd do was point out you had food in your teeth.

"How'd you go on the Porsche?" Jackson asks.

Drew beams. "Perfect. Here, I took some pics." He slides his phone from his back pocket and scrolls through it for a moment before turning the screen to Jax.

"Damn, she's beautiful," Jackson murmurs appreciatively.

Drew beams proudly. "I know. Look at this one." He scrolls through to another picture and once again holds it up for Jackson. I swear it's like they're gushing over baby pictures or something.

"Are we ever going to watch *Drag Race?*" Skyler pipes in, sounding bored.

"*Drag Race?*" Drew asks me, one eyebrow quirked.

I lift one shoulder in a shrug. "Skyler's choice."

He sighs. "Of course it is."

4

Tanner

I try to hold onto a polite expression as I stare at the two men sitting across the boardroom table: Monty Steele—the asshole who wants to buy my wife's company, gut it from the inside out and destroy everything Leah worked for, while putting hundreds of loyal employees out of work; and Sullivan Stapleton, the man who's trying to help him do it.

This meeting is the absolute last thing I wanted to kick off the week with, but these two are fucking relentless; it doesn't matter how many times I refuse whatever deal they're offering, they just keep coming back with something else they think will wear me down.

They just don't seem to understand that I'm not going to budge. Not on this. They could offer double what the company's actually worth—triple, even—and I still wouldn't want to let it go.

MesiTec was Leah's pride and joy while she was alive, and now it's her legacy. I know from a business standpoint it makes sense for me to let it go—I'm going to have to cut something if I want my media corporation to remain viable, and it's not as though they're trying to short-change me on the offer—but I just can't do it. She left me in charge and I can't let Monty Steele turn it into one of his cut and gut projects. Even if by some miracle he actually decided to keep the company in one piece, it won't be the same. It won't be Leah's. The whole point of the company is to invest in female media creators—predominantly in the gaming world, where the gender gap has always been shockingly disproportionate—but Steele won't follow through on that. All he'll see are profit margins, or lack thereof, and want to overhaul the entire company.

"Come on, Grimsay," Stapleton says, flashing a smooth smile that I'm sure must be kryptonite for most people. "Be reasonable. You haven't built a billion-dollar corporation without knowing when to make sacrifices. You've been in the game long enough to know how it's played—if you want to keep winning, you have to make some cuts."

"I'm happy with my roster the way it is," I bite back, keeping up the analogy.

He lets out a heavy sigh, shaking his head in exasperation. He turns to Steele and they lock eyes for a moment, some kind of silent communication playing out between them. Then Steele nods and Stapleton turns his attention back to me. "We can increase the offer. Another ten million."

I don't even blink. "I don't know how many times I can say it. MesiTec's not for sale."

Steele looks ready to fly across the table and strangle me, but Stapleton's only reaction is a tensing of his jaw.

Deciding I've had enough, I get to my feet and fasten my suit jacket, smoothing it down. "I think we're done here. Thanks for stopping by, gentlemen. I'm sure you can find your way out."

I stride out of the boardroom, hearing Steele muttering

the word "asshole" as I exit. I don't really care what he thinks of me, however; I have the same opinion of him, after all.

I'm supposed to be meeting with Grimco Media's director in a few minutes, but I need some time to myself first. Randy—or RJ as he prefers—is a good guy, and I'm hoping he might end up as my son-in-law at some point considering he's been dating my daughter Piper for about three years now, but despite the family ties, when it comes to work he's all business. Bordering on ruthless, if we're being honest. He's exactly what I need in a director: someone hungry and driven and focused, who I can trust wholeheartedly. But his passion does mean that meetings with him can be a little draining, and after my stand-off with Steele and Stapleton, I need a breather.

I smile gratefully at my PA, Joseph, when he hands me a coffee as I reach my office. "Thanks, I needed this," I tell him, taking a sip.

"No problem. RJ said to say he's running late, so he'll come to you."

I nod. "Okay, yeah, that's fine."

"Also, your wife called," he informs me, biting his lip and shifting around nervously. I don't blame him; I don't usually have much of a temper, but Natalia could make the Dalai Lama want to strangle someone, and poor Joseph has been witness to a fair few outbursts in recent years.

"*Ex*-wife," I grate out.

He arches an eyebrow at me and I scowl, grumbling to myself as I throw the door of my office open. The brief second of comfort I got from the coffee is gone, and now I'm agitated all over again.

It's true that technically Natalia and I are still married, but in reality I feel more like a man with a gun to his head every time I hear her name mentioned. As far as I'm concerned, we're nothing to each other. We haven't lived in the same house for more than three years, and for the past six months she hasn't even been in the country. The only reason I can think of for her to be calling me now is that she's run out of money. It's definitely not to find out how her daughter's doing, that's for sure.

I clutch the edge of my mahogany desk in a white-knuckled grip and take a few moments to breathe through the tension. I'm not going to lose it. I'm not going to let Natalia send me into a spiral. She doesn't have that power over me.

It doesn't work though. All I can think about are her threats to take Izzy from me and the fear of losing my baby girl, or subjecting her to a bitter custody dispute, is crippling. My chest starts to constrict and my vision blurs at the edges. I know I'm on the verge of a panic attack and I'm so fucking pissed at myself for letting Natalia get to me like this.

I manage to tear myself away from my desk and make my way to the bathroom in my office. I feel like I'm walking through quicksand; every step feels like an effort. Once I finally get there, I yank open the mirrored cabinet above the sink and grab the bottle of Valium I keep here for these—fortunately rare—situations.

I take the pill and splash some cold water over my clammy face. It's not instantaneous, but I can gradually feel myself returning to something resembling normal. I let out a groan of frustration. It's been a while since I've let Natalia get to me like this. I can only guess that my defenses were already worn down by the meeting with Steele and Stapleton.

I look like absolute shit so I decide to take a quick shower before meeting with RJ. By the time I emerge from the bathroom, dressed in a fresh suit, I'm looking a hell of a lot more like the owner of a billion-dollar corporation and ready to do business. I still feel like balls but RJ doesn't need to know that. Hopefully we can get this over and done with quickly, before the Valium really kicks in and I need to crash on my office sofa.

"How'd it go this morning?" he asks me as I step into my office.

I'm not surprised to find him already there, leaning against the arm of one of my sofas, glass of whiskey in hand. He's a fair bit older than Piper—in his mid-thirties —but I'm hardly one to judge on that count considering my ex is eighteen years younger than me.

"They offered another ten," I grumble. "I said no. Again."

He just nods and takes a sip of his drink. I'm grateful that he's not trying to push the issue right now—I really don't have the energy for it. RJ understands my reluctance to let go of Leah's company, but he also sees it as the most viable option for getting back in the red. And he's probably right; there are other companies I'd rather let go of, but we're not getting offers for those and we're not likely to.

"I want to set up a meeting with Carter Duncan," RJ declares, catching me off guard with the change of topic.

"Any particular reason?"

"I think we need to talk about making some changes at BCN."

BCN is the cable news network I bought back in 2000. It was a small East Coast broadcaster back then, but now it's a world-wide, twenty-four hour cable news network, and definitely one of the things I'm most proud of. Admittedly, it's not as profitable as it used to be—the climate has changed in recent years and people aren't as interested in watching the news on TV anymore—but I'm wary of the word "changes" coming out of RJ's mouth. If he mentions anything about TikTok, I'm out of here.

"What sort of changes?" I ask. "Programming or personnel?"

He shrugs. "A bit of both. Nothing too drastic, so you can calm down," he assures me, and I can tell he's barely containing an eye roll. "But I think we need to freshen things up a little. Look at Pax Greenwood for instance— he's been sitting at that desk doing the same show every night for fifteen years…"

"He doesn't do Saturdays," I point out, earning an actual eye roll this time. "And he's got the top rated show on the network."

"Tanner, that's not exactly hard."

Ouch.

I must not be able to hide my wince, because RJ sighs and shakes his head. "That came out worse than I meant it. I'm just saying we could be doing a lot better and Pax is a prime example of that. He used to do all these hard-hitting interviews and on the ground reporting, and it was great. But lately it's like he's been going through the motions. He's charming and likable, and he can still pull out some tough questions when he needs to, but it's not like it used to be."

I let out a heavy sigh, nodding in agreement. "That can happen when you're forced to hold your tongue for four years." Freedom of the press is great in theory, but it all becomes a bit complicated when you have to consider things like advertisers and ratings and the business dealings of the parent corporation. For the most part I think Pax has done a pretty good job of sticking to his principles and has made his views on certain issues clear. But it's true that he's become much more deferential, and his bite's not nearly as sharp as it used to be. "I wish I could give him free rein to do and say whatever he wants but it doesn't work like that," I tell RJ.

"Yeah, I realize that. But I've got some other ideas—I just want to run them by Carter."

I shrug. "Okay. I guess we could set something up." We usually only meet with the head of the network once a quarter, but it's not going to hurt to have a chat with him now. "What about Marion?" I ask, referencing the head of BCN's news division—AKA prime-time programming. Her we have much more interaction with as things are constantly moving and changing.

"Pax was just an example," RJ clarifies. "But, yeah, may as well loop her in too. I think prime time is probably where we should focus to start off with."

"They're not going to like us sticking our noses in," I point out. I've always made an effort to be as hands-off as possible and just let everyone who actually knows what they're doing do it. I like to keep informed of what's going on, but I don't usually butt in and make demands unless it's really necessary.

RJ holds his hands up. "They're only suggestions."

***

I WAS HOPING the stress of the day would ease off by the time I got home and spent some time with Izzy. But it hasn't.

I'm still all tense and agitated as I'm putting her to bed and reading a picture book to her; as much as I love holding her and hearing her giggle when I do the animal noises, the panic episode I had today is still fresh in my mind and I have to fight not to spiral again when the thought of losing this flashes through my mind. I know, logically, that the chances of that actually happening are slim, but that doesn't stop my brain from fixating on that dreaded 'what if?'

Once the story's over, I climb from the bed and tuck Izzy in. I carefully remove her adorable rainbow-framed glasses, setting them on the nightstand before bending down to give her a kiss on the forehead. "Night, baby girl."

"Goodnight, Daddy."

I gaze down at her for a moment, my heart clenching. Then I turn and stride for the door, turning off the light and closing the door over.

Fuck, I hate Natalia for putting this fear into me. It feels like every time I have a handle on it, she'll just swoop in to remind me what a fucking mess I am.

Forcing my brain away from earlier today, I think about what's waiting for me out in the kitchen. There's a whole pile of dishes on the sink from dinner, and the kitchen table is filthy because Izzy decided to try finger-painting with her spaghetti sauce. It'll probably take me about half an hour to clean up, which is good. Cleaning the kitchen of a nighttime always helps me to wind down, so tonight's a good night for it to be a disaster area.

When I get there, however, I see that the table is now clean, the dishes are gone from the sink, and the dish-washer is running. Kit is wiping a cloth over the island counter top, clearly just finishing up with the clean-up.

"Oh."

She glances up at the sound of my voice and smiles. "Thought I'd save you a job. You look like it's been a pretty stressful day."

Oh, the irony. I can't blame her, though. I've never told her about this particular quirk of mine, so all she would have seen is a huge pile of dishes waiting for me and decided to do a nice gesture.

I smile. "Thanks. It had it's moments."

I stretch my neck back and forth and roll my shoulders, attempting to ease the tension in my body, but it's not working. And, of course, it's not just my body—my mind is completely fucked right now and I know the odds are good I'll be getting an hour of sleep tonight if I'm lucky.

There's really only one thing I know of that's going to help me deal with this, and I'm frustrated to even be considering it. Not because I'm ashamed about it—I don't think I understand it enough to feel shame, if we're being honest—but because it's been barely a month since the last time and I shouldn't be needing it again so soon.

"Are you okay to stay with Izzy tonight?" I ask. "I think I'm going to go out."

Kit shrugs. "Sure, no problem."

I nod. "Cool. I'll probably crash at the penthouse, but I'll be home early—before six."

She smirks at me, eyes full of knowing amusement. "That's not a problem either. Have fun."

Yeah, she's not an idiot. She worked out pretty early on that when I go out and crash at the penthouse it means I'm getting laid. I doubt she's figured out I'm getting fucked in the ass by a random guy, though.

5

Deacon

"Hey, isn't that the sexy silver fox you have a crush on?" Skyler asks me, glancing over my shoulder.

I roll my eyes, assuming he's just stirring up shit like usual, but when I turn to see what's captured his attention, I almost pass out from shock. Because, for once, Skyler is being a hundred per cent serious. Tanner Grimsay is sitting at the bar, looking hotter than ever in dark jeans and a gray knitted sweater. "Jesus Christ," I mutter, swinging my head back around before he catches me watching him. "It really is him."

"Who?" Jackson asks, peering curiously around Skyler and me to get a look at the bar.

"A parent of one of Deacon's kindergarteners," Skyler informs Jax. "Deac's got a major crush on him."

"I don't remember using the word 'major'," I mumble.

Skyler just shrugs. "Well, at least you know one thing now—he actually is into guys."

I shake my head. "I don't know that. He probably came in here by accident."

Sky sends me a skeptical look. "Right. He just *acciden-*

tally wandered all the way to Brooklyn, and *accidentally* wound up in a gay bar, and *accidentally* sat down and ordered a drink even after realizing his 'mistake'." He lifts his fingers to form air quotes of condescension.

I fold my arms over my chest and issue him with a rueful look. "Okay, fine. It wasn't an accident. But just because he's in a gay bar doesn't mean he's into guys. Jackson's in a gay bar," I point out, gesturing to my very straight friend, who has dutifully endured several guys hitting on him throughout the evening just because Skyler was in the mood for cruising.

"Jackson got out-voted," he says in a grumble.

"And we thank you for your sacrifice," Skyler says with a grin, throwing an arm around Jax and planting a big, sloppy kiss on his cheek.

"You're never going to find someone to hook up with if you keep cuddling up to me," Jax says dryly.

Skyler just hugs Jackson tighter and rests his head on his broad shoulder. "I can't help it. You're so cuddly. Like a giant teddy bear."

A guy walking past stops to admire Jackson, taking in his broad, bulky frame, tattooed arms, and thick, black beard.

"Not that kind of bear," Skyler says to the guy, a hint of warning in his tone as he gestures for the guy to move along.

"Okay, as much as I *love* being objectified, I think I've hit my limit for the night," Jackson says, prying himself away from Skyler.

"It's still early," Sky says with a pout.

Jackson offers a wry smile. "Which means you'll have plenty of time to go chat up guys without worrying about me. Just don't forget you've got a paper due tomorrow."

Skyler rolls his eyes. "Yes, Dad."

Jackson lets out a chuckle then slaps me on the back as he passes on his way to the exit. "Bye Deac. Good luck with the sexy silver fox."

At his words, Skyler's pout forms into an excited expression that can only mean trouble. I groan inwardly as dread fills me.

Seriously, Jax—you just had to remind him…

"I think I'm going to get a drink," Sky says brightly.

I shake my head. "No, no, we don't need more drinks."

"Speak for yourself, I'm parched."

Fucking hell. I follow Skyler to the bar, and of course he makes a beeline for Tanner, making no effort to be discrete as he accidentally-on purpose bumps into his shoulder.

"Oh, I'm so sorry," Skyler gushes, reaching out a hand to steady himself. Arranging his features into a mask of surprised recognition, he flashes his attention back to me. "Oh my god, Deacon. Isn't this the parent you have a massive crush on?"

My face flames as mortification rushes through me. I send Skyler a hard glare but he just smirks back at me and stalks away, heading for the other side of the bar.

"I'm so sorry, he's not usually allowed out in polite society. It's all gone to his head."

Tanner lets out a wry chuckle. "Nothing to apologize for."

Damn, why are his eyes so god damned blue? It's like they have magic powers or something; it's pretty much impossible to tear my gaze away.

"Just so you know, you really shouldn't take anything he says seriously. He's a pathological liar."

Tanner arches a brow at me, his lips quirking with amusement. "So you don't have a *massive* crush on me."

Fuck, my face is so red right now. "I never said *massive,*" I confess.

"Ahh, so just a little crush then?"

I bite my lip in hesitation. Why am I even considering answering this? "That would be...inappropriate."

"That's not a no," he says, amusement dancing in his eyes.

Damnit. I need a drink. I need *something* to focus on other than his beautiful, mesmerizing face before I say or do something even more mortifying.

I order a whiskey and tap my fingers on the bar for a moment, wondering if I should just politely extricate myself from this conversation once my drink arrives and then pretend I never saw my student's dad at a gay bar.

"Don't worry, I won't tell," he teases.

"Huh?" I glance up at him, my brows furrowed in confusion.

"About your inappropriate crush."

"Oh...right." I let out an awkward chuckle. Fuck, when the hell did I turn into this bag of nerves? "Thanks."

"And I'd appreciate if you didn't mention my presence here to anyone..." he says, one eyebrow raised pointedly.

I shake my head. "I don't need a quid pro quo if that's what you're getting at. I'd never out someone."

He looks visibly relieved as he nods and takes a sip of his drink.

My whiskey arrives and I take a generous gulp, feeling the burn all the way down my throat. Shit, I really need to calm down. This situation doesn't warrant such a major freak out.

"You must think I'm such a coward," Tanner says wryly. "Being so worried about what people might think of me."

The stool to my left opens up so I claim it and make myself comfortable, figuring the window to exit the conversation has closed.

"I don't think that," I assure him. "It's everyone's own personal decision when—or even if—to come out. And I can imagine things would be complicated for you, with kids and your business and everything."

He lets out a rueful laugh. "You could say that. But, to be honest, I'm not even sure how I identify." He swings around on his stool and pins me with a an intense look. "How is someone supposed to identify when they're basically straight except for when they're really stressed and need a nice, big cock in their ass to relieve the tension?"

I sputter and cough as a sip of my drink goes down the wrong pipe. "Uh…I don't know," I somehow stammer out, desperately willing my cock to deflate before he thinks to look down.

He sighs. "I've tried dildos, and it feels good but it really doesn't give me what I need. There's too much work involved. The only thing that really works is being held down and fucked hard."

Holyfuckingshitballs.

I shift on my seat, any hopes of my hard-on deflating going out the window. "Okay, you really need to stop talking now."

He offers a wry smirk. "Sorry. I'm being *inappropriate*, aren't I?"

I nod and take another sip of my whiskey. "Just a bit."

He leans a little closer and I get a whiff of his incredible scent. Jesus Christ—is there anything about this man that *doesn't* send blood straight to my cock? "Do you always follow the rules, Deacon?"

I bite my lip, swallowing hard as I once again attempt not to drown in his gaze. "Pretty much."

"Is there a specific rule that says you're not allowed to fuck me?" he asks, one eyebrow quirked.

"Umm…I don't think so." My brain has officially stopped working; it's a miracle I can even form words.

"And do you want to fuck me?" he presses, eyes glimmering.

"I—"

He moves his hand to my thigh, rubbing it up my leg in a way that makes me shiver. "Because I *really* want you to."

I know there's supposed to be a reason for me to say no to this, but for the life of me I can't remember what it is. I mean, when the most beautiful man in the world asks you to fuck him, you just do it—right?

I drain the remaining swallow of my drink and slide off my chair. "Okay. Come on, let's go."

"Go?"

I arch a brow at him. "My place—I thought you wanted to be fucked?"

For a mortifying second I worry that in my lust-filled stupor I've somehow misconstrued or imagined the whole conversation we just had, but then a bright grin breaks across Tanner's face and he gets to his feet as well. "Lead the way."

6

Tanner

The moment I saw Deacon Stapleton at that bar tonight, I knew no one else was going to cut it. Yeah, he's right. It's inappropriate as hell for me to be getting in any way involved with my daughter's teacher, but the rational part of my brain is on hiatus for the moment. All I care about is getting naked and getting him inside me.

Thankfully, his apartment is only a few minutes walk from the bar, and once we get to his bedroom it's game on.

"Fuck, I need this off," Deacon groans, slamming me into his bedroom wall and tugging at my sweater.

I help him tug my sweater off, smiling as I see his eyes widen at the sight of my inked right shoulder and chest.

"Holy shit. Just when I thought you couldn't get hotter…"

"And you haven't even seen my cock yet," I say with a smirk. I know I sound like an arrogant bastard, but, come on, having a guy half my age ogle my body with this kind of heat in his eyes is making it difficult to keep the ego in check.

He grins and drops to his knees. "Well, that's about to

change." He deftly unfastens my jeans and shoves them and my boxer briefs down my thighs, letting my hard, pulsing cock spring free. *"Hello, beautiful,"* he murmurs with a playful smirk as he wraps his hand around the shaft and gives a couple of lazy strokes that cause my eyes to fall closed with bliss.

Then I feel Deacon's mouth close around the head and can't stop myself from letting out a groan of pleasure.

He sucks and licks and swallows me down with an eagerness that makes me think he's been wanting to do this for a while.

"Fuck," I groan. "You keep sucking me like that and I'm going to come."

He pulls away from my dick and looks up at me, the corner of his mouth lifting up. "You make that sound like a bad thing."

Not bad, necessarily. I don't usually let guys suck me off, but I definitely wouldn't mind making Deacon choke on my cum. Or maybe seeing his pretty face covered with it. That's not what led me to come home with him tonight, though. It's not what I need. "You're supposed to be fucking me, remember?"

"Right." He spares one last, longing glance for my cock before getting to his feet. "Get naked and get on the bed."

His heated gaze doesn't leave my body as I toe off my shoes and peel my jeans and briefs down the rest of the way.

"Fucking hell," he murmurs, once I'm completely bare.

I quirk a brow at him. "Something wrong.

He shakes his head. "Fuck no." He just stands there for a moment, his eyes sweeping up and down my naked body in a way I can't say I hate, before he finally snaps out of his trance and gestures to the bed behind him. "On the bed."

I hesitate, shaking my head. I can't do this on the bed.

It's way too intimate. "Not the bed," I tell him. "Right here. I want you to fuck me so hard against this wall we risk breaking through it."

A slow grin forms across his face. "I think I can do that."

He steps back and reaches behind his head to tug his t-shirt off, revealing a hard, muscular chest. I'm curious to know how a kindergarten teacher has the body of an Olympic athlete, but right now the why doesn't really matter. All I care about is that muscle equals strength. And power. And that's what I need right now.

He kicks his shoes off and then unfastens his jeans, giving me my first glimpse of his dick as he tugs them down.

My ass clenches at the sight of his hard, throbbing cock. It's nice and thick, and perfect for what I need tonight. I can already feel some of the tension from the past few days easing with the mere thought of being filled with that bad boy. Let's hope Deacon knows how to use it.

I give his naked body a quick once-over, but if I'm honest, I'm pretty much indifferent to the sight. It's not a turn off, but it doesn't have my mouth watering or my heart racing or anything like that. I'm interested in his fat cock and his hard muscles, because I know they can give me what I need. But that's as far as it goes.

Not all that surprising considering my general lack of interest in men, but after my strange reaction while he was blowing me I thought there might be something more going on here.

"Like what you see?" he asks with a smirk.

I arch a challenging brow. "Impressive. I hope you know how to use that thing."

"Don't worry. I'm well-practiced."

"I'll be the judge of that."

He lets out a soft laugh and strides over to his nightstand, retrieving the necessary supplies. "Turn around," he instructs. "Let me see the rest of the view."

I dutifully turn to face the wall, planting my hands against it and spreading my feet a little.

"Fucking hell," Deacon murmurs from close behind me. "I'd love to know how you stay in such good shape. This ass is incredible."

He runs his hand over said ass, slipping his fingers between my cheeks and making me shiver.

"Not exactly top secret information. I work out and take care of myself." I've always been relatively active anyway, but having a new baby in my forties definitely got me to up my game.

"Well I appreciate the effort," he says wryly. "Can't wait to get deep inside this gorgeous ass."

My hole pulses at his words, anticipation buzzing through me. "Then hurry the fuck up and do it," I growl.

"First thing's first," he says, and then I feel a slick finger probing at my entrance.

I groan as he thrusts it inside me, and can't help pushing back against his hand, needing more. He gives me what what I need, and before I know it, I have three of his thick fingers fucking me, stretching out my hole. And it's still not nearly enough.

"This is interesting," he murmurs in my ear, tugging on my earlobe with his teeth while his fingers twist around inside me, the overwhelming sensations making me moan and whimper in desperation. "You're a bit of a slut, aren't you? Listen to you, moaning like a whore, and I haven't even put my dick in you yet."

Fuck. What happened to the nice guy who was blushing and babbling at the bar? And why am I so damned turned on by his filthy words?

I can barely think straight, my cock is aching so desperately. And he's right; this is just the prep. This is usually the part that I just have to get over with before the actual fun starts. But clearly none of my previous male hook-ups have been doing it right if this is how good it can feel. Right now I just want more of Deacon's fingers stretching me. Fuck, I could probably take his entire hand, the way things are going.

But the reminder of his dick snaps me out of whatever spell his fingers have me under, and I remember what I really came here for tonight: that hard, fat cock filling me up, and Deacon's powerful body thrusting deep inside me.

"That's enough," I groan. "Just get inside me."

"That wasn't a very polite way of asking for something, Mr Grimsay," he taunts.

Fucking hell. "Please, can you fuck me now?"

"Much better."

He slowly withdraws his fingers, prompting me to let out a mortifying whimper at the sudden feeling of emptiness.

Any hopes that Deacon might have missed it are shattered when he lets out a putter of amusement, then murmurs in my ear, "Don't worry, you'll be stuffed full of my cock in a second."

I shiver at his words, once again noting the complete one-eighty from the guy I was chatting to earlier in the night. I don't have much time to contemplate the shift, however, because as promised, I feel the head of Deacon's cock lining up with my entrance a moment later.

My whole body is thrumming; my cock is aching, my ass is throbbing, even my legs are shaking slightly with the anticipation of what's about to come. I need this. So much more than I did earlier in the night when I first went out looking for a hook-up. I'm absolutely desperate for it now.

The finger fuck might have helped to take the edge off a little, but now I can see it was a mere substitute for what I really need. I'm like a junkie who managed to tide himself over with some morphine before getting his hands on the real thing.

And I realize that analogy kind of highlights just how unhealthy this coping mechanism I've developed for myself is, but now's not exactly the time to be analyzing that mental tangle.

"Come on," I groan, pushing back against Deacon's cock. "I need you in me, not just parked at my hole."

"Uh, yeah, I just realized I don't have a condom," he says. The cocky fucker who's been taunting me and teasing me has disappeared and the hesitant guy from the bar is back. "Is that a problem?"

I spin around, my eyes wide with horror. "What? How could you not have condoms?" And how could he only just be remembering *now* when I'm two seconds away from self-combusting.

His expression is apologetic but he lifts his shoulders in a shrug. "I don't need them. I'm on PrEP and get tested like clockwork."

I let out a grunt of frustration, lifting a hand up and thrusting my fingers roughly through my hair. I have no idea what PrEP is, but I can't remember the last time I was tested, which means it was too long ago. "Damn it."

"You don't have anything?" he asks hopefully.

"Not on me. I usually take hook-ups back to my place."

His eyes widen, telling me he hasn't forgotten that he's well aware I'm the parent of a five-year-old. "*Your* place?"

"Not my brownstone," I clarify. "I have a penthouse in Brooklyn."

"Oh." He nods, and then a thoughtful expression crosses his face. "Jesus, how rich *are* you?"

"Well, I'd happily fork over a hundred grand for a condom right now," I say wistfully.

He lets out a bark of laughter, then his eyes light up. "Hang on. I might have a solution." He strides over to a set of drawers and retrieves some sweatpants, tugging them on before brushing past me toward the door.

"What? Where are you going?"

"Give me two seconds. Don't go anywhere."

"Where the fuck am I going to go?" I growl.

Ignoring me, he exits the bedroom, closing the door behind him. A minute or so later, he's back, brandishing a little plastic packet. "We're lucky. It was the last one. I'll get shit from Drew about this tomorrow but I have a feeling it'll be worth it," he adds with a smirk.

Relief washes through me and I feel a burst of warmth at the lengths Deacon has gone to for my comfort. It's not just the risk of disease that bothers me—I'm sure with the precautions Deacon takes that would be low anyway—the fact is, I just don't feel comfortable having a guy's cum in me. Hypocritical, I know—I can let him fuck me, but not finish in me—but it's just how I feel and I'm not sure I should have to apologize for it. "Thank you," I tell him, offering a grateful smile.

"It's cool. And I'll accept payment in the form of a check," he teases.

I let out a wry laugh. "Well, it's Drew's condom, so…"

"But I went all the way over to his room to get it," he argues.

"What about payment in the form of a fuck?" I suggest. "Pretty sure this is a hundred thousand dollar ass." I turn around to give him a view of my backside, running a hand over my left cheek before giving it a little slap.

Deacon lets out a wry chuckle and then I sense him moving up close behind me. His hand replaces mine, his fingers giving my ass a firm squeeze and making me groan. "I don't know. Fifty grand, maybe."

I've lost the thread of the conversation because the feel of his breath on my skin and his hands on my body is making my bones practically melt. Lust and need sizzle away inside me and the only thought my brain can form is *Now! Now! Fucking hell, get inside me now!*

I manage to push through the haze and give a reply, but it's seriously one of the hardest things I've ever done considering his fingers are now sliding around my slick hole. And that's saying something considering I've built a billion-dollar corporation from the ground up and am raising three kids, one of whom has special needs. "I guess you'll just have to do it twice," I pant out. I was going for the same teasing tone as earlier but apparently I'm incapable of that now.

"Sounds like a fair deal," he murmurs. And then I hear the crinkle of plastic and the snap of latex that tells me we're good to go.

7

Deacon

I don't know what the fuck I'm thinking, agreeing to a second go around with Tanner. We shouldn't even be doing this one time, let alone setting up a repeat.

Whatever. Maybe it'll be horrible and he won't be interested in seconds. I doubt it, though. If the way he responded to me fingering him is any indication, he's going to love every second of my cock pounding inside him.

I do kind of wish we were doing this front on, because I'd love to be able to look at his beautiful face and take in his expression while I fuck him, but I wasn't about to push when he suggested this position. He's made it clear that his only real interest in men is getting fucked as some kind of stress relief thing; I can't quite say I understand it, but if that's his deal than I'm not going to judge. And I'm not going to push him into things he might not be comfortable with.

Pushing the thoughts from my head, I slather some lube on the condom and once again line myself up with Tanner's entrance. Fuck, I can't believe I'm about to be buried inside Tanner Grimsay's ass. Here's hoping it lives up to all the fantasies…

I push inside, hearing him let out a hiss as I breach his ring. I did the best I could to prep him, but my cock is quite a bit thicker than even three of my fingers. But it'll be okay, I'll just go slow and give him time for his body to adjust.

That's the plan, at least, but Tanner doesn't seem to be on board with it. Instead of waiting for me to inch in slowly, he pushes his ass back against me, causing me to bottom out in one deep thrust.

I let out a grunt at the unexpected onslaught of sensations. His hole is so fucking tight and the feel of his blood pulsing against my dick is making my head spin. The only thing that would be better is if I were bare right now, but that was another thing I definitely wasn't going to push.

The groan Tanner lets out is primal, and he lifts a hand to slap against the wall in front of him. I still don't quite understand it, but I think I have a bit of a vague grasp on what it is Tanner needs from me now. It's not just pleasure he's seeking. It's relief. Both physical and mental. And I think just having my cock inside him is helping a little. But it's not enough.

And that's a good thing, because this is definitely not enough for me. Now that I'm inside him, all I want to do is grab him tight and fuck him hard enough to wake the neighbors.

And that's exactly what I do.

I'm not sure about the neighbors part, but I wouldn't be surprised with the way Tanner's thumping against the bedroom wall with every hard thrust I drive into his body, or with the sheer volume of the grunts and groans and curses we're doing nothing to hold back. I did warn Drew to put his headphones on when I visited his room earlier, so hopefully we haven't disturbed him too much. Apart from that, I don't really care; we don't know any of our neighbors anyway.

I grab a fistful of Tanner's silver hair and yank his head back, grazing my teeth along his stubbled jaw, and then down the back of his neck. Fuck, he smells incredible. The scents of sweat and sex mingling in the air just make him even more delicious.

I really want to kiss him, but I think that's something I should wait for him to initiate. Instead, I settle for licking a few beads of sweat from his neck.

He lets out a soft groan as my tongue travels over his skin, and that prompts me to do it again.

"Mmm…you taste amazing. And that's just your sweat. Your cum must be a fucking delicacy."

"Doesn't' it all…taste the same?" he asks between panted breaths.

I drive in deep again, hitting him in the magic spot and prompting him to let out a string of curses, his palm slapping against the wall in front of him.

"Definitely not."

"Huh?"

I let out a soft chuckle at the bewilderment in his voice. Clearly hitting his prostate again killed a few brain cells. "Cum doesn't all taste the same."

"I wouldn't know."

I let out another laugh, shaking my head. "I figured as much." I dig my fingers in harder and speed up my thrusts. I can feel my orgasm approaching, but I need to clear something up before I really let it rip. "So can I?"

"Huh?"

Note to self—Tanner is not capable of holding up a conversation during sex. I'll take that as a compliment.

"Taste your cum," I clarify. I lean in closer so I can talk

right in his ear. "I'm going to come any minute, and when I do I want to get on my knees and suck on that beautiful dick of yours until you're exploding down my throat."

He lets out a soft groan, his eyes falling shut as though he's in pain. "Fuck...Deacon..."

"You okay?"

"My brain doesn't fucking work while your cock's in me—why would you think I could carry on an actual conversation?"

Reluctantly, I pull out of Tanner's ass, instantly missing the tight heat.

"Wha—I didn't mean for you to pull out," he growls.

"I need to know what you want," I say unapologetically —he's not the only one suffering here. "You seemed a little freaked out when I sucked you off earlier. But you also seemed to enjoy it. So now my instincts are off—are you cool with me finishing you off with BJ or not?"

"I don't usually do...that. With guys, I mean."

"Is there a particular reason why?" I ask warily. Does he not like doing *anything* with guys except using them as walking dildos?

Tanner shrugs. "I guess it's never come up before. Other guys I've hooked up with have been happy to get straight to the fucking."

"Other guys are idiots if they get a look of that cock and don't want to suck it," I say with an eye roll.

He lets out a snort of amusement before an uncertain expression crosses his face. "I did really like it, though," he admits. "Way more than I thought. I wanted to come down your throat." A faint blush touches his cheeks as he adds, "Actually, I wanted to come on your face."

I arch an eyebrow at that. Well, damn. I move behind him again and reach between his cheeks, my fingers sliding around his hole. My mouth quirks up as I feel his body shiver at the touch. "If I can't come in this beautiful ass, you can't come on my beautiful face," I tease. It's a bit of a dick move considering I'm a hundred per cent gay and perfectly comfortable with guys coming on me, but I'm in a bossy mood and want to set a boundary.

Besides, we have to save *something* for next time.

"But I can come down your throat?" he asks.

"Oh yeah, you can definitely do that."

Before Tanner has a chance to respond, I remove my fingers and thrust back inside him, driving in deep.

I snap my hips over and over, savoring the grunts and groans that fall from Tanner's lips as the fire starts to rekindle inside me.

"Keep going like this and you won't get a chance to suck me," Tanner grates out through panted breaths. "So fucking close. Need to fucking come…"

"Not yet," I growl, reaching around to put some pressure on the end of his dick and force the orgasm back. "Not until you're buried so far down my throat I can taste your balls."

He lets out a frustrated groan, his forehead hitting the wall in front of him. "Fuck…*Deacon*. Saying shit like that this isn't helping the situation."

"Shit like what?" I goad. "You don't want to hear about how I'm going to swallow your cock down until I'm choking on it? I can't wait to get my mouth around that gorgeous dick again, baby. Can't wait to get a taste of your cream…swallow it all down…"

The endearment just falls out amidst all the dirty talk, and I don't even think about it until I trail off and realize what I've just said. Fortunately, Tanner seems too wound up to even realize.

"I'm not going to last," he moans. "Please, just let me come. Please…I need to—"

"No," I say firmly, once again reaching down to squeeze the end of his dick. "Me first."

Deciding to put him out of his misery, I decide to let it rip. I dig my fingers into his hips and fuck him hard and deep, over and over as my climax approaches. I let out a fierce groan as it hits me, digging my teeth into Tanner's neck as I shoot hard into the condom.

I only give myself a moment to recover before pulling out and tearing off the condom. Then I grab Tanner's hips and turn him around, shoving him roughly back against the wall before dropping to my knees and wrapping my lips around the head of that beautiful dick.

I groan as I get a taste of his precum, my tongue lapping at the crown before I take him deeper, sucking him harder until he hits the back of my throat.

"Jesus, fuck," Tanner gasps, rocking his hips and driving his dick even deeper down my throat until I'm practically choking on it, just like I wanted.

I groan even more eagerly, loving the feel of him stretching my mouth and burning my throat. I grip Tanner's ass and squeeze firmly, urging him on as he thrusts harder. Deeper. His hands tugging roughly at my hair as he snaps his hips.

And I fucking love every second. I love the way he's using my mouth to chase his release. I can barely breathe and I don't even care, because every time I do manage to get some air in all I can smell is him. And it's so fucking hot.

I can tell when he's reaching the edge; his grip in my hair gets tighter and his body starts to tense up. At the last second he tries to pull away, but I don't let him. I want to swallow every last drop of his cum. I want to choke on it.

He lets out a loud groan as hot cum fills my mouth, half his load going straight down my throat and making me sputter. I slowly drag my lips down his shaft until his softening cock falls from my mouth. Then I take a moment to just savor the taste of him on my tongue before swallowing down my mouthful and grinning up at him, my tongue slipping out to slide over my lips. "Mmm…that was tasty."

"Fuck, that's an impressive gag reflex," he mutters, looking a little shell-shocked from the recent experience.

"Um…thank you?" I say awkwardly, clambering to my feet.

He offers a wry smirk. "I guess that's something you're well-practiced in too?"

I let out a breath of amusement. "Yeah, I guess you could say that. It's not always that fun, though."

Tanner's brows shoot up. "Fun? You looked like you could barely breathe. I—I didn't mean to get so carried away…"

"You didn't. Trust me, it was hot as fuck," I assure him, gesturing to my cock, which is already hard again after that epic BJ.

Tanner's eyes widen in obvious shock. "*Fuck.*" Then he wipes a hand over his face, looking suddenly exhausted. "I don't know what to be more unsettled about—that you got hard from something that looked like torture, or that you got hard *again* about ten minutes after coming. You really are a baby, aren't you?"

I cross my arms over my chest and issue him with an irritated look. "I'm twenty-seven, hardly a baby. I hope you're not about to pull the whole 'you're too young for me' shit, because one…" I hold my hand up and start counting on my fingers. "You've proved tonight that you can clearly keep up with me. You've probably got more stamina than a ton of guys my age. Two—I've well and truly learned over the years that age is completely irrelevant when it comes to sex. You're not even the oldest guy I've hooked up with. And three—this is supposed to be a one-night thing anyway, so what does it matter?"

Tanner's brows shoot up. "That was quite a passionate spiel."

I sigh, lifting one shoulder in a shrug. "I've had this issue come up before. Better to head it off at the pass."

The corner of his mouth quirks up. "Well I don't think you're too young. I was just making an observation. And, like you said, this is just a one-night thing anyway…"

I nod. "Right. Oh, and I'm not a masochist."

He blinks at me. "What?"

"You said you were concerned that I got hard from something that looked like torture," I remind him. "I got hard from something that turned me on. I'm not a masochist. I mean, I don't mind a bit of biting or a spank every now and then, but I'm not into full on S&M. Not that there's anything wrong or shameful about it," I rush to add. "Just not my thing. I'm more of an equal opportunist when it comes to power dynamics in sex. I prefer to switch things up. Sometimes I want to completely take charge and dominate, and other times I want to be used and just submit to someone else's power." Fucking hell, why am I still talking?

Tanner looks a little taken aback at the information I've just dumped on him, but then I see realization pass over his features and he nods, the corner of his mouth curving up in a smirk. "Right. I've got to say, though, even when you're submitting you're still pretty fucking dominant."

I offer a wry smile in return. "Likewise."

8

Tanner

I'm having trouble concentrating during RJ's BCN meeting. It's Wednesday afternoon and my ass is still tender from the pounding I got from Deacon on Monday night. That's not entirely unusual. A hard fuck means a sore ass; that's something I learned a long time ago and it doesn't bother me at all.

What *is* unusual is that I can't stop thinking about it. And by "it" I mean Monday night. Deacon's cock buried in my ass, pounding in hard while his fingers dug into my skin and his lips whispered filth in my ear. And that blow job... I don't think you could even call it a blow job, really. It was something else entirely. I mean, I fucked his *throat* for Christ's sake. I've never done something like that with a guy before. I'm not sure what possessed me to let Deacon go down on me in the first place—it just kind of happened and it felt too good to stop. And then when he was inside me and told me he wanted to finish me off with his mouth I couldn't agree fast enough.

Fuck, I can't believe I told him I wanted to cum on his face. What the hell was I thinking, admitting that to him?

Well, I guess that answer's obvious—I wasn't thinking. I was suffering from temporary insanity thanks to the pleasure he was wringing out of my body.

But if the insanity was only temporary, why the hell am I still thinking about it? And why do I still want to see that pretty face covered in my cream?

This definitely isn't supposed to happen. I'm not supposed to reminisce about the guys who fuck me. I never have before, that's for sure. All that has mattered in the past is how loose and…unwound I feel after a hard fuck. All my tension melts away and my mind seems clearer, and I can just feel normal for a while.

But I don't spend hours recollecting the details of those hook-ups. I don't get hard at the mere thought of a guy's cock. And I sure as hell don't zone out during meetings trying to work out if it might be possible to set up a repeat.

I *do not* repeat hook-ups. That's one of the rules my therapist helped me come up when I first started using this as a method of dealing with my anxiety. She wasn't exactly thrilled with the crutch I'd developed, but was still supportive and helped me to work out a system so that this weird coping mechanism I have doesn't turn into an unhealthy habit.

I've been incredibly diligent about keeping to those rules—only using sex when I absolutely need to, not combining alcohol and sex, not taking anyone home, et cetera…until Monday night when I broke one of the most important ones by hooking up with someone I already knew. Until then I'd been very strict about keeping it to random guys from bars or apps. I'm not sure why Deacon was the exception; I've met him a ton of times over the past couple months and never had an inkling of interest in him, although I've certainly sensed his interest in me. But when I saw him at that bar on Monday night—long before he spotted me—I knew it had to be him. No one else would do. And with the mood I was in, my rules didn't seem to matter all that much.

"So what do you think?" RJ asks, looking at me expectantly.

Shit, did I seriously miss his entire spiel?

I spare a quick glance at the other two occupants of the boardroom. Carter looks intrigued, while Marion looks concerned but not unhappy. Okay, so at least whatever RJ said has gone over okay. I decide to just bluff it out and hope I can trust he's not leading me astray. "I'm behind RJ on this one," I tell them.

They both nod. Carter looks like he's ready to get down to business, but Marion still looks hesitant.

"I'm not saying these aren't good ideas," she says. "But I can tell you right now it's going to be a hard sell getting Paxton Greenwood to agree to sharing the desk."

Wait. What?

"I've been through his contract," RJ says. "There's nothing in there about solo air time."

"It's called *The Pax Greenwood Hour,*" Marion says with a note of exasperation in her voice. "Not *The Pax Greenwood and Some Other Person We've Picked to Add More Diversity to Prime Time Hour.*"

Carter offers a wry smile. "She might have a point."

"And while you were going over his contract with a fine tooth comb, did you also happen to notice Pax doesn't have a non-compete?"

RJ arches a brow at her. "You seriously think he'd jump if he had to share time with a co-anchor?"

Marion shrugs. "I'm just pointing out the possibility."

I turn my attention to RJ. "Why don't we focus on some of your other ideas? We can talk about changes to Pax's show another time." I have no idea if RJ actually mentioned anything broader while I was zoned out, but he did tell me the other day that Pax Greenwood was just an example and that he had thoughts on changes that could be made in other areas of the network.

"Feel free to mess with daytime all you want," Marion says with a lazy shrug.

My lips curve into a wry smirk. There's no love lost between daytime and prime time at BCN, that's for sure. To be honest, we probably should have included Lee Kopek, the head of daytime programming, in this meeting, and if my head had been on straight over the past few days I probably would have insisted on it. But this is RJ's thing so if he wants to deal with Lee's bruised ego when he finds out he's been left out of this discussion, that's on him.

RJ frowns. "Sure, we could make tweaks to daytime, but that's not really where the audience is. I still think tightening up the prime time block is the best move for now."

"By pushing Paxton Greenwood out?"

"Jesus, Marion, no one's talking about pushing Greenwood out," RJ says, clearly growing frustrated.

I rub my hand over my forehead, tempted to just zone out again and daydream about Deacon's cock. But I've already let my dirty mind distract me for long enough this morning; it's time I actually contributed something valuable. "Everyone just take a breath. We are *not* pushing Pax out," I say firmly. "But RJ's right that prime time needs a bit of a shake up—and that's not a criticism of you, Marion."

She sighs and gives a nod of acknowledgement. "I guess we have gotten a little comfortable. What are you thinking?"

"I don't think a co-anchor would work for Paxton," I say. "He's been around way too long. He's too popular. Whoever we put with him would just be playing second fiddle. And if the co-anchor was female or a person of color it would have the exact opposite effect of what we're trying to achieve."

Marion flashes a dry smirk. "Or even better, a woman of color. There's nothing we love more than playing back-up dancer for an old white guy."

I let out a soft chuckle. "Watch it with the *old* talk. Pax is younger than I am."

"And prettier, but I wasn't going to point that out," she says with a wink.

"Not a co-anchor then," Carter pipes in, getting us back on track. "What have you got in mind?"

I shrug. "Give him some competition. Someone new in the nine o'clock slot—young, fresh, hungry. The way Paxton used to be before he got too comfortable."

Marion arches a brow at me. "You want to make him a warm-up act?"

"I wouldn't put it like that when you're selling it to him. We want the prime time block to be as tight as possible."

Carter leans forward, looking intrigued. "I'm not sure I understand how this would work—are you suggesting this person replace Lexi Haas?"

My eyes widen. "God no." Lexi Haas is the host of *Talking Points*, a nightly panel show that airs out of our Atlanta studio. She doesn't have the ratings that Pax Greenwood has, but she's still a big asset for the network. "I'm thinking we do something completely new. We could move *Talking Points* to ten, and move *Late News* to eleven." I'm totally making this up as I go—it's not even something I considered doing before now—but now that it's in my head, I can't help feeling like it's the right move.

Both Carter and Marion are looking a little shell-shocked now. RJ looks pleased, though. I wonder if this is something he's considered in his plan to shake up the network. It's certainly more dramatic than anything I'd anticipated before this meeting, but I think it could work.

"This would take a while to implement," Carter warns me. "And a significant investment. We could lose advertisers—they might not want to stick around at nine with a new face, or they might not want to follow Lexi to ten. Not to mention a new production team…"

I nod. "I'm well aware of what it takes to get a new show off the ground. This is just a suggestion I'm throwing out there for now, but if we go ahead with it you'll have what you need."

Marion raises a brow at me. "Not to be rude, but we all know Grimco isn't in a position to be throwing money around right now."

I smile at her. "We are definitely in a position to invest in our own news network. And we're working on consolidating and getting the profit margins back up. You don't have to worry about us."

"If we go ahead with it, will this be an Atlanta production?" Carter asks. "They won't like losing nine o'clock."

I sigh. "They won't, but if we go ahead I want it here."

Marion's brows shoot up. "You want us to do seven, eight, *and* nine?"

"You guys get to bed way too early," I tease, earning me an eye roll. "Look, if it's too much, we can move *BCN Tonight* to another studio—it can be aired just as easily out of DC or Atlanta as it is here. It'd be a case of figuring out what works best for Annie and David and their team." *BCN Tonight* is currently in the seven o'clock slot and generally considered the nightly kick-off for prime time news. The co-anchors, Annie Watts and David Dirdash have been working together for about fifteen years, even before they came to BCN, and they have a great partnership. That's probably another reason why a co-anchor on Pax's show wouldn't be the best idea—you can't recreate that kind of partnership by force.

"Well, you've definitely given us something to think about," Carter says, leaning back in his chair and sharing a glance with Marion. "I know you hate change, but—"

"I don't *hate* change. I'm just a believer in the phrase if it ain't broke don't fix it." She sighs. "But I guess things are a little broke at the moment, aren't they? I'm not all over every number and percentage and advertising dollar like you three are but I can read well enough to know audiences are down. Maybe they're done with TV news altogether. Or maybe changing things up a little might help. I guess we'll have to wait and see."

I offer a soft smile and then turn back to RJ. "Wasn't there something else you wanted to work on?"

He quirks a questioning brow at me. I'm sure he's noticed the difference in my levels of enthusiasm throughout the meeting, even if Marion and Carter haven't clocked it.

"Hard-hitting interviews," I prompt. "You mentioned we weren't doing enough of them."

He frowns in thought. "I mentioned a lot of the anchors seem to be pulling their punches a bit." He'd only mentioned Pax, but I'm not going to point that out. He *had* specified that was only an example.

Marion hits me with an accusatory look and I hold my hands up. "I know, I know. It's not as easy as it sounds when we're not giving you much slack."

"Or any," Marion grumbles, glancing away.

"It's a balancing act," I reason, hating how weak that sounds. It's pandering, pure and simple. "But I think there could be a way to add a bit more…*depth* without becoming attack dogs. Perhaps some more investigative specials, and feature interviews."

"You want this new ten o'clock show to be *60 Minutes?*" Marion asks, brows raised.

I let out a soft breath of laughter. "That wasn't exactly what I meant, but I guess it's somewhere to start."

We finally wrap up the meeting and agree to touch base in a few weeks to discuss everything in further detail and decide if this is a viable option for the network. And for Grimco Media. I'm sure the few million it will take to get a new program off the ground can be spared, but I also know that when RJ proposed some changes to BCN, he was anticipating making money, not spending it.

"Are you okay?" RJ asks me when we return to my office after the meeting.

I offer an expression of pure innocence. "Why wouldn't I be?"

He quirks a brow at me and I know I was right in guessing he would have noticed my strange behavior. "Well, you were completely out of it for the first half of the meeting, then completely in charge for the rest of it."

"I'm sorry for stepping on your toes…"

He waves a dismissive hand. "I don't care about that. It's a good idea. Bit of a gamble, but it'll definitely shake things up."

I nod. "BCN's given us a solid return for two decades, and it's been a while since we invested a significant amount back into the network. We've been relying on advertisers far too much." At RJ's skeptical look, I add, "I'm not saying we should roll back advertising—I don't think that's even possible at this point—but I think we could be doing more to support the network. This will be a good start."

"As long as we don't stretch ourselves too thin…"

"There are always up and down times in any business, RJ. The bigger the business, the better and worse those times seem. We'll be fine."

He sighs and gives a little shrug, no doubt deciding to leave this discussion for another time. "I haven't forgotten, you know," he says as he heads out of my office door.

"Forgotten what?" I ask, playing dumb.

RJ smirks at me. "About you daydreaming during the meeting. Or about you changing the topic when I asked about it."

"Don't you have work to do?"

He tosses back his head, letting out a hearty laugh. "Well, now I'm really intrigued. But yeah, I do have work to do—I need to go tell the finance team to find a few spare million in the budget they just spent two months putting together."

I wince, knowing it's going to cause more work for everyone, but this is what we have a finance team for, after all. "Make sure they know it's a simulation—we're not committing to anything just yet. And we don't know what our outlay will be."

"You know, we wouldn't be pinching pennies if—"

"Please don't finish that sentence," I tell him, rubbing my forehead in frustration. "It's not an option."

"I'm just pointing out that it'd be nice to have an extra two hundred million to play around with."

I'm more than aware of this fact, but it doesn't change my answer. I'm not selling Leah's company. I hit RJ with a hard stare and we lock eyes for a long moment before he finally backs down, sighing in defeat.

"I'll go talk to finance," he mutters.

"Thank you."

Once I'm alone in my office, I remove my suit jacket and hang it on the back of my desk chair. Then I roll back my sleeves and pour myself a scotch, taking it over to the sofa by the window.

I gaze out over Fifth Avenue as I mull everything over. I

don't like how distracted I was today—RJ was right to call me out on it. But it seems I managed to salvage the situation well enough, even if I have committed Grimco Media to potentially throwing millions it doesn't really have to spare right now at a venture that might not work. But it *might* work. And I have faith that Grimco will turn back around soon enough. I'm not usually a huge risk-taker when it comes to business interests, but many of my biggest wins have come from gambles with chancy odds. I guess we'll just have to see how it pans out.

And as for the other thing…well, I'm sure once the lingering physical effects of Monday night are gone, the daydream-inducing memories will disappear too…

I hope…

9

Deacon

I've been going insane for a week. Ever since last Monday when I brought Tanner Grimsay back to my place, I keep expecting to wake up *Wizard of Oz* style and discover the whole thing was a dream. A really, really, *really* good dream.

Because that's the thing that makes the most sense, right? Definitely more sense than the billionaire silver fox father of one of my kindergarteners propositioning me at a gay bar and letting me fuck him so hard he almost broke through my bedroom wall.

I haven't seen him since he left my place last Monday night. Every day since then, my gut twists and tangles with nerves as we get closer to pick up time as I wait to see if Tanner will show up to collect his daughter; but every day Isobel's been collected from school by her nanny, Kit. And I'm left torn between feelings of immense relief, and bitter disappointment.

It's not all that unusual for Kit to take Izzy home. In fact, it's probably the more common scenario—from what I can gather, Tanner's a pretty involved parent but he does have a billion-dollar business to run. Of course, that doesn't stop me from reading *way* too much into his absence over the past week.

I just can't help worrying that he's too embarrassed to face me or something like that. Not that he has anything to be embarrassed about—*believe me*—but I can imagine a guy like Tanner having a total freak out after what happened. He said he'd done it before, but what does that matter? That doesn't mean he's totally comfortable with it. And even if he is, I bet it's never been with one of his kids' teachers.

Fuck, I'm such an idiot. Why the hell do I let my dick make decisions for me? Just because Tanner's sexy, and smells amazing, and has gorgeous eyes, and ran his hand up my leg, and begged me to fuck him... okay, now I remember why.

But it was a mistake. Definitely a mistake. And clearly he thinks so too if he's been avoiding me all week.

Maybe avoiding me.

Fuck, I'm confused. Yet another reason why sleeping with a student's father was an incredibly dumb move.

School let out a while ago, but I have rugby practice tonight so there wasn't much point going home. Sully's office building is on the way to the park so I'm planning to meet him there in about half an hour so we can head down together. Knowing Sullivan, he'll be caught up with something or other and I'll be waiting in the lobby for at least fifteen minutes, so I don't feel the need to rush too much. I've been taking the opportunity to set up some projects for the kids tomorrow. We're doing the letter E this week, so they're going to be making some egg people. Should be fun, even if I have to listen to Daniel Kramer complain the whole time that egg people don't actually exist. I give a wry shake of my head as I finish organizing all the stuff we'll need. There's an obnoxious pain in the ass in every class; it's kind of a requirement. I'm pretty sure Danny will grow up to invent whatever saves us from global warming—or maybe invent an AI program that destroys the human race—so at least I can claim to have nurtured a bright young mind.

Once I've finished what I need to in the classroom, I grab my sports bag with my rugby gear and head to the staff bathroom so I can change.

Remembering I left my phone in my desk drawer, I head back to my classroom after I've changed, stopping in my tracks when I catch sight of a familiar, incredibly sexy figure standing in the hallway just outside my classroom door. He looks fucking incredible as always in his tailored navy suit, and I take a moment to greedily soak in the sight while his attention is diverted with something on his phone.

"Uh...hi." Wow, way to be original, Deacon.

Tanner snaps his head up at the sound of my voice and puts his phone away in the inside pocket of his suit. Then he takes a moment to scan his eyes over me, no doubt taking note of my gym shorts and hoodie. "You look very...casual today."

I offer a wry smirk. "I have rugby tonight."

His brows shoot into his hairline. "Rugby? With all the mud and tackling and no padding or helmets?"

"Yep, that's the one. I'm on a sevens team here in the city. We've got a tournament coming up so lots of practice at the moment."

He lets out a soft chuckle. "I'm not even going to pretend I understood any of that."

I nod. "Fair."

Fuck, I really want to know what he's doing here, but I'm too chicken to ask. Does this mean he's *not* freaking out about last week? Or maybe he wants to talk about Izzy and is mature enough to put what happened to the side. Yeah, that makes sense. "So what's up?" I ask, heading into the classroom and making a beeline for my desk.

"Ah…well, I came to get Izzy but I guess I got my days mixed up."

I turn back and arch an eyebrow at him, smirking when I see a faint blush touch his cheeks. *Liar, liar.* "Yeah, Kit picked her up. Almost two hours ago."

He offers a bashful smile. "Okay, fine. That's not why I'm here." He steps completely into the room and shuts the door behind him. Looking me squarely in the eye, he says, "I want a repeat."

I swallow hard, a shiver running through my body at the mere sound of the word 'repeat'. And fucking hell, those eyes. How are they so freakin' blue? And so intense? My cock is already responding to the power of that gaze; I really need it to just chill and not take over my brain again like last time. "You want to have sex again?"

"I want you to fuck me again," he says, making it clear he sees a distinct difference between his regular sex life and the anal sex he only seeks out when he needs to relieve a ton of tension.

Despite the action in my pants, a wave of doubt washes over me and I frown in hesitation. I think maybe if he hadn't provided that emphatic clarification, I'd have him up against my classroom door right now—screw the consequences. But now all I can think is that he doesn't consider sex with me—or any man for that matter—to be real sex. Just something he does when he needs stress relief, because apparently toys don't get the job done.

Maybe I'm reading too much into it—Skyler would definitely tell me I am—but I just can't shake that feeling of unease. And it's not only his comment just now; there were plenty of red flags last week as well. There's nothing wrong with Tanner's attitude, or his behavior; I'm certainly not going to judge him if this is what he needs. But I don't think I can be that person for him. I don't do casual flings at the best of times, and this is most definitely not that.

And then there's that whole other issue regarding me being his daughter's teacher. Let's not forget that.

I seriously deserve a medal for what I'm about to do. Maybe just one more time would be okay…? Fucking hell. I manage to shake the thought out of my mind, knowing that's just my dick trying to get its own way.

Before I lose all my willpower and give into the temptation laid out before me, I shake my head. "I really don't think it's a good idea."

He quirks an eyebrow at me. "Because of the rules?"

I shrug. "It's just not a good idea."

"It was a pretty good idea last week…"

I offer a wry smirk. "No it wasn't. I just wasn't thinking with the right brain."

He lets out a soft chuckle. "I guess you have a point there." He lifts a hand to rub over his forehead. "To be honest, this isn't something I usually do. Ask for a repeat, I mean. But then I don't usually hook up with people I know, so…"

"So why are you here then?" I ask curiously.

He shrugs. "Because I want your cock in me again. I kind of figured if I didn't see you for a while that urge to be fucked would disappear like it usually does. But it's been a week and I still really fucking need a dick in my ass."

Wow. Okay. Not going to lie, it's kind of weird having a conversation like this in a room with *a* giant *The Very Hungry Caterpillar* poster on the wall. Despite the less than sexy ambiance, hearing those words fall from his lips cause my cock to throb painfully. But my brain can't help catching on the words "a dick"…not necessarily *my* dick.

"So usually you don't need this whole stress relief thing that often?" I can't deny I'm incredibly curious about how this whole thing works. I mean, I can understand why the endorphins from sex would be great for getting rid of tension, but how did he even figure out anal is what worked for him if he's otherwise straight?

"Generally, it's at least a month or two between…" he trails off with a shrug. "It's really just a last resort option. I have some…issues, and I can usually cope pretty well with a bunch of other methods. But there are times when I just feel like I'm suffocating and everything is coming down on me, and none of my usual things are working. I need help letting it all go."

Okay, so a little more than run of the mill stress then. Although I imagine the pressures of a job like Tanner's probably don't help when he's going through periods like the ones he's describing.

"But you're saying last week didn't work?" I frown in concern. I'm not thrilled at the idea of being nothing but a coping mechanism, but I like the idea of him failing to get any relief from our hook-up even less. "You still feel like you're…suffocating?"

He shakes his head, suddenly looking a little lost. "No, it worked. This week's been great. There have been the usual stressors, obviously, but it's not like it was last Monday. And that's the really messed up part—I've never needed to be fucked at a time when I wasn't on the verge of a breakdown. Until this week."

Well, that's interesting. I think I'd be a little more excited if he weren't using words like "messed up" and wearing an expression that makes it clear how uncomfortable he is with this new turn of events. He might be here begging for me to fuck him again, but it seems that's only because it's what his body is telling him he needs. Not because his head or heart want it.

So I'm going to refer to my earlier objection. I'm sure Skyler would love a job as a walking sex toy, but it's not for me. It might sound crazy, but I need my partners to actually want more from me than my cock.

"I still don't think it's a good idea," I say gently. I hate that I have to deny him after what I've just learned, but it's not as though I'm the only guy in New York. I'm sure he'll find someone more than willing to fuck him in a matter of minutes on an app or at a bar.

My gut twists at the thought of someone else getting inside that incredible ass, but I know I can't have it both ways. I'm never going to have Tanner the way I want him, so I need to be okay with him being with other guys.

He lets out a sigh of obvious disappointment. I'm about to assure him that he'll find a replacement dick in no time, when he blurts out, "Is it because I made you wear a condom?"

My eyes widen, taken aback by the question. "What? You seriously think I'm that much of a dick?"

He lets out a breath of wry laughter. "No. You're the complete opposite, actually. But I guess you don't usually use condoms? And you seemed kind of disappointed not to…you know…"

"Come inside you?" I finish for him. I spare a glance for the drawings of rainbows pinned to the wall above Tanner's head, still finding it really strange to be having this conversation here. "I wasn't disappointed. I don't usually wear condoms because I'm on PrEP—HIV prevention. And I get tested regularly. But I promise, that's not even remotely a factor. I have this thing where I like to respect my partners' boundaries," I tell him with a quirk of my lips. "Anyone who gives you shit about suiting up doesn't deserve to get inside that incredible ass."

His lips curve up in return. "And yet…"

"Tanner, look where we're standing." I wave my arm around to gesture at my classroom. "This is your daughter's classroom. I'm her teacher. Even just having this conversation is so inappropriate. We shouldn't have gone there last week—"

"But we did," he interrupts. "The horse has bolted on the inappropriate factor, Deacon. And I really can't help feeling as though you're using that as a convenient excuse."

Damn it. He's too fucking smart. I avert my eyes from his shrewd, piercing gaze for a moment before glancing back. I feel as though the whole of what I'm feeling is a little too complicated to go into right now, and it'll put a ton of pressure on him that he doesn't need. So I opt for a half-truth instead. "Last Monday was a bit out of character for me," I explain. "I don't really do casual hook-ups. I'm more of a relationship kind of guy."

He gives a wry shake of his head. "Of course you are. But you made an exception last week?" he adds, one eyebrow raised.

"Like I said, I let my dick do the thinking last week."

At my words, his eyes stray to my crotch, where my cock really hasn't gotten the message that it won't be getting any action.

His gaze is full of hunger and need, and it makes me harden further, even as my brain acknowledges another sign pointing to the fact that he only wants me for my dick. The sight of the very obvious tent at the front of his suit pants isn't exactly helping the situation. I can still remember how incredible it felt taking him down my throat. And the taste of his cum…

Fucking hell, get a grip, Deacon!

"You've really got to stop staring at my cock like that, man," I tell him, shifting around awkwardly as my dick throbs under his scrutiny.

"I can't help it. It's like it's got a tractor beam pulling my eyes in. And it doesn't seem to mind me looking."

"Because you're staring at it like it's a tasty dessert and you can't wait to get your mouth on it and savor every delicious morsel." I smirk at him. "It really likes being...savored."

Tanner blinks rapidly and finally tears his gaze from my crotch, his cheeks tinted red. "I had something else in mind," he says awkwardly.

"I kind of figured." Okay, maybe it was a dick move to taunt him about going down on me, but it's not as though I would have asked him to do it.

"There's really no wriggle room on this?" he asks hopefully, arching an eyebrow at my erection in what I'm guessing is an effort to point out the very obvious fact that I'm attracted to him.

I sigh, running a hand through my hair. "Tanner, there are hundreds—probably thousands—of guys in this city who'd be more than happy to give you exactly what you want. Why do you need me?"

He shrugs. "I have no idea." *Ouch.* "When I realized this...whatever it is wasn't going away like I thought it would, I had a scroll through one of my apps but it was all...meh. Usually when I'm in that mood I don't give a shit who the guy is, as long as they're a top with a big dick who likes to fuck hard." Again...*ouch.* "But I just couldn't stomach doing anything with any of those guys. I need a dick in me, but for whatever reason, it has to be yours."

"Um...wow...I'm flattered, I guess," I say dryly, not sure how the fuck someones's supposed to respond to a declaration like that.

Tanner's gaze turns inward for a moment, then he gives a shake of his head. "Fuck, I'm sorry. I just realized how crass that all sounded." He lets out a heavy sigh. "Not exactly the best way to win someone over…"

I offer a wry smile. "Yeah, probably not. But you get points for honesty—I'll always take that over charm and manipulation."

He grins. "You'd get on well with my son. Honest to a fault—and I mean that literally."

Ah fuck, I wish his face didn't glow like that talking about his son. One of the first things that drew me to him —apart from the incredible smile, gorgeous eyes, and just all-around sexiness—was his amazing relationship with Izzy. I really don't need any more 'great dad' hotness hampering my ability to walk away from this situation.

"I'm sorry I can't give you what you want, Tanner."

"Need," he corrects in a soft voice.

I nod. Of course. He doesn't actually *want* me to fuck him, it's just something his body needs. Apparently. Gah. Yes, definitely better to put a stop to this before I go crazy.

I'm about to send him away when the tight reins I've held on my own desire finally snap and I find myself saying, "'I can give you something else, though."

His eyes widen in question. "Something else?"

I stride across the carpet, removing the distance between us until I'm right in front him, crowding him against the classroom door. "My mouth," I say, because apparently I'm a masochist after all. "I can give you that."

So there's no confusion over exactly what I'm offering, I reach down between us and palm the front of his pants, over his stiff dick.

Tanner lets out a soft groan at my touch, his eyes falling closed. "Like last week?"

"Like last week."

His eyes open and he hits me with a piercing look. "But you won't fuck me?"

"Just my mouth, Tanner. Take it or leave it."

I give his dick a firm squeeze through the fabric of his pants and he lets out a groan. "Fuck yeah, suck me. Want to come on your face."

He looks adorably shocked to have admitted that desire out loud, and I can't help smiling. I so badly want to tell him to go for it, but I've just remembered I'm supposed to be meeting up with Sullivan in about ten minutes. Not the ideal time for a facial.

"Maybe when I'm not at my place of work," I say wryly. Fuck, I can't even believe those words have left my mouth. I'm actually going to do this? Here? In my classroom?

Part of my brain is screaming that there's still time to turn back, and that if I really want to do this I can wait for a more opportune time and place, but it's being completely drowned out by the desire and anticipation curling inside me. My mouth is watering at the mere prospect of swallowing Tanner's dick again, and I haven't even taken it out of his pants.

"Did you want to go somewhere more…suitable?" he asks.

"We have about five minutes before I have to leave for practice," I tell him. "So you're going to fuck my throat right here and pray no one catches us."

"I see bossy Deacon's back," he says with a smirk as he hastily unfastens his fly and shoves his suit pants and boxer briefs down his thighs.

And that's how I end up on my knees on my classroom floor with Tanner Grimsay's cock down my throat.

10

Tanner

I still don't know how that all happened. One moment I'm convincing myself that whatever lingering thoughts and urges I still had regarding last Monday night would simply go away in time, and the next I'm tracking Deacon down at school, using some lame excuse about a mix-up with Izzy's schedule to explain my presence—like I didn't know full well that school had let out two hours earlier and she was well and truly home safe with Kit. And because that's not already mortifying enough, I just had to go and beg him to fuck me. Again. And watch him choke on my dick. Again. And ramble about coming on his face. Again.

Fucking hell.

The second I get home I head straight for my bedroom. I need to check on Izzy, but not just yet. I'm way too wound up right now; I need to calm down first so I can give her my full attention.

When I get to my bedroom, I start stripping out my suit, layers of designer businesswear falling to the carpet like a breadcrumb trail leading toward the ensuite. I wouldn't normally leave my clothes strewn all over the floor like this, but right now I just need to get into the shower and feel the hot water on my skin. And the mess will give me something to focus on later.

I get the shower running to the right temperature and step inside, letting out a sigh as the sharp pressure from the waterfall shower head causes the water to prickle all over my skin like hot little pin pricks.

I stand there for a moment as the water sprays down on me, relieving a little of the tension that's been building since I awkwardly tucked my cock back in my pants and slipped out of the classroom about thirty seconds after coming spectacularly down Deacon's throat.

Why the fuck did I go there? Why did I let him suck me? Did he expect me to help him get off as well? Does he think I'm a selfish dick now? Fuck, I *am* a selfish dick. He said he didn't want anything casual and I talked him into doing something anyway. And why the fuck do I keep asking to come on his face?

Fucking hell.

I let out a groan, my hand coming up to wipe my wet hair back from my face. So much for relieving the tension.

I shift sideways and rest my head against the tiles, closing my eyes as I breathe in some cooler air. The prickles of hot water pierce my back, and it feels nice; but I know I can't shut out reality forever.

I open my eyes and frown down at the thick erection standing up between my thighs. I don't understand why this keeps happening. I've never gotten hard in the aftermath of a hook-up before. Or in the lead-up to one. During one, sure—my anus is ridiculously sensitive so it really doesn't take much.

But I've been springing boners left and right whenever I've so much as thought about Deacon's dick over the past week. It's been strange, but I can understand it—at least to an extent. As I told Deacon, I have no clue why I'm reacting like this to him, but I do know his cock is what I want from him. His cock is what brings me pleasure and peace and relief, so it makes a weird kind of sense that I'd be aroused by the thought of it, even if that's never happened before.

But all I got to see of Deacon's dick tonight was the tent in the front of his athletic shorts, and even that was enough to turn me on.

Bur now I can't stop replaying the vision of him on his knees, lips stretched wide around my cock as I fucked his throat. He did the exact same thing last week, but for some reason the image is more potent this time. And not just because it's fresh in my head. Last week it was more of a sideline act, because I was already so riled up from the main attraction that it all just kind of happened in a rush. The fact that it occurred has crossed my mind on several occasions, but the memory hasn't induced angry, throbbing hard-ons like the one I'm experiencing now.

I let out another groan of frustration and reach down to take my dick in hand, giving it a little relief.

Fuck, I wish I could understand why I even agreed to let him go down on me in the first place. My mind wouldn't be such a fucking mess if I'd just said no. To be fair, he had his hand on my dick, and there aren't all that many guys who would turn down that kind of offer. But that wasn't why I tracked him down tonight; and when he told me that was all he could offer, I should have walked away.

I don't need blow jobs from men. I hook up with men because I need to be fucked. I only do it when I absolutely need to, and I don't give the guy a second thought afterward. The only thing I want from men is their cock. No fingering, no hand jobs, and definitely no blow jobs. If I sound like an asshole, so be it. They all know what the score is and I've never had any complaints so far.

Except for Deacon.

Why the hell is Deacon the one exception to all those rules? I've let him get so far beyond my comfort zone I'm not sure it even exists anymore.

The thought would usually send me into a spiral, but it doesn't—all I seem to be able to fixate on is my disappointment that now that I've let him in, he doesn't seem to want to be there.

I still don't understand any of it. I don't get why I can't stop thinking about him fucking me. Or sucking me. Or why I've sprung enough spontaneous erections in the past week to rival a fourteen-year-old. Or why Deacon seems more than happy to go down on me but won't give me his cock. None of it makes any fucking sense, and all I'm doing is twisting myself into tighter and tighter knots as I try to puzzle it out.

I straighten up, standing back under the water, and try to clear my mind using one of the boxing up thoughts exercises my therapist makes me practice. It's not an exercise I'm great with at the best of times, and having a throbbing erection incessantly reminding you of the thoughts you're trying to box up isn't exactly helpful.

I give up the exercise as a lost cause for now and grab my dick again. Unsurprisingly, it's the image of Deacon on his knees that comes to me as I stroke myself. I do my best to block out the confusion swirling in my head and just enjoy it.

Despite the strangeness of the situation, I think one thing is pretty obvious: I'm not done with Deacon. Not by a long way. I don't understand why, I just know I need a hell of a lot more from him than what I've gotten so far.

I can't give him the kind of commitment he wants.

Even if I were interested in dating a man, I'm not going anywhere near the word "relationship" after my disastrous experience with Natalia. But maybe I can convince him to bend his rules for a little while—just until I get past this fixation, or whatever it is.

11

Deacon

"What do you mean you sucked him off in your classroom?" Skyler hisses at me as we claim a tall table at Doyle's.

"I don't think I stuttered," I mumble.

"You couldn't have told me this yesterday?"

I arch a brow at him. "What? When we were surrounded by the entire team? They already know way too much about my BJ skills thanks to you."

He lets out a soft laugh, no doubt recalling his behavior last week. Then he fixes wide eyes on me. "It was seriously in your *classroom?*"

I sigh in exasperation. "Yes."

Skyler's lips quirk. "How very me of you. I'm impressed."

I roll my eyes. "I hope you're not expecting me to take that as a compliment."

"I'm offended you don't find that comparison complimentary," he says with an exaggerated pout. Jackson arrives at our table and Skyler turns cow eyes on him. "Deacon's being mean to me."

For once, Jackson doesn't pander to Skyler's whims, instead slumping down on a stool and letting out a heavy sigh, as though the weight of the world is on him.

Skyler instantly drops the kicked puppy act, his posture stiffening as he fixes an anxious gaze on Jax. "What's wrong?"

"The roof of the shop got damaged in the storm last night. Insurance isn't going to cover it, so we're out thousands—probably tens of thousands—from all the lost stock. And we've got no clue when we'll be able to re-open."

"What about the garage?" I ask, a wave of concern for both Jackson and Drew hitting me at full force.

He sighs. "Fine, thank fuck. We closed today and got an inspection, but it's all clear. Just the shop."

"You should have texted me," Skyler says, an angry scowl crossing his face, which I'm sure is more out of concern for Jax than any actual anger on his part.

"You had class," Jackson points out.

"Screw class, you're more important," Skyler huffs.

Jackson sends him a hard look. "I'll remind you of that when you fail the Bar." He sighs. "Besides, Drew and Tiff were there. We had it covered."

Skyler still looks put out, the way he always does when he feels like he's been overlooked—he's so fucking needy, especially when it comes to Jackson—but after another moment of pouting, he shrugs and lets it go.

I spot Drew moving through the crowd towards our table and pull another stool over from the table next to us so he can join us.

"I guess you told them?" Drew asks Jackson, looking just as wrung out from the day's events.

"You should have told me *hours* ago," Skyler grumbles.

I roll my eyes to the ceiling. So much for letting it go.

In typical Jackson fashion, he shifts closer to Sky and gives him a reassuring pat on the arm. "I promise the next time my business is ruined, you'll be the first person I call."

"That's all I ask," Skyler says.

I share an exasperated glance with Drew before getting back to the issue at hand. "You're really out thousands?"

He winces. "We haven't done a full inventory of the lost stock yet, but it'll be at least twenty grand."

"*Shiiitt.*" From what I understand, Jackson and Drew's business has been quite successful , but it's still a relatively new business and with all the operational costs plus their own salaries and those of the people who work for them, I can't imagine plucking twenty grand out of the budget is going to be easy.

I exchange a glance with Skyler. "You know, if you need money…" I venture, thinking of the multiple billionaires on our rugby team, any one of whom would be more than happy to give these guys the money they need to get the retail part of their business back up and running.

Drew gives a firm shake of his head. "No."

"Any one of them would be happy to help," I reason, Skyler nodding along with me.

"I'm not borrowing money from any of your billionaire friends," Drew says, his voice tight.

I glance at Jackson to see what he thinks about this, but he just shrugs. "We'll find another way." Then he fixes Skyler and me with a hard look of warning. "And you two better not tell them about any of this. You know what they're like—they'll probably pass around an envelope and fill it with ten grand bills or whatever."

"I don't think they make those," Skyler says, brow furrowed.

"It's okay, we won't tell them," I assure them. "But I still think you're missing an opportunity."

"I'm not taking money from billionaires," Drew repeats stubbornly, and I have to stop myself from rolling my eyes.

I guess I shouldn't be surprised he'd be so reluctant. He doesn't know the guys on our team as well as the rest of us do, having only met them a handful of times. And I have no doubt he's orchestrated it that way. I love the guy, but when it comes to money and class he's a fucking snob—in the sense that he instinctively assumes everyone who has money is a total asshole.

Drew definitely wouldn't be having any trouble staying away from Tanner Grimsay, that's for sure. If he were into guys, I mean.

Fuck, I really need to stop thinking about Tanner before I zone out of the conversation and begin a mental replay of our encounter at school yesterday.

"Can we just not talk about it for a while," Drew grumbles, wiping his hands over his face. "Come on…someone distract me."

"Deacon sucked off his silver fox in his classroom yesterday," Skyler blurts out. I send him a hard glare and he just shrugs. "What? You didn't tell me it was a secret."

So much for not thinking about Tanner.

Drew's brows are practically in his hairline. "Well, that did the trick."

"Seriously? In your *classroom?*" Jackson asks, face screwed up in obvious disbelief.

"Oh, and you've never hooked up at work before?" Skyler says.

"I don't work with kids."

"The kids weren't there," I clarify. Because *that* makes it okay.

"Yeah, I kind of figured that, given the lack of an arrest warrant out for you," Jackson says dryly. "But, still… for *you* to do something like that…" He shakes his head, looking completely bewildered. "You must really like this guy."

I let out a heavy sigh and rake a hand through my hair. "It's…complicated."

"In what way?" Drew asks curiously.

"Let's just say he's only interested in casual sex. And I need more…so I made it clear to him that we won't be hooking up again."

"Was this before or after you gagged on his dick in the same classroom where you teach his five-year-old daughter?" Skyler drawls.

I feel my face flaming, and not just at the reminder of what I did and where I did it. I screwed up, big time. I told Tanner over and over that it wasn't a good idea for anything more to happen between us, and that I wasn't interested in anything casual. And then I got on my knees and let him fuck my throat. No mixed messages there at all…

***

BY THE FOLLOWING night I'm starting to feel a bit better about the situation with Tanner. He hasn't contacted me since Monday, and he hasn't shown up unexpectedly at school again. So maybe he took my rejection to heart after all, even if I did contradict myself about five minutes later. Or maybe the blow job was enough to slake that lingering need, or whatever it was, that he said had been driving him crazy throughout the week.

Whatever the reason, I'm relieved that this little interlude seems to be over. It's for the best, even if not getting inside Tanner again when I had the chance is likely to go down as Life Regret #1.

I shake thoughts of Tanner from my head as I return to my apartment, a six-pack of beer in hand. I'm trying to cheer Drew up after yesterday's disaster, so tonight it's beer, Marvel movies, and Drew's tuna pasta, which I will dutifully eat even though I'm really not a fish person.

"Good, because I wouldn't want to lie to Deacon," I hear Drew saying as I swing the door of our apartment open.

I blink in surprise when I see my brother of all people standing there. Since when do Sullivan and Drew conspire about things?

"Lie to Deacon about what?"

Drew looks a little startled to find me standing in the doorway. Sully, meanwhile, spins around to face me, a broad grin on his face. "I found a solution. Drew here's coming to the wedding with me. He's going to pretend to be Andrew."

"I *am* Andrew," Drew says with a shake of his head.

Sully turns back to smile at Drew. "That's an excellent start."

Jesus Christ, I feel like I've been zapped into a Shakespearean comedy all of a sudden. When my brother admitted to me earlier in the week that he still hasn't told the rest of our family about his break-up with his asshole ex, I was curious to see how the situation would play out once we actually got to our sister's wedding and he was found out. I was definitely not expecting he'd resort to roping in my roommate as a rent-a-date.

"Alright, I'd better go. Deac, your jersey's over there," Sully says, nodding at the arm of the sofa, where my training jersey is neatly folded. He must have picked it up by accident on Monday.

"Thanks for bringing it back."

He shrugs and strides for the door. "Drew, I'll come by the garage tomorrow and we'll go suit shopping. Four pm."

"I don't need a new suit," Drew mutters.

But, of course, Sully just ignores him. "Four pm," he reiterates as he slips out the door.

I arch an eyebrow at Drew. "Seriously?"

He lets out a dramatic sigh. "It's for the shop. He's giving me twenty-five grand just to go to this wedding with him."

A slow whistle passes my lips. "Twenty-five grand? Dude, you got screwed. You know you could have gotten way more, right?"

Drew scowls. "I don't want way more. I just want what we need to fix the shop."

"What happened to not taking money from billionaires?" I can't help asking, one eyebrow raised.

Drew winces as though I've just punched him. "I know, I'm a total fucking sell-out. But at least this way I'm earning the cash instead of taking a hand out."

"So is Jax pimping himself out as well?" I ask with a smirk.

He rolls his eyes. "Hilarious."

12

Tanner

I can tell by Joseph's face when I arrive at my office on Thursday morning that I'm not going to like what he has to tell me.

"Spit it out," I tell him when he hesitates for a beat too long.

He winces and offers an apologetic look. "She's waiting on the phone for you."

There's only one "she" who would prompt Joseph to behave like this. My insides curl with dread and my grip on my briefcase becomes tight enough to turn my knuckles white. "Thanks," I say stiffly, before striding into my office.

This is really not what I want to be dealing with first thing in the morning; but at the same time, at least I haven't had a whole heap of work stress eating away at me all day. Things have been pretty good all week, actually. And by 'good' I mean, the usual levels of stress and anxiety I live with on a daily basis without too much extra shit piled on top of it. Stapleton and Steele still won't take no for an answer, of course, but if they want to waste their time barking up the wrong tree, that's their business. And the finance team was able to do some magic with the budget, so we can go into our next meeting with BCN on more solid footing, which is a huge load off.

To be honest, the thing that's been keeping me awake this week is the situation with Deacon. Unlike last week when it completely took over my life, I've somehow managed to switch it all off when I'm at work. But when I'm not at work? Jesus Christ… Ever since that blow job on Monday, I've been like a pendulum constantly swinging from anxiety and confusion to desperate horniness. The horniness just makes me more confused, which makes me more anxious; and I always want to fuck when my anxiety spikes, so that brings me back to horny. It's a vicious fucking circle. My brain's a mess, and I feel like my dick's permanently hard, and I've been using my dildos so much I ran out of lube last night and had to run out to the kitchen and grab a bottle of olive oil. That's how hard up I was. I put olive oil in my ass.

Which reminds me—I need to buy more olive oil. Because there's no way that bottle's going back to the kitchen.

But my anxiety over Deacon is a blip on the radar compared to what's waiting for me in my office. Fuck, I'd give anything to hear his voice on the phone instead of hers. He has a really nice voice. Even when he's using it to whisper filthy shit in my ear.

I let out a fortifying breath and pick up my office phone. "I'm busy, Natalia. What do you want?"

I know what she wants, of course, but I have to do this dance every few months anyway.

Through the glass wall of my office, I see Joseph put down the extension just as Natalia answers. "Aren't I allowed to call my husband to say hello?"

My jaw tightens in frustration and I have to close my

eyes and draw in a deep breath before I can respond. "*Ex-husband.*"

"That's not what my lawyers say," she chirps.

"What do you want, Natalia?" I repeat, not willing to let myself take the bait. I want her to just fucking ask for more money so I can agree and be done with her for a few months.

"How's Isobel?"

Fuck, was that a threat in her voice? I grab the edge of my desk in a white-knuckled grip, my heart thudding as a million worst-case scenarios race through my head at warp speed. Screwing my eyes shut, I take a breath and force myself to chill. It was just a question. She wasn't implying anything; not yet, anyway. "She's good," I say, proud of myself for the steadiness of my voice. "Likes school, likes her teacher." An image of Deacon pops into my head, but I shove it away; I really don't need to be daydreaming while I'm trying to hold up my end of this conversation.

"That's good," she says, but the disinterest couldn't be more obvious.

"Look, Natalia, I'm really busy, so…"

She cuts me off with a dramatic sigh. "You know I hate doing this, but things are expensive here…"

"In Bermuda? Yeah, no shit." She's not going to just hop off to somewhere more affordable, however. Not when she still has access to the Bank of Grimsay, albeit very limited and heavily-controlled access.

"You know, Tanner, you could make this so much easier on both of us if you just—"

"I tried to make this easy on us," I say, cutting her off. "You're the one who wouldn't accept my offer."

"Because it didn't give me what I deserve," she bites back. AKA twenty-five per cent of Grimco Media, as laid out in our pre-nup. The pre-nup that's only supposed to take effect after ten years of marriage, which we haven't got to yet.

I manage to hold in a groan, rubbing the tension from my forehead with the pads of my fingers. "I'll pay your credit card bill and put fifty grand in your cash account." I don't even want to think about how much she's racked up on that card. I had the company lower the limit to two-hundred grand when we first separated; that seemed like a pittance compared to the unlimited one she used to carry, and I guess at the time I wanted to make sure she'd have access to money if it took her a bit to get back into work and earning steadily for herself. I very naively assumed that would be something she'd want for herself; it didn't cross my mind that three years later we'd have gotten to the point of threats and intimidation just so she could continue living off my money while she does god knows what in the Caribbean, holding the gun that is Izzy's custody to my head while she waits out the ten-year clause in our pre-nup.

"*Fifty?* That'll last me a week here!" she exclaims.

"Then move somewhere more affordable," I say tightly, losing my tenuous hold on my patience. "Or get a job. You have a college degree, Natalia, maybe it's time you actually used it. I'm not filling your account with cash just so you can spend it all on booze and coke."

She lets out a derisive snort. "God, I forgot how fucking uptight you are. Maybe you should go get laid— that's what you do, right?"

"I'm done with this conversation," I grate out. "Good-bye, Natalia."

Before she can respond, I slam the handset down to end the call. I steady myself on the edge of my desk, gripping tight with both hands, as I draw in some deep, slow breaths.

I know I can't let this go on forever, with Natalia looming as a specter that could pop out at any moment, but I can't see any way through the situation right now. If I could give her anything else besides the Grimco shares to agree to a quiet divorce settlement, I would. But she doesn't want anything else. And I just can't take that risk of her having such a sizable interest in the corporation. I'm giving her the benefit of the doubt and assuming she's only after the money and influence the stake comes with, which would be bad enough, but with thirty per cent of Grimco's stock in public hands, Natalia getting control of twenty-five opens the risk of a hostile takeover.

***

"GOD, Dad, you need to stop giving that bitch money," my daughter Piper says with an exasperated sigh after I've told her about my call from Natalia.

We've just finished eating and Kit has taken Izzy off for her bath, so it's the first chance I've had to discuss the issue with Piper since she came over this evening. "What am I supposed to do?" I ask, feeling helpless. "You know what the alternative is."

She winces, understanding my meaning immediately. "But this approach isn't exactly solving anything. You can't keep doing this forever, so it's just…delaying the inevitable. And in the meantime, you're putting yourself through hell every time you have to talk to her. It's like the death of a thousand paper cuts."

She's right. It's definitely not a long term solution. In less than three years we'll get to that ten year mark, and Natalia will happily divorce me, walking away with a major stake in Grimco media. And these past years of hell will have been for nothing.

I run my hands over my face, once again mentally kicking myself for not trying to divorce her years ago, when Izzy was still a baby and too young to know what was happening. But the thought never even crossed my mind back then.

It was a shock for everyone when Izzy was born with Down's; it didn't come up on the tests Natalia had, and while the doctors expressed some concern about measurements in some late-term scans, it wasn't enough to warrant further tests. The heartbeat was normal, and the baby was growing, and Natalia was healthy. All really good things. But they warned us that the tests weren't a hundred per cent accurate, and that they couldn't always get a clear picture with the scans.

And I'm not going to lie, the shock of seeing Izzy and realizing the insanely challenging life she'd have ahead of her was panic-inducing. Literally. I knew absolutely nothing about Down's, except for common conceptions about a short life expectancy. And when you're forty-four and holding your new baby daughter in your arms and all you can think about is the likelihood that you'll outlive her, the fear and dread is crippling. I imagine it would be even for people without existing anxiety issues.

But even with all that going on, I loved her from the second I saw her face, and quickly became obsessed with learning everything I could about Down's, and doing everything I could to make sure Izzy's life is as long and fulfilling as possible.

Natalia didn't have that attitude, however. It's something I've thought about a lot, and I've come to the conclusion that it's very possible she would have struggled with postpartum even if Izzy had been born the healthy, abled child we'd expected. But I'm sure all the additional pressures of caring for an infant with Down's syndrome just made everything so much worse.

I kept thinking that in time she would adjust and start bonding with our daughter the way I had, and finally take an interest in all the plans and strategies I'd worked out for her future.

But that never happened. It just kept getting worse and worse.

And bit by bit, as Natalia grew colder, and harsher, and more distant, whatever sympathy I'd had turned to frustration, then resentment, then anger.

But I still hesitated about filing for divorce once we eventually separated. Whatever feelings I'd ever had for her had completely shriveled up and died by that point, but I guess in some way, even through the hostility that had developed between us I still felt...responsible for her, I guess you could say. And I wanted to see her back on her feet before dragging her into settlement negotiations.

If I'd imagined for even a second she would shoot down what was an insanely generous offer and callously threaten a custody hearing, there's not a chance I would have waited.

And now it's too late.

"You could just call her bluff," Piper suggests, taking a sip from her wine glass. "It's not like she actually *wants* custody of Izzy. She's just holding you to ransom by using your worst fear against you."

"I know that," I bite out through a tight jaw. And I know I could win custody if she fought me; but at what cost? Izzy would be put through an endless series of depositions, grilled by lawyers she doesn't know, who would likely have little sympathy for a child with special needs; the full contents of my life would be laid out for people to gawk at, including my mental health issues and certain…coping mechanisms I employ; Grimco would probably be under scrutiny as well, and the financial issues we're currently dealing with would surely come to light; and I'm sure Piper and Jazz would be under the radar as well. And frankly, after a judge hears all the shit that's likely to come out during the process, I certainly can't guarantee a successful outcome, even if getting custody isn't really Natalia's goal.

"I can't do that to Izzy," I tell Piper. "I can't put her through it. And, honestly, I'm not sure I'd cope with it either—you know how I get."

She offers me a sympathetic smile, her eyes full of understanding. "You cope with shit way better than you think, Dad. You should give yourself more credit." She sighs, leaning back in her chair. "As for Izzy…maybe there's some way she could be kept out of it? Surely they'd make an exception for a special needs five-year-old?"

"You know Natalia won't let that happen," I say wearily, rubbing my forehead.

ONCE PIPER LEAVES, I potter around the kitchen, making sure everything is sparkling clean and there aren't any stray dishes left around. Then I turn on the dishwasher and move into the living room, tidying up some stray cushions and wiping away a water ring from the coffee table—I'm pretty sure Piper always neglects to use a coaster on purpose simply to give me something to clean.

After I'm sure everything is in order, I head upstairs and peek into Izzy's room, checking that she's still asleep. My heart swells with love at the sight of her sucking on her thumb, her elephant stuffy clutched tight in her other arm.

I close her door over and head to my room to get ready

for bed, my hand thrusting through my hair in frustration the second I'm alone in my bedroom. God damn it, I need a fuck.

I need a hard, strong body holding me down while a thick cock fills my ass and pounds in deep. Over, and over, and over.

But I don't need some random, faceless guy's dick. I need Deacon's.

I turn and rest my forehead against my bedroom wall, breathing through the tension that's gripping my body. Tension from the exhausting day and that overwhelming conversation with Piper; and tension from the lust now coursing through me. I'm hard as fuck, and I know my dildos aren't going to cut it tonight. I need Deacon.

But he doesn't want me…

"Fuck," I groan, reaching a hand down to rub over my dick through the fabric of my pants. I need to convince him to be my stress ball. It's a fucking shit thing to ask, especially when he made it clear that he doesn't do casual sex. But I can't think of any other solution. For whatever reason, I've fixated on him and until I can get over whatever the fuck this weird obsession is, no other guy is going to work for me.

I grab my phone from my pocket and shift back around to lean against the wall. I pull up Deacon's number, glad that I had the forethought to save it when they emailed us the school contact information a couple months ago. Admittedly, I didn't imagine I'd be contacting him begging for sex, but here we are.

My brain catches as I read his surname. Did I know it was Stapleton? I don't think so. I've only ever known him as Deacon. I give a sharp shake of my head and push the gnawing thought aside—there is no way this nice, sweet kindergarten teacher is in anyway related to the asshole trying to take my company.

Me: *Should I send you that $50k via check like you asked?*

Deacon Stapleton: *Tanner?*

Me: *The one and only*

Deacon Stapleton: *What are you talking about?*

I let out a snort of laughter. If he guessed who it was based off the first text, it's pretty clear he knows exactly what I'm talking about.

Me: *You only got half your money's worth last week. So do you want a check for the other half? Or do you want to come to my penthouse tonight and get your payment in person?*

Me: *And by in person I mean your cock in my ass*

Deacon Stapleton: *We already talked about this…it's not a good idea*

Me: *I'd like to reopen discussions*

Me: *Like I want your cock to reopen my ass*

Fuck, I can't believe I'm typing this shit. If he took this to the press I'd be a laughing stock. But I really don't give a shit right now. Even just texting with him is helping me to relax and unwind—a pleasant distraction, I guess.

Deacon Stapleton: *Fucking hell Tanner*

Me: *Are you saying you don't want to?*

Deacon Stapleton: *I'm saying it's not a good idea*

Me: *Because you're Mr Nice Guy who doesn't break the rules* 🌚

Deacon Stapleton: *God you make me sound*

like such a square

I can't help grinning at the text. He's kind of adorable, which is a really strange thought to have about a guy I only want for his dick. Better than him being an asshole, I guess. Well, except for when he's buried inside me and turns into a domineering alpha with a filthy mouth. That was hot as fuck.

Me: *Only when you're being all rule-following and "appropriate"*

Me: *Not when you're pounding away inside me and spewing filthy shit in my ear*

Me: *Or when you're on your knees choking on my dick*

Deacon Stapleton: *Fucking hell. I'm out with friends, if I come in my jeans at the table there's going to be questions* 😳

I let out a soft chuckle, feeling my cock throb. As amusing as it is, the mental image of Deacon out at a bar somewhere, squirming in his seat and blushing furiously as he tries to hide his boner is also incredibly hot. Way hotter than I would have thought.

With my own erection now aching, I duck into the bathroom and retrieve the new bottle of lube I picked up today.

I'm still hoping Deacon will agree to meet me tonight —with Kit planning to stay over anyway, it's the perfect opportunity to duck out—but even if I can convince him, there's no way I can hold out that long.

This is new territory for me; I've never sexted with a guy before. I know it's the thought of Deacon fucking me again that has me so worked up, but it's still a little strange.

Brushing off my hesitation, I strip out of my clothes and stride over to my bed, retrieving one of my dildos from my nightstand drawer.

13

Deacon

Tanner Grimsay: *Are you hard?*

  Tanner Grimsay: *Because I am*

  Tanner Grimsay: *My cock is like stone right now and my ass is throbbing*

  Tanner Grimsay: *My fingers feel so good fucking inside me*

  Tanner Grimsay: *Love getting in my tight hole and stretching it out*

  Tanner Grimsay: *Wish I was stretching it out for your cock*

Fuck, fuck, fuck, fuck, fuck. *Why* did I check my phone? I was doing so well ignoring it. After I told Tanner I was out with friends, I put it back in my pocket, determined to leave it alone for the rest of the night, but the constant vibrations of texts coming through made me too curious not to check.

And now I'm a fucking mess. My entire body is trembling as lust and need and desire consume me, and the idea of my cock deflating any time soon is laughable. The only thing I can hope for now is that I don't *actually* cream my jeans. But, fucking hell, those texts...

I can't seem to tear my eyes from my phone as I read the words on the screen over and over again, my mind bringing up the image of Tanner lying naked on his bed, his legs spread wide, feet planted on the mattress, giving his hand access to that beautiful ass. I can practically hear the groans falling from his lips as he fingers himself, his other hand flying over his hard dick.

I somehow manage to tear my gaze from my phone and reluctantly bring my thoughts back to the present moment. I glance furtively around to see if anyone's noticed my strange behavior, but fortunately they all seem distracted.

As I told Tanner, now is really not a great time for this. If it were just Skyler and Jax, I probably wouldn't care too much, but it's Bryce's birthday so the whole team is out celebrating the occasion. I love them all, of course, but I'm aware that the older guys still see me as Sullivan's little brother. And that tends to lead to a combination of incessant prying, overprotectiveness, and merciless teasing, which basically means they're the worst people to be around while sexting with the almost fifty-year-old, pretty much straight, billionaire father of one of my kindergarteners.

Fortunately, a lot of this evening's focus has been diverted toward my brother, who's made himself the subject of a fair bit of teasing thanks to the whole fake boyfriend charade happening this weekend. There's a pool going to see how long it takes for their cover to be blown, and I'm sure if Drew were queer there'd be another one going to see how long it takes for them to hook up. Although considering Sully usually goes for pretentious, sleek and shiny twinks—AKA the exact opposite of Drew

—I would choose "never" even if my roomie weren't straight.

My phone buzzes again and, despite my better judgement, I read the text.

Tanner Grimsay: *So   fucking   full   of fingers*

Tanner Grimsay: *Want   to   be   full   of your cock*

Tanner Grimsay: *Need you to fill me up and fuck me hard*

Fuck, that was a big mistake. I let out a low groan, which fortunately goes unnoticed by most of the group, but not Skyler.

He arches a curious brow at me and shifts closer to sit right next to me. "Is it him? Sexy silver fox?"

I nod and let out an exasperated sigh. "He's sexting me. He really wants to hook up again—tonight, actually—but I've told him it's a bad idea. Now he's sending a text-by-text commentary of him jerking off."

Skyler's eyes widen slightly. "Okay, I'm not really sure which direction to take here. Is he a creep for sending you unsolicited masturbation texts? Or are you a dumbass for turning down a repeat?"

I blink at him. "Um…neither?"

Skyler lets out a dramatic sigh. "Dumbass it is."

"What?"

"Deac, if he's not a creep then you're a dumbass. Simple as that."

"How do you figure that?"

He ducks his head to peer under the table and I shift around uncomfortably as I sense his gaze on my crotch. He straightens back up, brows practically in his hairline. "*Damn,* I was going to ask if you were enjoying the commentary, but clearly…" He gives a little wave of his hand in the direction of my lower half.

"I'd prefer it if I weren't out in public surrounded by all my teammates," I grumble.

"I don't understand why you're so against fucking this guy again," Skyler says, sounding genuinely baffled. "You're clearly still into him. You sucked him off the other day for fuck's sake."

"Because——"

"Because why?" Skyler cuts me off. "You're not a Catholic priest. You don't need to deny yourself sex."

"This isn't about sex," I bite out, getting frustrated with him. "Or at least not in the way you think."

"Then tell me what it's about."

I shake my head. "You wouldn't understand. You never give a shit about anyone you sleep with."

"Ouch."

I can see from his expression that my words have genuinely stung, so I rush to clarify, offering an apologetic look. "Sorry, I just meant you only do casual flings and one-night stands. You don't expect anything from the guys you're with and they don't expect anything from you."

He shrugs, allowing the point. "Yeah, I guess that's fair. Okay, so…what are you saying?"

"I'm saying I'm not like that. You know I'm not. I can't do casual things. I can't do sex without emotions. I should never have gone there the first time," I finish with a heavy sigh.

"Or the second time…" he says wryly, eyes sparkling with amusement.

I grimace at the memory of Monday afternoon. Not because it was horrible—it was the exact opposite of horrible—but I've seriously gone and made everything so much more complicated now. "And…the second time," I agree. "I *really* shouldn't have done that."

"So he doesn't want anything more serious?"

I snort. "Skyler, all he wants is a dick to fill his hole. And I mean *literally* that's all he wants. He's not even really all that attracted to guys, but apparently having his brains fucked out is amazing stress relief. I'm surprised he hasn't just gotten one of those sex robots yet considering the only reason he goes out looking for dick is because dildos don't really cut it. He's rich enough for one."

"He's probably seen the end of *Ex Machina*," Skyler says, looking deadly serious.

I roll my eyes. I don't think there's anything Oscar Isaac's been in that Skyler hasn't seen at least fifty times. Even *Episode IX*, which takes commitment.

"How did he figure out being fucked is good stress relief if he's not into guys?" he asks thoughtfully.

I shrug. "We didn't really get to that part—my brain kind of fritzed two seconds later when he asked me to fuck him."

"I think you should talk to him," he says with a decisive nod. "Lay down some terms. If he wants your cock so bad, make him earn it."

I arch a brow at him. "Like what? Love me or I won't fuck you into a wall?"

"Okay, one…" He holds up his fingers, counting off. "That's not exactly what I meant. And two, that sounds really hot. I can see why he's so desperate for another go."

My phone buzzes again, and before I can grab it, Skyler snatches it from the table and reads the text.

"Holy shit! Damn Deacon, if you don't fuck this guy again I think I might have a go."

"Give me my phone, asshole," I growl, practically tackling him to the back of the booth.

"No! You had your chance to reply, now I'm doing it."

"Skyler!"

"You'll get it back in a second, and trust me—you'll be grateful."

There's a note in his voice that tells me he's up to something. And I know him too well to think it can be anything other than the exact opposite of what I would do.

He finally hands my phone back to me, a wicked smirk curving at his lips.

With great trepidation, I glance down at the screen.

Tanner Grimsay: *Just came all over my chest. Such a mess*

Me: *Sounds tasty. Send a pic*

Tanner Grimsay: *Only if you agree to come to my penthouse tonight. That barely scratched the surface—I need to feel that big fat cock of yours pounding away inside me again*

Me: *Okay you wore me down. But only because you called my cock big and fat* 😊

"Fucking hell, Skyler!" I growl, glaring at my best friend. "You better not have seen the picture."

He waves me away. "Relax, he didn't send it yet."

Sure enough, there's only one more text from Tanner, along with the three moving dots that indicate he's typing something.

Tanner Grimsay: *And thick and hard and perfect for filling up my tight hole*

Fucking hell.

Tanner Grimsay: *I've taken the pic but now I don't know if I should send it. I don't want it to seem like I'm bribing you or something*

Me: *You don't have to send it*

I debate whether to send the next text, but then decide to just go for it. As much as I would *love* to see that cumshot, I don't want him to think I'm some horny kid only interested in dirty pics. And I definitely don't want him to think I would base my decision on whether or not to see him again around receiving one.

Me: *You should know it was actually my best friend who sent the text requesting that pic. Sorry, he got a hold of my phone and thought he would be helping me by being an asshole*

Me: *Not that I wouldn't love to see it* 😊

Tanner Grimsay: 😳

Tanner Grimsay: *Is that the same best friend who "accidentally" divulged that you have a major crush on me at the bar the other night?*

Me: *I never used the word "major"*

Tanner Grimsay: 😏

Tanner Grimsay: *And do I take it this means you haven't actually changed your mind about meeting up?*

I can sense the disappointment coming through over the text and I really don't want him to feel that way, but at the same time I'm not sure what I'm supposed to do. I can't just demand for Tanner to develop feelings for me.

I rub a hand through my hair, letting out a frustrated grunt. I check the time on my phone; it's still relatively early—just after nine.

Me: *Where did you want to meet? Not to sound lame but I have a really big day tomorrow—can't be a late one*

Tanner Grimsay: *I have a penthouse in*

Brooklyn. And don't worry, you'll be home before you turn into a pumpkin 😉

Me: *Are you implying I'm currently a stage coach?*

Tanner Grimsay: 😅 *I messed that up, didn't I?*

Tanner Grimsay: *But I'm looking forward to you riding my stage coach* 😉 *And by stage coach I mean my ass*

I let out a burst of laughter, shaking my head. As turned on as I am at the moment, the amount of new ways he's finding to express how much he wants me to fuck him again is bordering on ridiculous. Not to mention it's a stark reminder that the only thing he wants from me is my cock.

Me: *Really? You want my dick filling your ass? Why didn't you say something earlier?*

Tanner Grimsay: *I'm sensing some sarcasm…*

Me: 😐

Me: *Also, that was a really terrible attempt at saving a fumble*

Tanner Grimsay: *It wasn't my best. My thinking thing in my head's already stopped working properly because I'm going to be getting your dick in my ass*

I roll my eyes. If I was in any doubt before now, that has definitely erased it. I need to sit Tanner down and talk him through my feelings on this whole thing. And this time I'm not going to crack and suck him off again.

Me: *What's the address? I can be in Brooklyn in a half hour*

I set my phone down and suddenly realize that Skyler

is basically breathing down my neck. I rear away from him. "What the fuck, Sky?"

He shrugs. "Couldn't help it. It was captivating."

I scowl at him. "Seriously? You were reading over my shoulder that whole time."

"Don't worry, I would have looked away if he'd sent the picture," he assures me, all innocence. Considering he wouldn't have known if Tanner sent the picture until it was actually there on the screen, it's not much comfort.

I sigh and slump back in my seat. "Whatever."

"Why so glum? You're going to be banging that gorgeous man again in less than an hour—you should be thrilled."

"It's not going to come to that," I say with a frown. "I have to talk to him, and I don't think he's going to like what I have to say."

Now that the distinctly un-sexy decision about my visit to Tanner's penthouse has been made, my horniness is melting away and my cock is *finally* deflating. Thank god, because it looks like everyone is getting ready to move onto another bar, and I really didn't want to stand up and attempt to explain the situation in my pants.

"So you're taking my advice," Skyler says, beaming with satisfaction. "You're going to lay down terms."

I wince. I'd actually forgotten it was Skyler who gave me the idea. When it comes to legal advice, he's as sensible as they come. Relationship advice, however... "I know I can't make him fall for me," I acknowledge, "but I can't go into every sexual encounter feeling like a walking, talking dildo. I want to be sensitive to his situation and not push him further than he's comfortable, but if all I'm ever going to be is a cock to fill a hole, I just can't do it."

"Even for mind-blowing sex?" Skyler asks, sounding

utterly flabbergasted that I'd be willing to turn my back on this opportunity.

I shrug. "It won't be mind-blowing for long without any emotion or intimacy to back it up."

"What if the emotions he feels are different to yours?" Skyler reasons.

"What do you mean?"

He fixes me with the kind of serious look he usually reserves for work stuff. "Look, I'm not saying what you do isn't important, because it is, and I respect the hell out of you for it. But it's not exactly the same as running a media corporation worth billions of dollars," he reasons. "Which, from what I hear, is in a bit of trouble right now…"

"It is?"

Skyler shrugs. "It's not anything disastrous—at least I don't think it is. But there's been some speculation about profitability of and viability and that sort of thing. There are a ton of assets within the corporation but only a few of them are real money-makers, the rest are starting to become dead weight. At least that's what I've heard some pundits saying—Sully would probably know more, it's his area of expertise."

I roll my eyes. "I am *not* talking to my brother about this."

He waves my comment away. "Whatever. All I'm saying is, you combine all that *plus* the fact that he's a single father with a special needs kid…it's no wonder the guy's in desperate need of some major stress relief."

Fucking hell. I don't know what exactly Skyler was trying to do—I didn't need him to justify why Tanner sought out that particular kind of relief, it wasn't some-thing I judged him for—but all he's accomplished is making me feel more for the guy than I already did. "You realize this hasn't helped at all, right?"

14

Tanner

I can tell by the expression on Deacon's face the moment I open the door of my penthouse to him that I need to adjust my expectations for what's about to happen here.

His familiar open, friendly features have made way for a tight, grim expression that immediately makes me wary. As soon as he sees me, his eyes move slowly up and down my body—currently clad in dark jeans and a white hoodie —and I notice a flicker of longing flash over his face, chased by a look of regret. Then his jaw hardens and he fixes me with a determined, resolved look. It's all very strange.

"Uh…do you want to come in?" I ask, feeling weirdly nervous. It's like I'm a nerdy high-schooler and the star quarterback has just showed up at my door. What the actual hell?

He nods and steps inside the apartment. I close the door behind him before leading the way through to the living area. As far as penthouses go, this one's not huge— only two bedrooms—but I certainly don't need anything bigger. For the record, I didn't buy this place just so I'd have somewhere to get fucked by random guys. It was originally an investment property, then the kids used it as a kind of base when they were out with friends and didn't want to be coming home in the wee hours and disturbing Izzy. And I guess that's how I got the idea for its current purpose.

"Are you okay?" I ask Deacon. "You don't seem all that…enthusiastic to be here."

He winces and his expression turns apologetic. "I'm sorry for leading you on tonight. Trust me, it's not that I don't want to have sex again—I swear, I changed my mind about this about five times on the way over here—but we just can't."

"Because it's inappropriate?" I ask, arching a skeptical brow. I don't really understand how the text exchange earlier is okay, and sucking my dick in his classroom is okay, but fucking me is crossing a line.

Deacon shakes his head. "No. I mean…yeah, they don't exactly encourage us to get involved with parents, but that's not what my real issue is."

My brow furrows in confusion. "So what is it?"

He lets out a heavy sigh. "You don't actually want *me*. You just want my cock."

My lips curve in a wry smirk. "It's a really great cock. I'm actually starting to think it might have magic powers or something given the way it's been invading my thoughts lately. Never had that happen before."

"Yeah, Tanner, I know," Deacon grates out, thrusting a hand through his dirty blond hair in obvious exasperation.

I stare at him in confusion. "You're upset that I'm complimenting your dick?"

He closes his eyes for a moment, letting out a slow

breath, before opening and hitting me with a look of...
disappointment? Is that what I'm seeing right now?

"I tell you that I don't want to have sex again because
you're only interested in my dick, and you respond by
waxing lyrical about my dick."

I just stare at him, feeling confused as hell. All this talk
about his cock is making my brain function fritz out. "So...
you don't want me to like your cock?"

He lets out a soft breath of amusement, shaking his
head. "I don't care if you love my cock, Tanner. Dream
about it all you want. Write poems, paint artwork, name a
fucking constellation after it if you want to."

Okay, let's not go that far. I'll settle for having it in my
ass again, though.

"What I care about," Deacon continues, "is that you
only want my cock. That you only want cock, period, and
at the moment it just happens to be mine you're fixating
on."

I frown at him. "Well, yeah. But you knew that already.
I told you before anything happened with us I just need to
be fucked sometimes."

He nods. "I know. And I'm not saying you hid
anything. I knew what the deal was and I wanted to have
sex with you anyway because I've been attracted to you
since the first time we met," he admits as a tinge of red
colors his cheeks. "But like I said the other day, it's rare for
me to do stuff like that."

Crippling disappointment floods through me. He did
mention the other day that he doesn't usually hook up; that
he prefers to stick to relationships. But after the blow job
he followed that spiel up with, I'd hoped there might be
some wriggle room.

I rub my fingers against my forehead as the tension
starts to build. "I can't do a relationship, Deacon."

"I know," he says gently. "I'm not asking for that."

"Then what the hell *are* you asking for? Because you really seemed to like fucking me last week."

"*Sex*, Tanner. Call it sex," he demands, sending me a hard look. "Not fucking. Not getting a cock inside you. *Sex.*"

I frown at him in utter confusion. "Why is that important?"

He takes a step closer, an intense expression on his face as he asks, "I want to know—do you consider what we did last Monday night to be sex? The same way you'd consider penetration with a female partner to be sex."

Sex? God no. Maybe when I was a kid I thought sex was simply about getting tab A into slot B, but as a grown man? Hell no. There's way more to it than that: kissing, and touching, and foreplay…

Why is Deacon even asking me this? Of course I don't consider being fucked from behind like a dog in heat to be in any way similar to regular sex. I shake my head slowly, still feeling baffled. "I'm not gay."

"But *I* am," Deacon says, speaking slowly as though I need the fact reinforced for some reason. "And being a man who sleeps with other men doesn't mean I don't crave intimacy, and connection. I love a good hard fuck as much as anyone, but I'm not a freakin' robot you can just turn on whenever you want a dick. When I'm with someone, I want them to actually want to be with *me*, and not just a part of my body. So as much as I loved having *sex* with you," he says, emphasizing the word to make his point, "I can't be your walking dildo."

And it finally sinks in, making me feel like absolute shit. How could I not have realized sooner this is what the issue was? And tonight—he had to spell it out to me, what, about eight times? I can go on and on about how I've never had complaints from other guys and that I'm always upfront about what I want before a hook-up. But Deacon was always different; from his talk of inappropriateness, to the way he rushed to his knees the second he glimpsed my cock, and the way his hands roamed all over my body. Even finding a condom to make sure I was comfortable moving ahead...it was completely different. He's completely different. And he definitely deserves to be treated better than the way I have been lately.

Deacon must see the change in my expression, because his own tightly-held features soften and he hits me with a gentle smile. "Tanner, just to be clear, I'm not judging you. I mean...I don't really understand the whole stress relief thing, but if that's something that helps you, then so be it. I just can't be your stress ball anymore."

I nod. "I get it. And I'm sorry for how...insensitive I've been. I suppose it doesn't mean anything to you that it's not just the thought of your dick in my ass that's been running circles in my brain lately. I keep thinking about those blow jobs as well. Especially since Monday..."

A sheepish expression crosses Deacon's face. "Yeah, I really shouldn't have done that. I totally sent some mixed messages, didn't I?"

I shrug. "Yeah, but I'm not complaining."

He lets out a soft chuckle, and then sighs. "I should probably go. I guess I'll see you around school."

"Or you could stay for a bit?" I suggest, suddenly realizing I really don't want him to leave, even if fucking's not on the table anymore.

He lets out a sigh, a weary expression crossing his face. "Tanner—"

"Not to f—have sex," I clarify. "Just... stay. Hang out for a bit."

His brows shoot up. "You want to...hang out?"

Fucking hell, now I sound like the nerdy teenager asking the quarterback if they want to "study." And I can't blame him for doubting my motives; I've made it abundantly clear, over and over, that there's only one thing I want from him.

But apparently that's not actually the case. Right now, I seriously just want to stay in his presence. Maybe it's because he's such a nice, genuine guy and I feel…safe with him. Or maybe it's because he's completely removed from the rest of my world. Maybe it's both.

"I'd like for you to stay," I say with less hesitation. "I enjoy your company. Even when our clothes are on."

He eyes me skeptically. "I'm not going to fuck you."

I hold my hands up. "I already said sex was off the table." I wouldn't mind if it was on top of the table, but I'm not going to say that out loud and send him packing.

He hesitates for a long moment, then finally nods. "Alright then. What do you want to do?"

Despite my efforts to behave, my brows shoot up suggestively, prompting Deacon to roll his eyes.

"Tanner…" he says in warning.

"Okay, okay—why don't you just decide," I suggest.

His eyes sparkle with curiosity. "You could tell me about your…um…stress relief system? I've got to admit, I've been fucking dying of curiosity since last week."

Huh. Well that definitely isn't where I thought tonight would be going. The only other person who knows about this coping mechanism of mine is my therapist, Dr Cho. I'm not sure why I even mentioned it to Deacon last week; I think maybe instinctively I knew I could trust him.

"Okay…have a seat on the sofa," I tell him. "I'm going to need a drink for this—you want something?"

"I'd better stick with water. I've got a—"

"Big day tomorrow," I finish, remembering his text earlier. "Of course."

"Big weekend, actually. My sister's wedding," he explains. "I have to drive to Long Island straight after school, then it'll be non-stop all weekend."

"Sounds like fun, though," I comment as I bring his water and a glass of merlot to the sofa. I'm finding myself strangely curious about his life. "Big family?"

He shrugs. "I guess so. I'm one of five."

I let out a soft chuckle. "Yeah, that's more than plenty. Your parents must have a lot of patience."

Even with the large age gap between Jazz and Izzy, it's still hard to keep up with my three kids at times; I couldn't imagine having another two on top of that.

"We're supposed to be talking about you," he reminds me. "My turn for questions now."

I sigh with resignation and lean back against the sofa, shifting around a little so I'm facing Deacon. "Alright then, fire away."

"How did you know?" he asks, staring at me with a curious expression.

"Hmm?"

"How did you know that getting fucked is good for stress relief or whatever?" he clarifies. "If you're not into guys, I mean. It seems like a pretty wild leap."

I'm thoughtful for a moment. I've never had to explain this to anyone before—mainly because every other guy I've hooked up with has been a random stranger and has likely made the assumption that I'm gay or bi or whatever. But considering Deacon's the one I want to use as a stress ball, he probably has a right to know. And I have to wonder whether any of his hesitation is wrapped up in him not being able to understand my "system" as he called it.

Maybe if he understands things better he won't feel so used.

Or maybe the complete opposite will happen.

"Okay, first of all—I don't really know what my attraction to men is, but it's clearly not zero. I mean, I've watched gay porn before and didn't get so much a twitch of desire, but then if I'm at a gay bar and I see a guy who looks like he'll be a good fuck, I can definitely get aroused. I might not get fully hard until I see his cock, or until he's inside me, but things will start happening." Except with Deacon, when I got rock hard from just watching him across the bar. I should have twigged then that something weird was going on.

"But you only go to gay bars when you're really stressed, right?" he presses. "Do you get that reaction normally—like, if you're feeling good and not all stressed out would you still see a hot top and get hard?"

I want to laugh at the notion of me not being stressed out, but I can see what he's getting at. "To be honest, I only really go out when I really need to hook up. Otherwise I prefer to stay at home with my family."

He nods, and I can see a flicker of disappointment in his eyes. "Right. So it probably is just the stress thing."

I shrug. "Like I said, I don't know. But one thing I should clarify is that I'm not using this to deal with run of the mill stress. I have Generalized Anxiety Disorder, and I've got a ton of techniques and methods I use to help me deal with it. And this is one of them. Sometimes I have days where everything just feels like it's spiraling out of control and my mind's a fucking mess, and I need to clear it out. This helps with that."

He nods, brows knitted in concern. "Okay. I can definitely see how it could help. How did it start, though?" he probes, reminding me of the original question.

I take a fortifying sip of my wine before offering Deacon a small, wry smile. "It was after my wife died. As you can imagine, it was an incredibly difficult time…"

"I'm sorry," he says, eyes full of sympathy as he reaches out to grasp my hand.

"Thanks," I say with a soft smile, before drawing in a steadying breath. "During the year straight after Leah's death I was…well, I think 'basket case' might be a pretty accurate term. I've had issues with anxiety in the past, but after the accident it felt like I was on board a capsizing boat in the middle of a storming sea. I kept bailing out water and then twice as much would be dumped back in. It felt like I'd never see dry land again." I glance to Deacon and offer a wry smile. "Sorry, that was a bit melodramatic."

"It doesn't sound like you were a basket case," he murmurs, squeezing my hand gently. "It sounds like you were coping the best way you could with an impossible situation. And you made it through the storm, which is more than can be said for George Clooney."

My brows draw together in confusion. "Huh?"

He just blinks at me, as though unable to comprehend my confusion. "George Clooney dies in *A Perfect Storm*— you haven't seen that one?"

"No, but I guess the ending's ruined now."

He rolls his eyes. "The movie's almost as old as I am. I think when you hit the twenty-year mark spoilers are fair game."

I shrug. "Fair. But for the record, I haven't seen *Gladiator* yet either and I don't want to know the ending."

Deacon stares at me, dumbstruck. "What the hell were you doing in 2000?"

"Well, we were in the process of acquiring BCN and I had a newborn daughter, so free time was limited."

A bright grin spreads across Deacon's face, his dark eyes lit with amusement. "Okay, you win. But your *Gladiator* virginity is something we shall have to remedy."

I quirk a brow at him. "That's a line from *Braveheart.*"

He lets out a dramatic sigh, one hand held over his chest. "Oh, thank god. There's hope for you yet." Turning serious, he sends me a soft glance. "You don't have to tell me the rest if you don't want to."

I shrug. "I've started now." I try to remember where I left off before we went on that wild tangent. Right, my anxiety. "My therapist wanted to put me on meds for the anxiety," I tell him. "But I was on my own with two young kids and I didn't want to take anything that could fuck up my brain chemistry, or make me all drowsy and out of it. I have Valium for emergencies, but that's as far as I'll go." He gives me an encouraging nod and I go on. "What I needed to do was to figure out ways to cope with my triggers and reduce my stress. My first move was to change therapists because the other one seemed way more interested in trying to medicate me than actually talking to me, then I hired a director for Grimco and pretty much halved my work load; I brought in a team to help me handle the management of Leah's estate and business interests; but probably the best thing I did was talk to my kids. They were so young, I thought I was protecting them by keeping them out of everything and by making it seem like I was fine, but kids are way smarter than adults give them credit for—especially my kids—and they could tell that I wasn't okay. All I was doing by keeping them out of everything was pushing them away. Once we started talking, we were like scattered puzzle pieces being put back together. There'll always be a piece missing, but you can see the picture." I give a sharp shake of my head, letting out an exasperated huff. "Fuck, I really need to stop with these lame analogies."

"I like your analogies, they're cute," Deacon says with a grin.

Fucking hell. A twenty-seven-year-old is calling me *cute*.

"Anyway…I gradually started doing better, but I was nowhere near back to my normal self. And after about a year, one of my buddies started suggesting I try to get laid. Sex has always been a good outlet for me—I mean, it's sex, it gives you endorphins, I'm pretty sure most people get some sort of relief from a good orgasm—so it was a valid suggestion. But I wasn't ready to be with another woman —not at that point, at least." I send Deacon a hesitant glance. "I'm not sure you're going to like the next part…"

"Well, now I'm intrigued," he says with a smirk. Perhaps sensing my unease, his expression softens and he gives my hand a reassuring squeeze. "Tanner, I'm not going to judge you for doing whatever you needed to do to get through your wife's death."

"That's not really what I'm worried about," I murmur. I sigh and decide to just get it over with. I'm about to justify all the reservations he came here with tonight. "I've always been into anal play—mainly fingering—but I took it to another level after Leah died, with dildos and beads and stuff like that. It just felt better to be doing stuff we hadn't done together."

"Like, you would be cheating on her otherwise?" Deacon asks, brows furrowed in thought.

"Not exactly. I can't really explain it. It just didn't feel right to be fucking a Fleshlight, or even my hand." He nods, and I continue, "And it helped…a little. With every-thing being so chaotic at the time, it helped to have this nightly wind-down routine to help my mind settle so I could sleep. You know, clean the kitchen, tidy up after the kids, get ready for bed…and then I just threw in 'fuck myself with a bright pink, six-inch dildo.'"

Deacon lets out a strange noise that sounds halfway between a laugh and a groan. "It was really pink?"

I smirk at him. "Yep. And very…girthy. I can show it to you if you'd like?"

He gives a sharp shake of his head. "Nope. No, I'm good. I think I need to hear the part of this story that I'm apparently not going to like."

I arch a curious brow at him, but then my eyes catch sight of his crotch, where his hard dick looks ready to tear through his zipper. Fuck, I want to ride it. "Right. Yeah…" I tear my gaze away and give a shake of my head, forcing my mind back on track. "Well, as pleasurable as stuffing myself full of a six-inch dildo is—"

"Fucking hell," Deacon mutters, thrusting a hand through his hair.

"It was getting to the point where it wasn't really enough. A solo session is fine for settling down for the night, but it's not going to help me unwind in the way a proper fuck is. And it seemed like the more stable and together I started to feel, the more I was craving it. So one night, after a pretty nightmarish day where a ton of shit hit the fan, I went to a bar and looked for a woman to hook up with. All I could think about was getting laid—I knew it wasn't going to magically fix all the shit going on at work, but for the first time in ages I'd be able to just relax and let go and lose myself in someone and not have to think. But there was a problem…"

"You didn't want a woman?" he guesses.

I shake my head. "I wasn't ready. I flirted with at least ten beautiful women that night and not one of them sparked any interest. At that point I genuinely thought I might never have sex again," I admit. "But then I went home and went through the usual routine. And just after I came, it occurred to me that maybe I didn't need to find a woman to fuck, maybe I just needed to find someone to fuck me." I glance at Deacon, but I can't read his expression. He doesn't look pissed off, but he doesn't look pleased either. He's a complete closed book. "You were right when you said I saw men as walking dildos," I admit. "That's all it was. I figured if I could get off from having a fake cock in me I could probably get off from a real one. And at least with a real one I wouldn't have to do the work. I knew there was a good chance I wouldn't be able to get it up for a guy, but that didn't really matter—once I had a cock in me I'd be fine."

"Are you expecting me to be mad about this?" he asks, brows drawn together.

"You seemed pretty mad earlier," I point out.

"I was frustrated," he clarifies. "Because I didn't understand. And I don't like being used. But I do understand now, and you telling me all of this—trusting me with your story—that makes me feel anything but used."

I blink at him, a little startled. To be honest, I hadn't really intended to divulge so much when I started talking, it all just sort of…came out.

"Can I ask…what does your therapist say about this particular coping strategy?" he asks, a mix of curiosity and concern in his tone.

I sigh and lean back in my seat. "She's not thrilled," I admit. "But as long as I'm safe and responsible she'd prefer this to something else—like alcohol or drugs."

He nods. "Fair point. What does she mean 'responsible'?"

"I don't ever bring guys to the house. I always make sure someone's at home with Izzy. I'm never out the whole night. I don't drink alcohol on nights when I'm hooking up. I don't give out personal details," I list off. "I don't hook up with the same guy twice…usually."

The corner of his mouth quirks up. "Why the hell am I the exception?"

I shrug. "I've already told you. I have no idea. You've imprinted on me like a baby duck."

He lets out a burst of laughter that lights up his entire face. "Maybe my dick is magical."

"I'm pretty sure it is. You might want to have it studied for science."

He offers me a wry smile. "And I guess you'd be the first one to volunteer your services as a test subject?"

"Well, if it's for the good of science I just don't think I'd have much of a choice."

He smiles indulgently before tugging his phone from his pocket and groaning when he sees the time. "Fuck, it's nearly twelve. I really need to get going."

I really don't want him to leave, but I did promise to have him home by midnight.

We get up from the sofa and I walk him to the door. I'm about to open it for him, but after how considerate he was while I shared my story—and after glimpsing that boner he sprung while I talked about dildos—I just can't resist taking one more shot. "I know I sound like a broken record, but is there any wriggle room that doesn't involve an actual relationship?"

Deacon eyes me thoughtfully for a moment. "I guess that depends on you."

"Me?"

He steps forward and brushes a kiss to my cheek, taking me completely by surprise. "If you want my cock, you get my lips as well," he murmurs in my ear. "They're kind of a package deal."

He steps back and I stare at the lips in question as they form into a wry smirk.

Is he saying…that he wants us to kiss? On the lips?

"What…what does that mean?"

"I mean you don't get to be Julia Roberts anymore. Sex *is* personal, and if you want it from me, that's my price."

My brows shoot up. "Do you have a movie reference in your back pocket for every situation?"

He lets out a soft laugh. "Just about. But I mean it, Tanner. This is your choice—if the thought of kissing me is too gross then you should just go find some other walking dildo to be your stress relief. I'm not going to be with someone who just wants me for my dick." He lets out a breath and starts to back toward the door. "Take however long you need to think about it and let me know when you've decided."

He turns for the door and my mind suddenly snaps back into gear.

I catch up to him in two large strides, blocking his exit. "Wait—"

Deacon's brows shoot up. "We both agreed it was time to call it a night."

"How am I supposed to decide if I want you to kiss me if I don't know whether you're a good kisser?"

"I am a *fabulous* kisser," he assures me.

"Well I don't know that," I argue. "Where are your references?"

He lets out a soft chuckle. "Should I be carrying around a resume?"

"I think a sample would be a good idea."

"A sample?"

I nod. "Yes. You can give me a kissing sample and then I'll decide if I want more. Like a free trial."

"You've already had the free trial, babe." He waggles his eyebrows suggestively. "With all the extra features."

"And I'm definitely interested in signing up for the full-access plan. But I want a kissing sample first."

His lips curve into a smirk and he nods. "Okay, then." He leans forward, and I brace myself for the kiss, but he bypasses my lips to whisper in my ear instead. "Just so you know, I kiss the way I fuck."

Before I have a chance to figure out what he means, his lips are on mine. Hard and demanding, like nothing I've ever experienced before. And now I understand what he meant; the kiss is full of the same power and dominance he had over my body last week. I can't fight the onslaught. And, surprisingly, I don't want to…

I've never thought about kissing a man before—not even Deacon, until the condition was laid out on the table —so I can't really say whether this is how I expected it to be. But I'll admit that when he gave me the ultimatum, I figured it'd be something I'd just have to put up with; I wasn't expecting it to be something I'd actually enjoy. I didn't think it would be so…hot.

And I definitely couldn't have imagined it would turn me into this: a groaning, whimpering mess, clinging tight to Deacon as desire rages through my body.

He finally tears his lips from mine and I draw in some much-needed oxygen. My mouth feels lonely now, and all I can think about is how much I want his lips on me again. Which is completely ridiculous. Clearly my brain has been deprived of oxygen for too long, and all my blood's rushed to my cock. No wonder I'm thinking up absolute nonsense.

"Are you ready to sign up?" he asks me, his hungry, heated gaze flicking between my eyes and my lips.

It takes me far too long to figure out what the fuck he's

talking about, but then I dredge up the conversation from before the kiss and let out a soft chuckle. "Fuck, yes."

A wide grin spreads across his face. "Thank god." Then he yanks down the zipper of my hoodie and hastily shoves it off me, before grabbing the hem of my t-shirt and tugging it up over my head. Then his lips come crashing back against mine for another fierce, demanding kiss as his hands blaze trails of heat over my bare torso.

15

Deacon

I know, I know, I was supposed to be leaving—big weekend ahead and all that—but there's no way I can go now. Not after that kiss.

I attack his mouth as my hands run over the hard, lean muscles of his chest. I didn't get to explore his gorgeous body as much as I would have liked to last week, and now I just can't help myself.

Tanner grips onto my hair, holding my mouth against his and kissing me back just as eagerly. I'm not going to lie, his response to my kisses has definitely caught me off guard—but in a good way. I'm not entirely sure what I was expecting to get out of my little ultimatum, but it wasn't this.

I'm sure he's even more surprised than I am, but he's not freaking out about it. And I love that. I love that he's just going with the flow and letting himself do what feels good. Who knows, maybe he'll freak out tomorrow once everything sinks in, but we'll deal with that if it happens.

I snap my hips forward, grinding my hard dick into his

and prompting him to groan into my lips, his grip on my hair even tighter.

"Fuck, Deacon," he gasps. "Please tell me you're going to fuck me."

"Of course I'm going to fuck you."

Apart from the fact that I desperately want to be inside him, I'm not just going to get him all riled up and then leave him hanging. He respected me earlier when I explained my reservations, not pushing me despite his obvious disappointment. And he was willing to step out of his comfort zone to give me what I needed; it's my turn to give him what he needs now.

"Thank god." His smile is one of relief, but his eyes are full of fiery anticipation.

He starts to turn around but I grab his shoulder and force him back against the wall. We're doing this front on this time. And there's going to be kissing. Lots and lots of kissing.

"No," I growl. "You're on the Deacon plan now, and we're doing things my way."

"Deacon…"

"Pick a word," I tell him.

"What?"

"Any word at all. Something completely random and not sex-related."

His brow furrows in obvious confusion. "Uh…vikings?"

I let out a breath of laughter. "Hot—I like it." I crash my lips back to Tanner's, kissing hungrily as I rock my hips forward again, seeking that delicious friction.

"Why do I need a word?" he gasps, sounding adorably bewildered.

"Because I'm in charge now, and there are things I

want to do. Things I've been fantasizing about since the first day I ever saw you."

"What things?" he whispers, a note of wariness in his voice.

I graze my hands down his sides as I list off some of my fantasies. "I want to have you spread out underneath me on a bed. I want to run my lips over every inch of this beautiful body. I want to eat your hole until you're trembling and desperate and begging to come. I want to cover you in my cream and make you stink of me... And if there's anything you don't want or aren't comfortable with, all you need to do is say that word."

"Vikings," he murmurs. "No cum. I'm sorry. I don't want cum on me...or in me."

"You don't have to apologize, Tanner," I say gently, fixing him with a sincere look. "That's why there's a safe word."

He nods, looking a little more relaxed.

I lift a hand to his cheek and run my thumb over the silver stubble. "Was there anything else I said that you weren't comfortable with?"

"Maybe just...go slow," he suggests. "That was a lot of stuff."

I offer a wry smile. "I can do that. My first priority is fucking you against this door." Then a thought hits me and I scrub a frustrated hand through my hair in realization. "We're going to need a condom, though."

"Um...actually..." Tanner reaches into his back packet and pulls out a condom, handing it to me. "I assumed you were coming over for sex, so I thought I should be prepared."

I quirk an eyebrow at him. "How prepared?"

An adorable blush colors his cheeks. "Well, I didn't

clean off after…before." When he was using his dildo and sexting me about it.

I grin and lean forward to briefly press my lips to his. "That's handy. Now we just need these off," I say, tugging at his jeans.

He gets with the plan and hastily unfastens his jeans, sliding them down his legs and tossing them away on the floor. I do the same with my own and then stand there for a moment once we're both naked, staring hungrily at Tanner's hard, throbbing cock. I'm so tempted to drop to my knees and take him down my throat again; I've sucked a lot of dicks over the years, but there's something about Tanner's that is just so addictive. That's not on the cards tonight, though. Tonight is all the kissing.

I snap on the condom and pinch the tip. I'd prefer to have some lube to get really slicked up, but this one's a little lubricated already, and if Tanner had a dildo in him earlier then he's going to be plenty stretched out and slicked up.

Tanner starts to turn his back on me again, but once again I grab his shoulder and push him back against the door. It occurs to me that he's probably never had sex with a guy front-on. Well, this is going to be an interesting experience for him, then.

"I don't—how are you—"

Before he has a chance to finish the question, I grab his thighs and hoist him off the ground, thrusting forward and driving deep inside him.

Tanner lets out a strangled groan, his head falling back against the door with the thud.

"Do you want to use your safe word?"

"God, no. Just fuck me," he groans, wrapping his legs around my waist like a vise and urging me forward.

I crash my mouth to his, kissing him with a wild, desperate hunger as I fuck him hard enough to make the door rattle. I hope the hinges are good quality, because otherwise we're screwed.

He feels just as incredible wrapped around my cock as he did the first time. I'd love to be bare inside him, but I fully respect his wishes on that matter, and even with the latex barrier, sex with Tanner Grimsay is just so much fucking better than sex with anyone else. I'm not sure why, exactly; maybe just because I've wanted it for so long.

The sex we had earlier in the week was phenomenal, but this…it's just next level. It's so much *more*. I know that the level of intimacy I'm feeling right now is completely one-sided. Tanner couldn't give a fuck about us being face to face, and clinging to each other, and sharing kisses like they're full of oxygen we need to survive. But I care; I need this. And I appreciate that he's giving it to me even if he'd prefer a hard, rough fuck from behind where he didn't have to think too much about the fact that the cock buried inside him was actually attached to a man.

"Deacon…shit…I don't…I don't…"

Concerned by the thread of his words and the desperation in his tone, I pause my movements and look at Tanner. "What is it? Are you okay?"

"Deacon…"

"Do you need your safe word? It's Vikings," I remind him.

He shakes his head. "No. Don't stop…don't stop. I just…I don't…"

"Tanner—"

"I don't understand," he murmurs.

"Understand what?"

He shakes his head. "Just fuck me," he rasps out. "Don't stop. Fuck me."

His arms tighten around me and he drops his head to the crook of my neck. I'm surprised but encouraged when

I feel his lips against my skin. Kissing and sucking in a way that makes my body shiver.

I'm not sure what's going on, but he's specifically told me not to stop, so I don't. I speed up the tempo again, snapping my hips hard and driving in deep.

Fuck, I want to go farther, deeper, but this position's not really the best for that and I'm not about to change it up now. Not when Tanner's wrapped around me like a koala bear and sucking on my neck like I'm a watermelon *Jolly Rancher*.

"Fuck, I need to come," Tanner groans, finally tearing his head from my neck and slamming it back against the door, his expression pained with desperation. "So close."

"Grab your dick, babe," I tell him. "Get yourself there."

He nods and drops his left hand from around my shoulders to reach between us and stroke his angry, throbbing cock.

I claim his lips again, devouring his mouth as I continue to thrust hard inside him. I'm so close to the edge; I can feel the heat building in my belly, the tingling in my balls. I'm sure I'll get there before Tanner does, which wouldn't be a bad thing—maybe I can finish him off with my mouth after all.

It doesn't turn out that way, however. He flies over the edge first, groaning into my mouth and gripping my shoulder hard enough to bruise. His hole clamps down around my cock like a vise and it's enough to trigger my own release. I come hard into the condom, accidentally biting Tanner's lip in the process.

I draw away from him, offering a sheepish smile as I try to gather myself. "Sorry about that."

"Huh?" He looks completely out of it and it's fucking adorable. I realize he's more than two decades older than me, but that is exactly the right word to describe his bewildered, blissed-out expression right now.

I just give a wry shake of my head and take a moment to survey the situation before me. I'm going to have to pull my dick out of Tanner and get rid of the condom soon, not to mention my legs are trembling and my arms are aching—this position is not exactly the most sustainable, especially when the bottom is relatively tall and leanly muscled—but I just need a moment. I notice Tanner's hand is covered in his cum, and that gives me the motivation I need to finally set him back on the ground, letting my cock fall from his ass.

Once my arms are free, I grab his left hand and bring it to my mouth, cleaning up the tasty mess with my tongue.

"What—did you just lick cum from my hand?" Tanner asks.

I glance up to see him staring at me with wide-eyed surprise.

I grin at him. "It would have been a shame for it to go to waste."

"You seriously like cum that much?" It's not exactly judgement in his tone, more just a general confusion.

I shrug, offering a smile. "I seriously do."

He glances away, a frown touching his features. "You must think I'm such a prude—not wanting your cum in me."

"Tanner, I've already told you, you don't have to apologize for stuff you're not into," I say firmly, seeing as how it didn't seem to take the first time. "But, likewise, I'm not going to apologize for or try to sensor anything that I *am* into. I'm a gay man—I'm going to be into stuff that you might balk at. That's why you have the safe word."

He nods, still looking a little unsure.

"Speaking of…I'm sorry I didn't check with you about

the position *before* I actually put my cock in you. I know you told me not to stop, but I got the impression you weren't a hundred per cent comfortable with it?"

"It was…different," he allows.

"Did you feel…um…emasculated?" I ask warily. "Because that really wasn't my intention." It's not something I even considered; most bottoms love to be manhandled, but, of course, Tanner's not like most bottoms.

He lets out a wry breath of laughter. "I'm plenty secure in my masculinity. You don't have to worry about that. But…it was a lot. I liked it, obviously. But it was just…" He lets out a breath as he gathers his thoughts. "Overwhelming, I guess. And with the kissing as well…I liked that too, but now my head's all messed up. I want to kiss you, but I don't understand what's happening." He lifts a hand to rub at his forehead, as though trying to massage the thoughts out. "This used to be simple."

"So basically, I've done the opposite of what you needed. Instead of helping you relieve your stress, I've just added to it."

"I—no—I'm not…" He sighs and lifts one shoulder in a shrug. "It was a really fucking good orgasm…"

But it wasn't what he needed.

I can't say I'm surprised that Tanner's freaking out a little, but I was expecting something more along the lines of, "I'm not gay, I don't kiss men, yada yada yada." The fact that he clearly enjoyed what we did tonight is just adding to his confusion and that really pains me. I don't want to be the cause of any feelings of anxiety or overwhelm that he's experiencing. I'm supposed to be the cure for that.

I feel weird standing here completely naked while we have this serious conversation, so I grab my briefs and jeans from the floor and tug them on, taking up a position leaning against the hallway wall. Tanner does the same, leaning back against the opposite wall. He's left his jeans unfastened, however, and it's incredibly distracting.

I manage to tear my gaze from his crotch and look at his face, finding his eyes glimmering with amusement. "What do we do now?" I ask. "Because I don't want to be a trigger for your anxiety."

He offers a rueful smile. "Trust me, there are far more stressful things I have to deal with in my life than whatever confusion I have over...all that," he says, gesturing at the door.

I frown, not really liking the sound of that. "I don't want to add to it. Especially not when the point is supposed to be stress relief."

"Well, I don't want to stop fucking," he says simply. "You're way too good at it."

I let out a breath of amusement, my lips curving up. "Thanks."

Tanner eyes me levelly, and I can see him hesitating for a moment before he speaks. "Would you consider...doing things like we did the other night? I know I said yes to the kissing, but..."

"It's too much..." I let out a sigh as a stab of disappointment hits me, shifting my gaze toward the door, where not that long ago I seriously thought we had it made. I've never questioned my sexuality before, so I can't imagine what Tanner must be thinking right now. But it's clear that his cock had full control of the reins just before and now that his mind's back in charge, he's having a really difficult time adjusting to the new reality. It might not seem like much of a change considering he's been comfortable letting guys fuck him for years; but what we did tonight was very different—I made sure of that, didn't I?

"So...you need distance, and I need intimacy," I finally say, shifting my gaze back to Tanner.

"It's a deal-breaker then?" he asks, wincing with obvious disappointment.

I thrust a hand through my hair in frustration. "I don't want it to be." And I sure as fuck don't want him going out and finding other walking dildos to help him with his stress relief. I think it over a little more before coming to decision. I glance up at Tanner and nod. "Okay, we can fuck the way you want to, but I want three things."

His brows shoot up. "Have you considered getting into the corporate world? You're quite the negotiator."

I screw my nose up. "I spend enough time around suits thanks to my brother and my buddies. That's more than enough for me, thanks."

Tanner looks stunned for a moment and I wonder for a second if I've insulted him by shitting on the corporate world, but then he gives a little shake of his head and hits me with a questioning look. "What are your terms?"

"I want to hang out sometimes without having sex."

He quirks a brow, but nods. "I think I can manage that. But you'll have to keep your hands to yourself as well."

I offer a wry smile and continue, "The second thing is I don't want to *only* have sex when you're in desperate need of stress relief. I'm happy to help you with that, but I don't want to just be your stress ball. And it'd be nice to be with you on a day when you're actually relaxed and happy."

He eyes me curiously. "So you want us to spend time together *without* having sex, but you also want us to have sex more often?"

I think back over my conditions and feel myself blushing. Shit, it sounds like I'm trying to manipulate him into a relationship. "Yeah, basically. But only when it's convenient obviously."

He lets out a soft laugh. "I'm sure we can make it happen. Especially if more sex is on the table." His brows creep up in question. "What was the third thing?"

I fix him with an intent look, trying to communicate my sincerity as best as I can in regards to this last condition. "This is temporary. I'm not going to pressure you, but I need you to figure out all your thoughts and feelings about all that," I say, gesturing toward the door. "Work out why you're so overwhelmed and anxious about something you clearly enjoyed, and whether or not it's something you can get past. I think we could be really good together, Tanner, but there are things I need from a partner and you need to figure out whether you're able to give them to me."

He nods. "I get it. And...I'm sorry."

I step forward and cup his cheek. "How many times have I told you not to be sorry?"

He gives a soft smile and I awkwardly drop my hand, remembering I'm supposed to be putting distance between us. This is going to be fucking hard; the dam has burst now, and I've got all these intimate and affectionate instincts I have to fight to keep to myself.

"Alright, now I really should be going," I say with a wry grin. "The field trip tomorrow's going to be a nightmare."

I quickly gather my t-shirt and shoes from where I discarded them earlier and put them on. Then I check that I've got my phone and wallet, and make my way toward the door.

"Can you come over this weekend?" Tanner asks, just as I'm pulling the door open.

I glance back, offering a rueful smile. "I'll be on Long Island all weekend for my sister's wedding. Free all next week though."

"*All* next week?" he asks, one eyebrow arched suggestively. "I'm going to hold you to that."

"As long as you remember rule number one."

He smiles and taps his his temple. "It's right up here. Along with rule number two."

I let out a loud chuckle and swing the door open. "I'll see you next week."

16

Tanner

"Was there ever a point where you thought you were interested in girls?"

Across the table from me, Jazz's face screws up. "Dad, we did all this when I was twelve. Remember? I told you I was gay, you were cool with it. End of discussion."

I let out a sigh and run my hands over my face. "Sorry, I should have clarified. I wasn't asking specifically about you. I just…thought you might be able to give some perspective on a particular issue. It's…queer-related."

He arches a skeptical brow. "Then why the fuck were you asking me about girls?"

I shrug. "I don't know. Sorry, it was a bit of a silly question." I shouldn't have even brought this up; I know Jazz has experienced confusion about his sexuality in the past, but it was the confusion of a child. I doubt he could offer much perspective on my current issue. And do I really want to give him the details of my unorthodox sex life? It's not exactly the ideal topic of conversation for Saturday lunch.

But it's been on my mind pretty much every second

since Deacon walked out of my penthouse in the wee hours of yesterday morning, and I've gotten to the point where I feel like if I don't talk to someone, I'll explode. I don't blame Deacon at all for laying down his ground rules; if he's willing to go against all his instincts to give me casual, low-intimacy fucking while I figure my shit out, then I need to fucking figure all my shit out. I don't want him to have to hold anything back when he's with me…I just need time to understand what I'm feeling.

Jazz rolls his eyes and gives a casual shrug of one shoulder. "What's the issue?"

I shake my head. "It's not important. A friend of mine has been going through an…interesting situation recently. I thought maybe you could give some perspective but I'm now thinking it's probably a bit inappropriate to involve you. I should respect his privacy."

Jazz nods. "Fair enough. But you don't have to tell me who it is. You can just give me the broad strokes."

"Okay…" With the shield of my "friend" to hide behind, I'm able to relax a little, although I'm still very aware that we're in a crowded bar with several of Jazz's employees liable to move within earshot at any moment. Not much that can be done about that, I guess.

I take a moment to string my thoughts together before launching into my dilemma. I don't feel great lying to my son—we've always been totally honest with each other, even about uncomfortable matters—but I think in this particular instance it's necessary. Maybe one day, when I've figured everything out, I'll tell him the truth. For now I'm just happy to be able to talk in this way. "My friend is straight, but he has sex with men sometimes."

I wait for Jazz to object to this claim of heterosexuality, but he just nods. At my blank look, he says, "What?"

I shake my head. "Nothing, I just thought you'd say

he's kidding himself for thinking he's straight when he has sex with men."

Jazz shrugs. "There are a lot of straight men who have sex with other men."

I blink at him. "There are?"

"Sure. I've probably fucked more straight men than gay men." He's thoughtful for a moment and then shakes his head. "Okay, that's probably not true. But there have definitely been a fuck load of tourists."

I wince, rubbing a hand over my face. It's hardly news to me that my son is incredibly…active. But I don't need it shoved right in front of me. Jazz, meanwhile, just gets back to his burger, casually chewing away as though we're talking about baseball or something.

"Tourists?" I ask warily.

He swallows his bite before answering. "Straight guys who just want to experiment. Generally just for a night or a weekend or whatever. Usually they want to try it with a guy because they want to be overpowered by someone stronger than them, so that's fun."

I shake my head in exasperation. This is far more than I needed to know. "I don't think he's a tourist," I say, getting us back on track. "He's been doing this for years."

Jazz eyes me skeptically. "Are you sure he's not just closeted? He might be bi—nothing wrong with that."

"I don't think so…he's not actually attracted to men, he just likes…um…anal sex sometimes in very particular circumstances." I can feel my face heating but I know Jazz won't read anything into it.

"Like when he's drunk?" he drawls, rolling his eyes as he brings his soda to his lips for a sip.

"No—apparently it's good stress relief," I say with a shrug.

Jazz nods. "Ah, yeah. I can see that working. Sounds like your buddy's a bit heteroflexible."

"What the hell does that mean?"

He shrugs. "Straight guys who do gay things under very particular circumstances. Like Jace—he loves sucking cocks when he's high."

"I really didn't need to know that," I grumble, rubbing my fingers into my forehead. Jace is one of Jazz's best friends and I've known the kid and his family since the boys were about five.

"Which part? The sucking cocks or the getting high?"

"Take your pick," I say dryly.

"Was that all you were trying to figure out?" Jazz asks. "How your friend should identify? Because you know it's really his choice—if he says he's straight don't be a dick about it."

I let out a soft laugh, shaking my head. There's never any sugar-coating with Jazz. "Thanks, but no, that wasn't even the crux of the issue."

I pick at my chicken salad as I attempt to explain the situation with Deacon, being as vague as possible while still getting the main point across. I'm not sure what insight I can possibly hope to get from Jazz when he only has half the information, though. Maybe it just helps to get it all out there, even if it is in the guise of me speaking on behalf of a friend.

"So he kissed a boy and he liked it, but then he freaked out afterward?" Jazz summarizes.

"That's the gist of it, yeah," I say awkwardly.

"And what? You told him you'd check with your gay son to see if this makes him gay now?" he asks with a snort.

I roll my eyes. "Of course not. I definitely won't be telling him I spoke to you about it. But it might help to have some insight if he wants to talk about it again. I was a bit caught off guard the first time."

Jazz nods in understanding and it makes my gut clench. I'd much rather see more of his glib side, or even his abrasiveness, because those are his factory settings. The gentle, caring Jazz rarely peeks through the surface for anyone but Izzy, and I feel as though I'm squandering this rare sighting by lying to him.

"Alright, well I don't really know what sort of insight I'll be able to give—I've never freaked out after kissing a boy before." He thinks for a moment and then says, "There have been a couple guys who got all weird after kissing me, though. And, trust me, there is nothing wrong with the way I kiss. If you ask me, they only got weird because they were so into it. It sounds like that might be your buddy's problem as well," he adds thoughtfully.

Well, that's something I could have figured out on my own.

"Why would someone freak out, though?" I press. "If they liked it, I mean. You'd think that'd be a good thing?"

Jazz shrugs. "I guess if you've always thought of your-self as being one way, and then suddenly this happens to change things, it's going to come as a fucking shock. And kissing is one of those things...I mean, yeah you can still kiss someone you're not that into but it's never going to be as explosive as when it's with someone you're actually attracted to. That makes it different to things like BJs and anal, because they're always awesome."

I think his words over, applying them to my situation. Is it possible that I'm actually attracted to Deacon—as an entire man, and not just for his cock? I liked kissing him. No, I *loved* kissing him. It was just as Jazz described—explosive. But I'm still not sure if this is the right explana-tion for all my confusion and mental gymnastics.

Realizing I need to say something before Jazz starts getting too curious, I nod. "Right. I guess that makes sense."

"It's irrelevant," Jazz says firmly.

I return my gaze to his, finding hm staring at me intently. "What is?" I ask, my brow furrowed with confusion.

"The fact he's been taking dick every now and then for however long. That's what you were thinking, right?"

Um, no it wasn't, but I'm not about to correct him. "Why is that irrelevant?"

"Because the circumstances are completely different," he says with a shrug. "If the info he's given you is right, all the other times he's been with a guy have been completely random and impersonal. More like a really, really fun deep tissue massage than actual sex. But things are different with this new guy, so there must be something about him that your friend likes?"

I shrug, offering a wry smile. "I guess there must be."

"So if he wants to talk to you about it again, maybe that's something you could say—forget about everything from before and just focus on this guy, because there's obviously something there."

I smile fondly at my son. "That was quite insightful, after all. Thank you."

Jazz shrugs casually. "No worries. Maybe next time ask Reddit. Then I wouldn't have this merry-go-round thing happening in my head with all your friends' faces. I'd prefer not to know that one of them likes to get fucked to relieve stress."

"And I'd prefer not to know that Jace likes to give blow jobs when he gets high," I quip back. "At least I kept mine vague."

He lets out a heavy sigh. "Fair."

Yeah, definitely a good idea not to go into specifics.

We finish up lunch and then I stay for a couple drinks and watch Jazz's afternoon guitar set. He's decided to go to LA after all, so this will be my last chance to see him for a while. I don't think there's a huge chance that he'll actually stay out there, but you never know. He's got a lot of friends in LA, and I can't help thinking that it's only a matter of time before he changes his mind and decides he wants to do something meaningful with his musical talent.

And if that's what he decides, I'll support him. But, selfishly, I just want all my kids right here with me where I can keep them safe.

17

Deacon

Watching Sullivan and Drew play the happy couple at my sister's wedding is...surreal, to say the least. Between Drew's aversion to the whole money thing, and Sully's tendency toward open affection with his partners, I really hadn't expected Drew to last all that long. And let's not get started on the fact that, for some reason, Sullivan decided to tell my mom that Drew is a vegan. I'm pretty sure my buddy was more freaked out about the prospect of going animal product-free for the entire weekend than he was when the entire dinner table started calling for him and Sully to kiss at dinner last night.

The weirdest part of it all is how my family seem to be buying the whole charade. Drew is so far removed from the perfectly polished, smarmy twinks my brother usually goes for it seems insane to me that none of them have questioned it. But I guess the fact that everyone in my family has hated most of Sully's previous boyfriends, they're just happy to see him finally branching out.

My phone buzzes in my pocket and I step away from the conversation between my sister Willow—the bride to be—and our cousin Laura. I haven't really been paying that much attention, but I think it was something to do with the honeymoon.

It's not the first text that's distracted me this weekend, and I doubt it'll be the last. I know it's kind of rude to be preoccupied with my phone while I'm a guest at an event —particularly when it's my sister's rehearsal dinner—but if I don't check I'm only going to be distracted wondering about it, so what's the difference?

My brow creeps up as I read it. It's not as dirty as I was expecting. Or dirty at all, really. But it's no less intriguing.

Tanner Grimsay: I asked my son about my… situation - he's gay so I thought he might be able to shed some light

Me: You told your son you de-stress by getting fucked in the ass?

Tanner Grimsay: 😳 *God no. I told him I was asking about a friend*

Me: Ahh, I see. Like the "friend" I had who wet his bed til he was nine 🤭

Tanner Grimsay: 😏 *Yeah, that sort of friend.*

Me: And did it help?

Tanner Grimsay: I have no idea. Pretty sure Jazz is twisting his brain inside out trying not to think about which of my buddies I could have been talking about. And I learned some things about one of HIS friends that I'd really prefer I didn't know. But for me…I'm not sure. I feel like a mess of contradictions

I let out a sigh. Selfishly, I wanted Tanner to work everything out really quickly. But I knew that wasn't a realistic scenario. He's dealing with an onslaught of feelings and sensations and desires that he's never felt before and doesn't understand. It's going to take him time to figure out what it all means and what he wants.

Me: *That's okay. You'll get there.*

Tanner Grimsay: *There was no judgement though. Jazz is not exactly the type to hold back his opinions so I wasn't sure what to expect, but he took it all in stride (albeit without knowing we were talking about me)*

Me: *I'm not surprised. You're a really good dad so that kind of tracks*

Me: *Is his name seriously Jazz?*

Tanner Grimsay: 😄 *Jasper. But only his grandmother gets away with calling him that.*

"Ah-he-hem."

I glance up at the sound of someone dramatically clearing their throat to find my sister Blair—the middle child and the rebel of the family—staring at me with an arched brow. I slip my phone back in my pocket and offer a soft smile. "Hey, what's up?"

"Who's the new guy?" she asks, blue-painted lips curved in a knowing smirk.

I blink at her. "Excuse me?"

She rolls her eyes. "Please, you've been pretty much glued to your phone all weekend. And you've got this whole sex glow thing happening." She waves a hand over me, as though she's pointing out an interesting feature in a work of art or something.

I let out an exasperated groan. "Jesus, did you and Skyler both go to some Jedi sex school or something?"

Her brows shoot up. "No, but let me know if you hear of one because it sounds fabulous."

"What do you even know about sex anyway? You're ace."

"And you think that means I don't enjoy sex?" She shakes her head in mock disappointment. "Little brother, you need some education. I might not be sexually attracted to people, but trust me I can get just as horny as anyone else."

"So...what...you have sex with people you're not attracted to?" I ask warily, not sure why I'm continuing with this conversation. "You don't just...um...take care of things yourself?"

She gives a dramatic eye roll. "Well I can't exactly lick my own pussy, can I?"

I cringe and turn away. *Why* did I ask that question? My brain is obviously broken. "Fucking hell, Blair. I really didn't need to know that."

"Too bad—you opened the door, and now that I know just how patchy your knowledge is, you're going to sit here and listen to my spiel." She grabs my arm and leads me across the room to a corner where there's a little sofa. The party's pretty much winding down now so there aren't too many people around.

Damn it, I just want to go up to my room and sext with Tanner. Why the hell did I start down this road? I really don't want to sit here and listen to the intimate details of my sister's sex life. Before now I always thought of Blair as the safe one, but I guess I've fallen victim to popular misconception—and maybe a little wishful thinking. Apparently asexual does not equal celibate.

"Alright, so—"

"Blair, come on, I don't need to hear all this," I groan, thrusting a hand through my hair.

"I had to listen to Sullivan's very graphic description of

life as a gay man when I was about seventeen, so you're hearing this."

"This isn't a pay it forward situation," I grumble. "Why don't you go find Sully and torture him?"

"Because you're here now, and you're the baby, and you asked," she says with a casual shrug.

I let out a heavy sigh and slump back into the sofa. May as well get comfortable, I guess. When Blair decides on something, there's no talking her out of it.

"Alright, it's time to introduce you to the fascinating world of asexuality. And stop looking at me like I'm about to smash your kneecaps in," she adds with a scowl. "Don't worry, I'm not going to make you sit here while I bust every ace myth out there—there are way too many of them and I don't have any wine. So let's just skip to the sex stuff... There are definitely a ton of aceys who are totally repulsed by sex—some might never feel any kind of arousal, and others might get a bit horny sometimes but have no interest in engaging with a partner. There are others who are kind of indifferent. They might not be super into it, but they're not repulsed by it. There might be particular acts they enjoy more than others, and they might be more open to it if they're in a serious relation-ship. And then there are others that do enjoy sex with others, and will generally seek out a partner when they get horny. That might not be that often, or it could be on a frequent basis. And there are a bunch of people who fall somewhere in between all of those as well," she explains, waving her hands as though to demonstrate a line in the air. "Asexuality has absolutely nothing to do with libido—it's purely about sexual attraction, or lack thereof."

"Okay...I think I've got it. Can I go now?" I practically beg.

"No," she says, tugging on my arm to pull me back down as I try to rise from my seat.

I let out a heavy sigh. "Can you please at least keep the specifics to a minimum."

"So I'm one of the people who enjoy having sex with a partner when I get horny," she says, completely disregarding my request. "I mean, jilling off is fine and it does the job when I can't really be fucked going out to hook up. But like I said, I love getting eaten out, so I need to find a girl for that when I'm in that sort of mood."

My head jolts up in sudden confusion. "Girl? I thought you were straight...no—" I try to think of the right word for an ace person who dates their opposite gender and am immensely proud of myself when I manage to pull it from the back of my mind. "I mean heteroromantic."

Blair groans. "Oh my god, you're still not getting it. I don't give a shit who I'm having sex with. I mean, I have certain standards obviously, but other than that it doesn't matter. I go for women because they know what they're doing down there. Finding a guy who wants to eat pussy is a fucking dice roll. I mean, they might do it, but it's usually only for about five seconds before they try to put their dick in you."

"Please, god, make it stop," I groan. "I'll tell you what you want to know, just make it stop."

"I only hook up with guys when I really need a dick in me," she continues.

"Blair, *please,*" I beg. "I'm scarred for life."

She shakes her head. "God, you're such a fucking prude. You realize Willow and Summer have way more sex than I do, right? I mean, Willow and Dean are probably up in their room fucking right now."

I glare at her. "I hate you." As far as I'm concerned, none of my sisters have sex. Neither do my parents for that matter, except for those five times back in the late eighties and early nineties.

Despite my better judgement, I find myself asking, "If guys are so horrible, why do you date them instead of women?"

"Guys aren't *horrible*," she says. "They're really sweet. Well, not all of them, but the ones I've dated were. And a relationship is completely different to a hook-up. You have time to learn about each other and figure out what works." She screws up her face as she continues, "Girls are fucking bitches. I could never date one."

I feel like my brain is about to explode from both the influx of information and the effort it's taking not to think about my sister's sex life.

"Okay, now it's your turn," Blair says brightly. "Who's the guy?"

I groan, tossing my head back against the wall behind me. "No. We're not getting into this."

"You said you'd tell me what I wanted to know," she argues.

"Yeah, if you stopped the torture. Which you didn't."

"God, you're such a baby," she grumbles. "And I can't believe you didn't tell me about Sully and your roommate!"

I shrug. "I didn't know myself until recently."

"How is that possible?"

"Well, unlike you, Sully doesn't share the excruciating details of his sex life."

Blair rolls her eyes. Then her expression morphs into one of curiosity. "A bear cub though? That's such an interesting development when you think about all the bony little twinks he usually goes for."

She's definitely not the only member of my family to make such an observation since Sullivan and Drew arrived here yesterday. Weirdly, the fact that he's so different to the guys Sully usually dates seems to have endeared Drew to my entire family instantaneously. They're so happy for Sully not to be dating some ultra-smooth, shallow asshole who's only interested in him for his money and connections that they've completely fallen in love with Drew already. I'm pretty sure Mom will cry for a week when they 'break up'.

Blair taps a finger to her chin in thought. "I'm really not getting the sub vibe from Drew, which is really interesting because I always thought Sully was super toppy in like a dom way."

"I'm really uncomfortable talking about this," I grumble.

"But Drew just so doesn't look like the kind of guy who likes being told what to do. Like, ever," she says, once again completely ignoring me. "So does that mean Sully's not a total dom?"

"Do you realize how creepy you sound, speculating about your brother's sex life?"

"Are you seriously saying you're not the least bit curious about this?" she says, fixing me with a skeptical look.

Okay, to be fair, if I didn't know Sullivan and Drew were totally faking then I might have some of the same questions. But I wouldn't be sitting around trying to puzzle them out; there's a line between curious and creepy, and I'm pretty sure that's it.

"Okay, I need to remove myself from this conversation before I go insane," I mutter, getting to my feet.

"You never told me about your guy," Blair protests as I start walking away.

I turn my head back. "Don't be such a creep and maybe I'll tell you things."

She rolls her eyes and sticks her tongue out at me.

I let out a soft chuckle and make a break for it, leaving Blair behind at the party and heading upstairs to my room.

When I get there, I find Drew hovering awkwardly in the hall outside the door to his and Sully's room, looking completely out of character in dress pants and button-down shirt, and with his hair styled neatly for a change.

"You okay, man?"

His head snaps up, eyes wide in obvious surprise to find me standing there. "Yep. Good. All good. Nothing weird happening at all."

My brows draw together in concern. Drew is *not* a rambler. "You sure?" I step a little closer and lower my voice. "You know, if you're not super comfortable sleeping in there with my brother you can crash in my room. You can just say you had a fight or something. Or sneak back in before anyone gets up tomorrow." It'll put a bit of a kink in my sexting plans, but I guess I can sacrifice an orgasm to help out my buddy.

He gives a sharp shake of his head. "Nope, I'm good. All good." Then he draws in a deep breath and opens the door to his room, slipping inside.

I shake my head in bafflement but decide to let it go. If he says he's okay, he's okay.

I step inside my own room and retrieve my phone from my pocket.

Me: *Party's finally over. Time for bed*

Tanner Grimsay: *I hope "bed" doesn't mean "sleep"*

Me: *Definitely not* 🫠

18

Tanner

The moment Deacon enters my penthouse on Sunday night, he's on me, tugging my sweater over my head and roughly shoving me into the hallway wall before unfastening my jeans and shoving them down. My cock quickly grows hard in his hands and I let out a harsh gasp, my head falling back against the wall.

"What—what happened to just hanging out?" I somehow manage to ask.

"It's been three days since I've had your ass and I need to be in you," he says simply, before dropping to his knees and wrapping his lips around my dick.

Fucking hell. This definitely wasn't what I was expecting after Deacon made such a point about this not just being about sex. It was something we stuck to over the weekend—for all the sexting we did, there were a bunch more random texts with little stories about Deacon's family that I found very amusing—and I suppose I assumed the same would apply for tonight.

But I'm not complaining about this turn of events, that's for sure. If Deacon wants to barge into my place and start sucking on my dick, I'm never going to turn that down.

I thread my hands through his hair and gently rock my hips, marveling at the way Deacon groans with eagerness as he takes me deeper into his mouth, as though my cock's the best thing he's ever tasted. And, fuck, it feels incredible. I swear, if they gave Olympic medals for blow jobs, this guy would be on top of the podium.

"Fuck, Deacon…Jesus." The words fall from my lips in a strangled groan. If he keeps going like this, I'm going to shoot down his throat. I can already feel the orgasm approaching.

Perhaps sensing it as well, Deacon drags his lips away from my dick and gets to his feet.

I can't help letting out a whimper of frustration at the loss of his mouth.

"Bedroom," he says in a stern voice. "On the bed. On all fours."

I just stare at him blankly for a moment, feeling a little dazed.

"Now, Tanner," he growls.

Damn, he's got his bossy pants on tonight. I like it.

Snapping out of my stupor, I quickly tug my jeans off the rest of the way and make my way to the bedroom, Deacon following after me. I can hear clothes falling to the floor behind me and, sure enough, when I get to my bedroom and glance behind me, I see Deacon is now completely naked. My eyes rake over his tan, muscular body, fixating on his thick, hard cock. A shiver of anticipation runs through me, and I feel my hole throbbing with the need to be filled.

I might not have been expecting sex tonight, but that doesn't mean I haven't been absolutely fucking desperate to have this man inside me again since the moment he walked out my door on Thursday night.

He steps closer to me, right up in my space, and ducks his head. For a second, I think he's going to kiss me and I'm torn between excitement and dread. But he doesn't make a move for my lips, he just stares into my eyes, his gaze full of fire and dominance. "I thought I told you to get on the bed? Or am I going to have to throw you on there myself and give your ass a spanking until you remember to do what I ask?"

I smirk at him. "I don't think I'd mind that."

The challenge leaves his eyes and suddenly Mr Nice Guy is back as he lets out a soft laugh, shaking his head wryly. "Just get on the fucking bed, Tanner."

Figuring the sooner I comply, the sooner he'll be inside me, I don't bother putting up any more of a challenge. The only reason I delayed in the first place was because I was too caught up staring at his cock, so it's really his fault.

I get into position on the bed, feeling a little exposed with my ass just hanging out in the air like this, but I did ask for less intimacy so I can hardly complain now. "I'm not prepped," I warn him. "I really wasn't expecting this."

"Good," he says, his voice bordering on a growl. "That's my job. It was handy the other night, but I don't want to come here again and find you already stretched out." His hand lands on my ass, sliding gently over my left cheek before his fingers tease my crease, prompting me to gasp. "I liked hearing you moaning like a slut while I fucked you with my fingers. I don't want to miss that again. Got it?"

I nod. I'm already denying him so much of what he needs, I can give him this one simple thing. "Got it."

"Good."

My brain is starting to fritz from the sensation of his

fingers teasing my crease. I'm so fucking sensitive in that part of my body, even this light touch is driving me crazy. "Lube and condoms in the nightstand drawer," I tell him before my mind completely fogs over.

"I'll get to that," he murmurs. "But first thing's first. You remember your safe word?"

"Yeah."

"Tell me."

"Vikings." In my bewildered and horny state the other night, my brain clearly just reached for something that's been on my mind lately. The book I'm reading at the moment is a history of Vikings and their influence in Europe. I'm sure if it'd been a month ago the word would have been "Churchill." I doubt Deacon would have found that as sexy.

"Good," Deacon says. "Don't hesitate to use it if you need to."

I'm curious to know why he thinks I might need it, because I thought we'd set out some pretty clear boundaries in regards to what I'm comfortable with the other night. Maybe he's just being cautious...

Now that he's confirmed that I remember the safe word, I'm expecting to hear him rummaging in my nightstand drawer. But I don't. Instead, I feel him take a firm grip of my ass cheeks, spreading them apart. And then something hot, and wet, and incredible slides over my crease and around my hole, and I almost collapse onto the bed from the shock and the intensity of the sudden pleasure.

He's licking my hole; swirling around the rim and thrusting inside. And it feels so fucking good I can't even be freaked out by the fact that he has his mouth...*there*. My mind is blank. All I know is pleasure; intoxicating, all-consuming pleasure.

I'm vaguely aware that pathetic little whimpers and moans are falling from my lips, but I can't bring myself to care. Deacon is fucking me with his tongue, and I'm powerless against the onslaught of overwhelming pleasure.

Am I pushing my ass back against his mouth? Fuck, I didn't even realize I was doing that. My limbs are trembling so badly they can barely hold me up, and yet I can still shove my ass into Deacon's face like a greedy, desperate slut.

I finally get a reprieve when he pulls away, but it's only to replace his tongue with his fingers, thrusting two of them in deep and causing me to let out a strangled groan.

"Fucking hell, Tanner, the noises you make. I swear, I could eat this ass for hours if you're going to keep begging like that."

I was begging? My mind's such a scramble, I can't even remember. But I probably shouldn't be surprised considering the way my body has been responding—why shouldn't my mouth lose control as well?

"Deacon…shit…Deacon…" I don't even know what I'm trying to say. I don't know what I want. I'm desperate to have his tongue back inside me, even though it'll probably be the end of me; I'm not sure how much more of that intense, overwhelming pleasure I can take, but I'm greedy for it anyway.

But I'm also desperate for Deacon's cock. I want him buried deep inside me and fucking me hard. It'll be a different kind of pleasure, but one I'm not less greedy for.

"What do you want, babe?" he asks, his fingers twisting inside me and making me moan. "I could give you my tongue again if you want? I can eat this hole until you've collapsed on the bed in a puddle of your own cum. Or would you prefer my cock? That's what you usually want, isn't it? My dick buried deep inside you?" There's no challenge in his tone. It's just a question. "Or I could put you on your back and swallow that gorgeous cock again," he suggests. "It must be getting pretty painful by now."

I let out a pathetic little whimper, because yes, my cock is fucking aching, and I can't even lift a hand to attend to it because if I move a single finger I'm going to collapse.

"So, what'll it be?" Deacon presses.

"I don't…I can't…" I can barely even manage to think let alone talk.

"You can't what?" he asks, a note of concern in his tone.

Fuck, now he thinks I'm about to freak out again.

"I don't know," I manage to rasp out. "Can't decide."

"Ah, so it's my choice," he says, and I can hear the note of anticipation in his voice. I can picture his eyes gleaming with excitement. "In that case, I choose all of the above."

Before I have a chance to wonder how he's possibly going to get through that list, his fingers are gone from my ass and I only have a second to breathe before his tongue is back.

On cue, the whimpering and moaning starts again and I can feel the vibration of Deacon's laugh against my ass. Part of me feels completely pathetic to be reduced to this keening mess, but at the same time I know that Deacon enjoys it and I like making him happy, even if it's completely against my will.

"Deacon, please…"I beg. "Please, fuck…I need…"

I don't even know what I'm begging for. I have no idea what I need right now. My mind is a complete haze and my body has once again taken over, pressing back against Deacon's mouth.

He seems to know what I need, however, even if I don't, and a moment later his tongue thrusts inside me, sending bolts of that intoxicating pleasure coursing through me. It's just as overwhelming and unbearable as earlier, but I still don't want it to stop.

My arms finally give way and my front half collapses onto the mattress. I bury my head against the comforter, moaning and gasping as my body trembles.

Deacon pulls away from my ass and I hear him let out a soft chuckle. "That happened quicker than I thought. You didn't come as well, did you?"

"No," I gasp out. "Need to."

"You're going to come down my throat once I'm done with you. We already decided this."

We did? Fuck, why is my brain not working?

I feel Deacon's hands gripping my waist, and then I'm being shoved over onto my back. He straightens up and stares down at me, dark eyes full of lust. "Jesus, you're a fucking mess."

"Your tongue's been in my ass for days," I groan. Fuck, I want it back there. After that onslaught of overwhelming intensity I feel completely bereft now.

Deacon flashes a wry grin. "Not quite that long, but you're giving me ideas." He turns to the nightstand and opens the drawer, retrieving the box of condoms and tube of lube I keep there.

I watch him as he rolls the condom onto his hard cock and then adds some lube, glad to have a brief moment to collect myself.

"Do you think you need more prep?" Deacon asks me, holding up the lube.

I shake my head. "I'm good." There's no way I could handle having his fingers in me right now, and I think a bite of pain as he enters me will probably be a good thing in my current state.

"I was going to keep you on your hands and knees, but I don't think you're up for that," he says with a smirk.

"Don't worry, though, I remember the deal. And you can close your eyes if you need—I won't take it personally."

I offer a grateful smile, once again marveling at the seamless shift from the bossy alpha to the sweet, caring guy who's always so sensitive to my needs, even when they conflict with his own.

I don't have much time to dwell on those thoughts, because Deacon swiftly moves into action. He climbs up onto the bed and grabs a pillow, stuffing it under my back. Then he spreads my legs out and kneels in front of me.

"You don't have any groin or hamstring issues do you?" Deacon asks me once he's satisfied that I'm positioned where and how he wants me.

My brows shoot up. "No."

"Good," he says with a smirk. "I'd hate to do anything that might put you out of action. I've got big plans for you."

Before I have a chance to wonder why he's concerned about flaring up an old injury, he grabs my legs and tosses them over his shoulders, almost bending me in half as he leans forward to drive inside me.

"Fuck, fuck, fuck," I groan. The burn as he thrusts into me is worse than I'd expected, but it's not unwelcome. After all the new and intense sensations from earlier, I feel like I'm back on familiar ground. For the most part, at least. The sensation of being filled and fucked is one I know well, and with Deacon in particular I feel like I get to know him better every time we're together. Each time has been completely different, but the way he feels inside me is the same. The way he moves is the same. The connection between us is the same.

I snap my gaze open so I can look at him, realizing that even though I've admired his powerful, muscular body before, I've never actually seen it in action. I've felt it, but never actually *seen* it.

I'm surprised to find his own eyes closed, his face a mask of tension. Is he trying to hold back an orgasm? Or maybe this is how he always looks during sex? The only other time we were face-to-face we spent the whole time with our mouths fused together.

I brush the thoughts away and take the opportunity while I'm unobserved to soak in the sight of Deacon's hard muscles straining and flexing as he fucks into me in hard, powerful strokes.

The slight burst of clarity the burn of his entry brought me is fading as my brain is once again scrambled by pleasure from the way Deacon's cock keeps bumping my prostate. It's probably a good thing I don't have sex all that often or I wouldn't have any brain cells left.

Deacon lets out a soft laugh and I see his eyes are on me, glimmering with amusement. "You're too smart as it is. You could do with some brain cells dying off."

Fuck—I actually said that out loud? "That's embarrassing," I groan. "Didn't mean to say that."

"You don't ever have to be embarrassed with me," he says with a reassuring smile.

Jesus, how is he capable of switching into nice guy mode even when he has me folded over like a birthday card, with his cock buried deep inside me?

I move my hands from his hips to slide over his torso, feeling the muscles strain and pull underneath my fingers. I want to touch every inch of his skin, get to know his body, feel the way it moves as fucks me…but I have enough brain power left to know that's not fair. Not after the deal I've made him agree to. So I reluctantly slide my hands down his back and settle on his ass, gripping firmly and urging him forward. Deeper.

"Fucking hell, you're relentless," he grunts. "Such a needy bottom."

"For your cock," I rasp out. "Definitely."

"And my tongue apparently. In your ass, at least." He says the words wryly, but I see a flicker of disappointment cross his features and I'm confused for a moment. And then my sex-addled brain supplies me with the answer and I'm left with a tide of guilt. The truth is, I *am* needy for Deacon's kisses. Desperate for them, even. But I'm still too confused about that whole situation, I'm not about to open that door now. I doubt correcting him would be any comfort anyway. The result is the same.

I toss my head back with a loud groan as he hits my prostate again. "Fuck, Deacon...keep it up and I'm going to come."

"No you're not," he growls, his bossy pants clearly back on. "You're coming down my throat, we already decided."

"*You* decided," I correct him.

"You gave me the authority," he quips back.

I let out another wild moan as he once again hits my prostate. Desperation is coursing through me now; there's no way I can hold off this orgasm for much longer. "If you don't want me to blow then stop fucking hitting my prostate," I groan.

"Stop moaning like a whore when I do it and I'll give you a break," he says with a smirk.

The moan leaves my lips before I can help it, causing Deacon to laugh with obvious delight. The nice, sweet guy has officially retreated and the alpha is back. I'm getting whiplash.

"Deacon, please..." I gasp out. "Please, I need to come."

"No."

"I'm going to blow," I groan, tossing my head back.

"No you won't."

I wish I had his confidence…

Deacon leans forward and starts speeding up his thrusts, pounding in hard, over and over. Fortunately, he's not deliberately aiming for my prostate anymore, but I'm still fighting what I'm sure will be a losing battle to hold back my climax. It's just too good; the feel of his thick cock filling me, hitting me deep in those hard, powerful strokes is just too fucking incredible. And I'm going to blow any second.

Then Deacon stops, his whole body tensing as he lets out a deep groan. His expression looks pained for a moment, and then it clears to reveal eyes clouded with lust and a lazy, satisfied smile.

His breathing still rapid, he wastes no time in dropping my legs back to the bed and then bending over me, taking my raging cock between his lips.

It takes barely ten seconds of his hot mouth on me before I'm arching off the bed and coming hard down his throat.

He straightens up, licking his lips and offering me a bright grin. "There we go. All of the above."

"I don't remember collapsing in a puddle of my cum," I point out dryly.

He shrugs. "There were some necessary adjustments."

19

Deacon

"Urgh, this is fucked." Skyler cries, jumping to his feet and tossing his game controller onto the sofa, a frustrated scowl crossing his face. "Why are you two ganging up on me?"

I smirk at him. "Because it's fun to beat you at something for a change." Skyler's one of those people that just has a knack for things, and his ultra-competitive nature means that no one else even gets a look in. Unless, of course, they can level the field by playing two against one like we've been doing tonight. Three games in and Jackson and I are staring down the barrel of an unprecedented clean sweep.

"*Jackson,*" Skyler pouts, stamping his foot like a toddler. I swear, sometimes I can't help thinking that's exactly what he is. A sex-crazed, twenty-seven-year-old toddler…who's only months away from earning a law degree, with a job at one of the best firms in the city waiting for him once he passes the Bar.

But despite being totally wrapped around Skyler's little finger, it's actually pretty rare for Jax to indulge this kind of bratty behavior, so I'm not too surprised when he just smiles and shrugs. "Call it a lesson in humility."

Skyler's scowl grows darker, and I can't help letting out a soft chuckle. "Are you going to throw tantrums like this when you lose in court?"

He waves me away. "Don't be ridiculous, I'm not going to lose in court. Look at this beautiful face—" He gestures through the air around his face, which I'll admit is a very pretty one even if he's not at all my type. "No jury is going to vote against a face this gorgeous and a body this hot," he says with absolute confidence, moving his hand down to wave over his entire body.

I exchange a look with Jackson. "I'm a little worried about the law program at Columbia if that's what you're walking away with after three years."

Skyler just rolls his eyes and flops down onto the sofa with a huff. "Where the hell's Drew anyway? He's been a total ghost lately, He didn't even reply to my *Modern Family* GIF yesterday. No "ha ha" or anything. Just dead air."

God forbid. In Skyler's world, if you don't reply to a text, especially a funny one, there must be something seriously wrong.

"I guess he's just busy," Jackson says with a shrug. "Cool of him to come on Saturday, though."

Saturday was our rugby tournament, which we actually won, much to everyone's delight and—dare I say— surprise. We worked incredibly hard for it, but there were a ton of teams competing so winning the whole thing was huge. Spencer's main goal each year is always to get further in the tournament than a team which has been our "enemy" since before I ever came on board. Coinciden-tally, Spencer's boyfriend, Will, is best friends with the guy who's dating the captain of that other team; I'm not sure how much that's done to thaw tensions, however. Not if Saturday was anything to go by.

"Yeah, that was kind of weird," Sky mumbles. "He hates hanging out with the team."

"Drew and Sully are fucking," I blurt out. My eyes widen as I realize what I've just done. This isn't something I should be telling my buddies like it's a piece of interesting gossip; because a) I don't a hundred per cent know how far it's gotten yet; and b) I do know Drew's struggling with how to identify and even if he weren't it's insanely uncool to out someone, regardless of whether the people I'm telling are two of his best friends or not. I run a hand through my hair, my face tight with regret. "Shit, forget I said that."

"How the hell are we supposed to forget you said that?" Skyler demands.

"You mean just...like, the whole fake thing, right?" Jackson asks, clearly baffled.

Skyler lets out a snort. "*Fake* fucking, Jax? How do you fake fuck someone? Unless you're an actor doing a full-on sex scene with the whole cock sock thing. I swear that must be the most awkward thing ever, with everyone watching, and the director telling you exactly what to do every five seconds. I think I'd just rather stick it in and tell them to roll camera."

"Pretty sure that's called porn," Jax says dryly.

I let out a rough sigh and lift my head up. As Tanner would say, the horse has bolted now. I may as well just tell them what I know. I'm hoping it won't be secret for much longer anyway.

"Alright...I don't know for *sure* that they're...you know," I clarify. "The last update I got was on the way home from the wedding. Drew told me they'd done some stuff, but not full on sex."

"What kind of stuff?" Skyler asks, eager for details.

"I didn't ask for specifics," I grumble. Between my traumatizing conversation with Blair, the frequent comments people kept making to Willow about the wedding night, and then this thing with Drew and Sully I was well and truly done with hearing about my siblings' sex lives. Thank god Summer is still a virgin. Despite the barb Blair threw out there, that's something I'm sure of. A thirty-two-year-old virgin. Definitely.

"They were together at the wedding?" Jackson asks incredulously. "Over a week ago?"

I shrug. "I guess so." I still feel like a total dumbass for thinking Drew's odd behavior outside his room after the rehearsal dinner was because he didn't want to sleep in the same room as my brother. In my eagerness to get to bed and share some texts with Tanner, all I saw was him hesitating in the hallway; it wasn't until breakfast the next morning when I saw Drew blush bright red and shift around nervously when Sully kissed him on the cheek that I remembered him doing the exact same thing the night before.

And then there was the staring during the ceremony, and the slow-dancing at the reception. Needless to say, by the time we all left Long Island, no one had any doubts that Drew and my brother were madly in love.

"And now…?" Skyler presses.

I sigh. "I don't know. I haven't exactly been home much…"

Skyler smirks and Jackson rolls his eyes. They both know exactly why I've barely slept in my own bed since the wedding weekend. With Tanner's free time so limited and sporadic, it's been simpler for me to just hang out here at the penthouse in the evening rather than try to schedule times to meet up. Sometimes he comes by straight after work and we have dinner together and hang out for a bit before he goes home, and other times he doesn't get here until ten or eleven, but can stay until early morning.

It's not the ideal situation, obviously, but it's working okay for now. I'd still love to have more intimacy sex-wise, but I said I'd give him some time and I meant it. And I guess at least this way we've been able to spend time together both in and out of bed without it feeling forced, or like a booty call.

The fact that Tanner's completely cool with me having my friends over is a bonus. And Skyler and Jax have been very appreciative of the giant TV, four-player PS5, and well-stocked fridge.

I haven't actually slept here overnight yet; even on the nights where Tanner can stay, I always leave once the sex is over so he can get some sleep. It's not as though we can cuddle anyway, so what would be the point of staying?

"So you know that *something* happened, but you don't know for sure if anything else has happened since then?" Skyler asks.

"I'm pretty sure it has. Based off some…things."

"Things?" Jackson asks, one brow arched.

I cringe, wishing I'd never started this conversation. "I'd rather not go into it."

"I think you'll have to," Skyler says.

I let out a heavy sigh. "Urgh, fine. Things like…I noticed Drew washed his sheets three times last week."

Skyler's brows shoot up. "Jeez. You'd think Sully would have a few tricks for avoiding a wet spot. I mean, it's not that hard to come on a guy's chest. Or, better yet, in his mouth." He brings his hands together to mime dusting them off. "No mess, no stress."

I roll my eyes. "Thanks. I desperately needed that advice."

Jackson folds his arms over his chest, looking mildly amused. "What other clues have you gathered, Detective Deacon?"

Why do I get the feeling that nickname is going to stick? "The only other physical evidence was a tube of lube I saw in the kitchen when I got home on Friday night."

Skyler gives a nod of approval. "Kitchen. Nice. Although they could have mixed things up a little—so many other options for getting slicked up right there in front of you. Olive oil, butter, mayonnaise…"

"Mayonnaise?" Jackson asks, expression incredulous.

Skyler shrugs. "It's oil-based."

"You seriously put mayonnaise up your butt?"

Sky rolls his eyes. "Jax, I don't put anything up my butt."

"Well, this sounds interesting," a familiar, sexy voice says from the doorway.

I snap my head up to find Tanner standing there, an amused expression on his face. He's taken off his suit jacket, but still has his vest and tie on and looks absolutely edible, especially with his shirtsleeves rolled back to reveal those toned forearms.

"I keep forgetting how hot he is," Skyler whispers to me.

"Back off," I growl, before turning back to Tanner and flashing a bright smile. "Hey! I didn't think you'd be here until later. Hope you don't mind these two being over here again."

He shakes his head, smiling fondly. "Not at all. What are you guys up to?"

"We were just talking about—*omf*" Skyler cuts off as I elbow him in the ribs to stop him from blurting out what I've told them about Drew and Sullivan. It's bad enough I spilled the beans to these two, I don't want it going any further. I trust Tanner, of course, but that's not the point.

"Jackson and I were just kicking Sky's ass," I say, holding up the game controller.

"Only because it's two against one," Skyler says with a scowl.

"You want to even the field?" Tanner asks him.

Sky's brows shoot up in skepticism. "*You* want to play?"

Tanner chuckles. "Don't look at me like that. I've been playing video games since before you were born."

"I don't doubt it," Skyler says under his breath. But he shrugs and holds up the spare controller.

Tanner strides over to us and takes the controller from Skyler's hand.

"Do you know how to use it?" Sky asks. "This button here—"

"You realize this is *his* PS, right Sky?" I say with an eye roll.

Tanner's lips twitch with amusement and he gives Skyler a nod. "Thanks, I'm pretty sure I've got it."

We start the game, and it only takes about twenty seconds for me to realize that letting Skyler and Tanner team up together was a big mistake. Rodeo Drive sales girl huge.

It's an absolute slaughter, and the glee Jackson and I were feeling over our earlier victories has been completely sapped away.

The only positive thing is that Tanner is at least more dignified in victory than Skyler. Although that's not exactly hard…

"Wooh! *Yeah!* Suck on *that*, bitches!" Skyler cries, getting right up in our faces.

I slap a palm over my face, shaking my head. Why am I friends with him again?

Next to me, Jackson just stretches out his body and gives a massive yawn. "You want to go hit a bar?"

Sky's eyes light up. "Yes! I'm *so* in the mood to fuck right now."

I roll my eyes. "When are you *not* in the mood to fuck?"

He shrugs. "I just give the people what they want."

Jackson gets to his feet and starts maneuvering Skyler toward the door. "Come on. Let's get going. Did you want to swing by home to put on tighter jeans first?"

"Yeah, obviously."

"Have fun," Tanner says, offering a wry smile as he waves goodbye.

"Oh, I always do. If you ever want to trade up—"

"*Goodbye*, Skyler," I say firmly, getting up from the sofa and stalking over to the door so I can usher them out faster.

Skyler's cackle of laughter echoes in my head as I finally close the door and turn back to Tanner, letting out a sigh. "I'm sorry about them. *Him*, really."

Tanner's brows shoot up. "Skyler? Why?"

I shrug. "I know he can be a lot to take. He's a good friend when it counts though."

"I'm sure he is," he says with a wry chuckle, then he hits me with a questioning look. "I've told you about my son, right?"

I frown in thought. "I think you've mentioned him a couple times. Jazz, right? Hard name to forget."

Tanner grins. "Yeah, well, imagine Skyler multiplied by about a thousand, then add in scathing honesty and unrepentant abrasiveness. That's Jazz."

I let out a snort and walk back to the sofa. I love how warm and affectionate Tanner's voice is, and how his eyes sparkle with happiness at the thought of his son, even when describing some qualities that I'm sure a lot of people would find less than charming. "And what about your daughter?" I ask him, settling onto the sofa next to him. "Not Izzy, obviously."

He grins. "Piper? She's…I think *high maintenance* is probably the best way to describe her. She can be a little catty sometimes, but she's got a really good heart. Both of them do. And they both absolutely dote on Izzy. They've been amazing with her."

There's a touch of regret in Tanner's expression, but I can't bring myself to prod at it. I'm still curious about what the deal is with Izzy's mother. At first I thought all his kids had the same mom, and that Izzy was just a late arrival. But when Tanner was telling me about his wife's death a few weeks ago, I'm sure he mentioned having only two kids, and that they were both young. Piper and Jazz would have had to be in high school at the very least by the time Izzy was born.

I shelve my questions for now and instead tell him a bit about my crazy family. I gave him a few tidbits while I was away for the wedding, but there's always more to tell.

"Baby of the family, huh?" he asks, eyes shimmering with amusement. "Do they all try to protect you or do they tease the hell out of you?"

"Both," I grumble. "Or corrupt me."

He lets out a huff of laughter. "They clearly don't know you as well as I do if they think you need corrupting."

20

Tanner

"RJ's waiting for you to start the BCN meeting," Joseph tells me when I stride past his desk on my way to my office on Wednesday morning.

I stop short and just blink at him for a moment. "BCN's tomorrow morning."

He shake's his head. "Nope. Wednesday."

I groan. Fuck. How did I mess that one up? I rarely need reminding of what's on my schedule, and I can't even remember a time when I mixed up days or times of an important meeting. Clearly all my brain power has been taken up by something else recently…

"Right, thanks." I pivot around and start walking in the opposite direction, toward the boardroom.

"Oh, hang on, Tanner," Joseph calls after me. "Sullivan Stapleton—"

"No," I growl, holding my hand up to cut him off. "Tell him no."

I hear Joseph let out a sigh from behind me. I'm sure he's just as tired of this merry-go-round with Monty Steele as I am.

I try not to cringe as I think of my conversation with Deacon last night. He told me all about his family, including his investment banker brother. That was my opening to say, "Oh, yeah, I know Sullivan—he and his asshole client won't accept that 'no' means no." But I didn't take it. I felt like if I mentioned something I'd be putting Deacon in the middle, which I doubt he'd be comfortable with. Not to mention, I wasn't sure I could talk about Stapleton without insulting him; and considering Deacon seems to be under the impression that his brother is some kind of sweet, fuzzy teddy bear I doubt he'd want to hear some of the names I have for him.

But now I can't help thinking that staying quiet might not have been the best idea. If Deacon and I actually start dating then the truth's bound to come out and I'll look like a total ass.

I pause in my step as shock rolls over me. *Dating?* Did I actually just think that? I don't—that's not what I want…is it? I love spending time with him, and the sex is phenomenal; but I still haven't figured out any of the stuff he told me to figure out. And we haven't kissed since that first night at my penthouse.

I give a sharp shake of my head and continue walking, ignoring all the people in the office giving me curious looks. No, we're not dating. Yet.

Yet?

Fuck. I hate my brain.

I breathe a sigh of relief when I get to the meeting, glad for the distraction from my whirling thoughts. But the relief only lasts a moment, because as soon as I enter the room, it dawns on me that Joseph was actually trying to issue a warning, not pass on a message. And I completely brushed him off.

"Sorry, I'm—" My words cut off as my gaze lands on

Sullivan Stapleton sitting comfortably in one of the board-room chairs. "What the fuck are you doing here?"

"Tanner," RJ hisses at me, and I realize just how rude that phrasing must have seemed, particularly to Marion and Carter who don't know how tense my dealings with Stapleton have been recently.

Even so, I want to know what the fuck he's doing here.

"Pax invited me," he says with a dazzling smile, reaching to his side to give Pax Greenwood a pat of acknowledgement.

My brows shoot up, because as far as I'm aware, Paxton Greenwood wasn't invited to this meeting either. Scanning further down the table, I see another uninvited guest on Pax's other side: Charlie Campbell. Why Pax felt the need to drag an overpriced corporate litigator to the meeting, I have no idea, but my confusion makes way for horror as I catch sight of the guy sitting next to Charlie. Skyler.

With his dark hair neatly styled and a pair of black-framed glasses on, he looks very different to the guy hanging out with Deacon at my penthouse last night. But it's most definitely him.

When my eyes land on him, he gives me a wink that fills me with trepidation. Is he about to blurt out to the entire boardroom that I'm sleeping with his best friend? Or is he trying to reassure me that I have nothing to worry about?

I send an incredulous look down the table at Marion and Carter. "I thought this was a developmental meeting? What the hell is the jock squad doing here?"

I hear a snort of laughter that's quickly disguised as a cough, and when I shift my gaze back at the unexpected meeting attendees, I see Skyler wearing a bashful expression. I have to bite my lip to keep them from twitching in amusement; it's difficult not to like this guy.

"I mentioned the proposal to Pax the other day and he expressed interest in being involved," Marion says, shifting awkwardly in her seat as I fix my gaze back on her. "He's been at the network for almost as long as you've owned it, Tanner. He could have some useful insight for this new…venture."

I nod and turn my gaze back to Paxton. "I appreciate that, Marion. And I'm aware of how long Pax has been at BCN. I remember meetings like these where we developed his show. I don't remember any veteran anchors attending. With a retinue, no less."

Pax flashes me the dazzling smile that's had BCN viewers charmed for fifteen years. "I'm just looking to stay abreast of things, that's all."

I quirk an eyebrow at him. "And you've brought along a litigator, an investment banker, and…" I pause when I get to Skyler. I'm not supposed to know he's in law school, am I? "Clark Kent?"

Skyler doesn't attempt to disguise his snort of laughter this time, earning him a quiet reprimand from Charlie Campbell. "Sorry, but he's funny," Skyler sputters.

"This is my paralegal, Skyler Mason," Charlie says with a lazy gesture.

My brows shoot up in faux surprise. "A litigator *and* a paralegal. Is this a secret deposition? I thought you needed a subpoena for those?"

"Charlie's here to represent my interests," Pax says smoothly.

I arch a brow at him—*"stay abreast of things" huh?*—before turning my gaze on Stapleton. "And you?"

He lazes back in his chair as though he's a king who expects the world around him to bow down to him. "I'm the money," he says, arms held out as though presenting himself as a generous offering. "Pax told me there was a new venture happening at BCN and thought I might be interested in the investment opportunity."

I offer a bland smile. "How generous of you. I had no idea you'd taken an interest in news broadcasting."

He shrugs. "I like to keep different avenues open."

If Sullivan Stapleton is looking to personally invest in a news program then I'm a fucking flamingo. There's no way someone as financially savvy as this guy would take that risk in what is essentially a dying market. My guess is he's trying to work out just how vulnerable Grimco is, and whether BCN could be ripe for the plucking sometime soon. I'm sure he has a few clients who'd love to get their hands on such a prized asset.

As for Greenwood? I honestly have no clue. Maybe he genuinely is worried that the changes will ultimately result in him being pushed aside or something like that, but this definitely isn't the way to handle that. Work it out in contract renegotiations, don't bring it into my boardroom.

I let out a sigh and pin Pax with a level look. "Paxton, I realize you're a drama major, but I'm really not in the mood for a Shakespearean farce today. It really wasn't necessary to bring the Dream Team here to *represent your interests*, because, frankly, you don't have any interests here. If you'd like to provide some productive ideas, then by all means we'd like to hear them. But whatever we implement will have no bearing on you or your program. And as for the poorly disguised Trojan horse here," I say with a wave in Stapleton's direction, "BCN is not for sale, so you're wasting your time sniffing around."

"I don't really look like a Trojan horse do I? Stapleton grumbles to Pax.

"Just your ass," Pax says with a smirk.

I run my eyes back down the foursome and land on Skyler, who's no longer even trying to hide his amusement. The second he feels my eyes on him, though, he jolts to attention and makes himself look as though he's been jotting down notes the whole time. "You're a paralegal?" I ask him, as if I don't already know all the details of Deacon's friends' lives. "Full-time, or are you studying?"

He blinks up at me for a moment, then says, "Almost done with law school. Take the Bar next year."

I nod and then gesture to Charlie. "Are you planning to keep working for him once you graduate?"

Skyler casts a sideways glance at Charlie and shrugs. "That's the plan."

I click open the briefcase I'd set down on the chair in front of me when I first came in, and locate a crisp white business card in the index sleeve. I reach across the table to hand it to Skyler. "Here's another option. If you want some actual legal experience, that is."

"What the hell, Grimsay? You're poaching my employees now?" Charlie demands.

"Well you're not exactly using him, are you?" I say with a shrug. Then I turn my gaze on Marion and Carter, who have been relatively quiet while I said my piece to the interlopers. "I think I'm going to leave it here. Unlike these three, apparently, I don't have endless time in my day to waste. RJ can fill me in on everything."

I give a brief nod to everyone and start backing out of the boardroom.

As I exit the room, I hear Skyler say, "Can we go back to the part about Pax being a drama major?"

When I get into the hallway, I see RJ has followed me. "Sorry about that—I thought Joseph was going to warn you…"

"He tried," I say wryly. "I didn't let him finish."

RJ nods. "That explains it, then. You want me to come get you once those idiots have left?"

I shake my head. "It's fine. You can get me if there's anything really crucial that comes up but otherwise I'm okay for you to handle it. You know where we stand on everything."

He gives a brief nod and slips back into the meeting, while I return to my office. I start pacing my office, forcing my brain through the monotonous boxing-up exercises to clear out the mess. I think I handled myself pretty well in there given the unexpected circumstances, but it could have easily gone the complete opposite way. I could have completely broken down...over absolutely nothing. Nothing major, anyway. And now I can't stop thinking about what *could* have gone wrong; how I *might* have fucked up. In front of a boardroom full of some of New York's most influential business people. I would have been a laughing stock. This whole corporation would be.

Why do I always feel like I'm hanging on by a tether?

Box it up. Put it away. Clear it out. Box it up. Put it away. Clear it out.

"Hard at work?"

I pause in my step and glance up at the sound of the familiar voice, finding Charlie Campbell at the threshold of my office, a wry smirk on his face.

I arch a brow at him. "You don't pace when you're trying to work out a problem?"

He shrugs. "Sometimes. I have more fun ways of clearing the mind, though." The innuendo in his tone can't possibly be missed. Oh god, please don't tell me Charlie Campbell and I have something in common.

"Why are you here?" I ask him.

He sighs. "I wanted to apologize. You were right—we shouldn't have ambushed your meeting like that. It was...

unprofessional. Also…" he glances behind him for a moment, then looks back at me, a bewildered expression on his face. "Skyler wanted to *thank* you for giving him Leona's card. I told him he should actually meet Leona before considering it a favor, but whatever."

"Uh…okay, then. Is he out there? He can come in."

Charlie gestures behind him and a moment later, Skyler appears in my doorway. The pair stand there awkwardly for a moment before Skyler says, "Can't a guy thank another guy in private anymore?"

Charlie's brows shoot up, but he shrugs and walks away from the door, still looking utterly baffled.

Skyler steps farther into my office and closes the door.

"He's going to think something nefarious is going on," I say with a twitch of my lips.

Skyler shrugs. "Yeah, he'll probably be like "Oh my god, Skyler, tell me you did not try to seduce Tanner Grimsay" and I'll be like "Who, me? Of course not. You know I don't catch, and that guy doesn't look like a guy who'd take it." Which is funny if you know the truth," he says with a snort.

"How about you just don't speculate on it at all?" I suggest wryly.

He nods. "Yeah, and about that—I just wanted to tell you I didn't mean for you to get blindsided today. I only found out about this meeting this morning."

I wave him away. "That's okay."

"Deacon has no idea you and Sully hate each other, does he?" he asks, brows raised in curiosity.

I wince. "Hate's a strong word. But no. I haven't mentioned this to him. He seems to have a very different relationship with his brother than I do. And for the record, I didn't even know they were brothers when everything with Deacon started. They definitely aren't anything alike as far as I can see."

"Yeah, well, you only know the asshole businessman Sully. Real life Sully's way cooler. He's actually a lot like Deac…all nice and sweet and shit."

I screw my face up in disbelief. I just don't buy it. That asshole from the boardroom today is *nothing* like my Deacon.

My Deacon? Jesus Christ I'm turning into a sap.

Skyler nods adamantly. "Seriously. He's like a…eskimo pie."

"Cold and tasteless?"

"Umm…I was going for hard on the surface and soft underneath. You'd have to ask Drew how he tastes, I really can't vouch for that."

"I'll keep that in mind," I deadpan.

"I should go or Charlie really will think we're hooking up," he says with a grin, turning for the door. Looking back at me he says, "Did you really mean for me to call your lawyer about a job, or was that just part of the thing with the others?"

I shrug. "A bit of both. Today aside, I'm sure you're getting some great experience working for Charlie, but it definitely won't hurt to see how things work at different firms. And if Leona knows she's poached you from Charlie, you'll get the star treatment."

"Well, I do like being the star," he muses.

"How very surprising to hear that," I deadpan.

He grins and holds up the business card. "Thanks, Tanner. And make sure Deacon goes easy on you tonight. My first thought when you walked into that meeting was that you looked like you'd been ridden hard and put away wet. Which I guess isn't far from the truth," he adds with a chuckle, before pushing the door open and almost concussing RJ who was on his way in.

The pair look at each other for a long, awkward moment, before RJ finally says, "Uh…your boss said to say to meet at DeLuca's when you were done…um…striking out."

Skyler rolls his eyes. "He has no faith in me."

"Well, you did strike out," I joke.

He gives a dismissive wave. "I didn't even swing. This is what we call a walk."

"A walk implies you got to first base," I point out.

He nods. "True. Not even Deacon can get there."

I wince. The words aren't meant as any kind of taunt, just a statement of fact, but they sting nonetheless, because I know how much my hesitation over the whole kissing thing has been costing Deacon.

"I feel like I'm missing something," RJ says, looking utterly baffled. "Do you two know each other?"

Skyler's eyes widen as he realizes he's said a bit too much.

I wave him away. "It's fine, Skyler. Go meet up with the others."

He casts one more regretful glance back, then strides out my office door.

Once he's gone, I'm left to deal with RJ's expectant face.

I sigh in resignation. I guess this was inevitably going to come out sooner or later if it just kept going on… "Yes, we've met before today. He's friends with the guy I'm… seeing," I finish off awkwardly.

RJ's brows knit together for a moment, before shooting up into his hairline. "You mean…as a couple? Romantically?"

"Erm…" God, how do I even explain this without him wanting to chop his ears off. "It's not really that…official."

"So it's just sex?" he asks matter-of-factly, as though the notion of his boss and potential future father-in-law being in a no-strings gay sex arrangement is totally normal.

I wince. Since when did the idea of me and Deacon being described as something so casual seem so…wrong to me? "I'm not sure I'd put it that way. We hang out and do other things, and have meals together, and just talk sometimes. And…"

"And you've met his friends," RJ finishes for me. Then he shrugs. "Sounds like a romantic relationship to me."

Maybe he's right. Maybe it is a romantic relationship… But when did that happen?

I suppose the answer to that isn't all that important. The main thing is…I've realized the thought of actually being with Deacon isn't something that scares me anymore.

21

Deacon

"Can I ride you?"

I can still hear those words ringing in my ears even now while I gaze up at the incredible sight of Tanner straddling me as he wantonly rides my dick. The request was definitely a bit of a surprise, and needless to say I said yes immediately.

I've noticed Tanner showing a little more initiative in our sexual activities recently, but it's been baby steps, with him gradually growing more comfortable with things that I'd completely taken for granted with previous partners. Eye contact and reciprocal touching, for example.

The touching is something I'm especially enjoying; it started with light brushes of my body, running his hands gently over my abs and biceps, before turning into more confident glides over my skin and grabs of my ass as I pounded inside him. And tonight he actually touched my dick. I'm not even sure if it was a conscious thing or not; for all I know he was imagining one of his sex toys as he carefully lined the head of my cock up with his hole. But that didn't stop me from nearly blowing my load the second I felt the grip of his fingers around me.

I'm not sure even the most pragmatic part of my brain could imagine he's ever ridden one of his dildos the way he's moving right now, though. The expression on his face as he fucks up and down and swivels his hips around is pure bliss, lips parted slightly, cheeks flushed, eyes closed.

I wish I could reach for him and pull him down against me, then wrap my body around him and just kiss and kiss and kiss as we move together. But he still hasn't given the okay for that yet, so I settle for gripping his ass as I meet his movements, and soaking in the sight of his beautiful body, with all his lean muscles straining and flexing and his hard, leaking cock tapping against my abs as he bounces around. Definitely not a bad second prize at all.

I already know—I have for a while, actually—that I'm not going to hold him to the time limit ultimatum I set a couple weeks ago. I'm going to be that idiot who waits around forever for the guy who might not ever commit to an actual relationship. But he *might.* So I'll wait. If there's even the slightest chance of something real with Tanner, I'll give him however long it takes. I've gone and completely fallen in love with him, and there's no going back now.

"Jesus, Deacon," he murmurs, gasping and panting with what I'm guessing is a combination of exertion and pleasure. "Why does it always feel so good with you?"

The confusion and apprehension I used to see in his eyes when he ventured questions like that isn't there right now. Instead what I see in that captivating blue gaze is a wry acceptance combined with the fiery heat.

"Because I'm the best," I say with a quirk of my lips.

His eyes sparkle in amusement. "Well that much was obvious. Where's bossy Deacon tonight?"

I let out a soft chuckle that turns into a groan as he fucks down again, taking me in deeper. "*Fuck,*" I gasp out, casting an amused look at a very proud-looking Tanner. "Bossy Deacon's enjoying the show," I murmur. It's adorable how he's nicknamed the different sides of my sex demeanors "Bossy Deacon" and "Mr Nice Guy." To be honest, I didn't even know there was that much of a difference until Tanner joked about it last week. "You're on top tonight, babe. You get to be the boss."

He arches a curious brow. "*I* get to be the boss?"

I nod. "Uh huh."

He's thoughtful for a moment. "What kind of powers do I get?"

I grin. "Bossy ones."

His eyes flood with heated anticipation and I can't help wondering what he has in mind. Is there something he's been holding back on asking me for? Maybe he wants to top? Actually top, I mean, not just ride me like he is now. It's not something I usually do, but I don't hate it. If he really wanted it I'd be on board.

"What's bossy Tanner thinking?" I tease.

He offers a soft smile and releases his grip of the headboard, moving his hands down to my chest instead. "About how much I want to do this."

I let out a soft groan as his fingers slide over my skin, leaving fire in their wake.

We lock gazes for a long moment, and he must see the question in my eyes because he nods. And then I finally let myself move my hands over Tanner's body as well, greedily roaming over smooth, pale skin and hard, lean muscle. I just can't stop my hands from moving; it's not as though I haven't touched Tanner before now, but I haven't been able to touch him *like this*, and now it feels like my fingers are making up for weeks of lost opportunities in the space of a few heartbeats.

"You didn't have to be the boss for us to do this, babe," I tell him, feeling like I'm in a daze.

"No. But I think maybe I did to do this...so you know I really mean it."

And before I can take a beat to work out what he's talking about, he's leaning so far forward he's practically draped over my body. And his lips are sealed against mine.

I'm stupefied for a moment, before my brain suddenly screams *TANNER IS KISSING YOU! MOVE, YOU IDIOT!*

So I move.

Part of me is wondering whether maybe I've fallen asleep and started dreaming as my fantasy starts playing out in real time: I wrap my body around Tanner's and we just kiss and kiss and kiss as we move together.

I let Tanner set the pace with both our bodies and our tongues—he's the boss at the moment, after all. It's slow, and intense, and incredible. I keep waiting for him to freak out and declare kissing once again off limits, but he doesn't; he just continues exploring my mouth like it's a new and wondrous place while our bodies keep perfect time.

"Tanner, shit" I gasp, as our lips break apart for a moment. "This is...oh my god, this is amazing. But I need..."

I hate to even suggest moving from this position—I'd happily die like this—but I can feel my orgasm approaching, and the urge to chase it down is getting way too overwhelming.

Tanner lifts his head a little and offers a wry smirk. "Does Bossy Deacon need to enact a coup?"

I arch an eyebrow at him. "It was a free and fair election."

"I don't remember voting," he teases.

I let out a wry huff and decide to enforce my rule—democratic or not, it's what the people want. Within seconds, I have Tanner on his back, with his knees pressed back against his body and my cock driving deep inside him. He has a split second to let out a rough groan before any further sounds are stolen by my lips. And, fuck, it feels incredible. The only thing that could possibly make this better right now is if I were bare, but that's an insignificant blip compared to what I've just been handed.

Kissing. Intimacy. Connection. All the things I asked for. I'm getting ahead of myself if I'm thinking this suddenly means wedding bells or some shit, but it's a start. A sign that Tanner cares about me enough to take my needs into consideration and that he's genuinely been using the past couple weeks to figure out what his interest in me is.

"Deacon," Tanner gasps, his fingers digging in hard to my ass cheeks. His entire body is all but trembling and I know he's going to hit his climax before me, despite how hard I've been chasing mine down.

"Look at me, beautiful," I tell him. "I want to see it."

His cheeks color at the endearment, but his eyes flutter open and he stares back at me, eyes intense with pleasure and need and trust.

Fuck, I love you. By some miracle, I manage not to say it out loud.

Instead I reach a hand between our bodies and wrap it around Tanner's straining dick, stroking firmly as I continue to thrust inside him. "Just keep your eyes on me, baby," I tell him, staring deep into those intoxicating eyes. "And I'll take care of you."

It doesn't take long for him to hit the edge, and then

topple over, his body tensing and a harsh groan escaping his lips as cum spurts between us.

The heady sensation of his hole clamping down around my cock is all I need for my own climax to come rushing up in a forceful wave. I grunt and shudder as I fill the condom, only realizing once the haze of the orgasm has passed that my abs are streaked with jizz.

I was too focused on watching the expression on Tanner's beautiful face as he orgasmed to consider trying to catch his load in my hand or something, so we've both ended up pretty well-covered. Fortunately, it only seems to be other guys' cum that Tanner has an aversion to, so this shouldn't cause him to freak out. I hope.

I smile down at him; he still looks completely blissed-out and it's adorable. I lift my hand and brush a thumb over his cheek. "God, you're perfect."

"I'm a fucking mess," he groans.

I'm not sure if he's referring to the literal mess on his stomach, or his struggles with his mental health. Knowing Tanner, probably the latter. Actual messes, he's okay with —they give him something practical to handle and direct his focus.

"So is "Bohemian Rhapsody". So are all of Jackson Pollock's paintings. And Picasso's." I offer a gentle smile. "Perfection is boring as shit, babe. You're a masterpiece."

I can see my words have affected him by the movement of his throat and the emotion swirling in his eyes; I'm glad, but I also don't want him to feel like he's under a micro-scope, with me just hovering over him watching his every reaction. Also, there's an important matter to attend to. "Okay, I'm going to have to take my dick out of you now," I tell him. "Otherwise you might end up with a cum-filled condom stuck in your butt."

Tanner's eyes widen in alarm. "Ah, okay. Yeah, we should probably avoid that."

I *really* don't want to leave his body, but it's not really an optional situation. So, with great reluctance, I finally pull out and duck into the bathroom to take care of the condom.

I return to find Tanner still lying on his back, his palm over his face as he draws in slow, even breaths.

"You okay, babe?" I ask warily.

He nods, but doesn't move his hand. "Yeah."

"Would it help to clean this mess up?" I suggest. "In the shower?"

Tanner finally moves his palm and looks up at me, brows knitted together. "What mess?"

I gesture to my abs first, then his. "That mess."

His lips twitch and I'm thrilled to see a sign of amusement touch his features. "It might."

22

Tanner

Deacon thinks I'm having an anxiety episode. I don't know, maybe I am; but it's not what he thinks. I'm not freaking out because of how intimate and intense our sex became. Or about the kissing. All of that was incredible. I've been needing a closer connection for a while now, but I haven't really had the courage to pursue it. I kept worrying that I'd spiral like I did the last time things got so intense and I'd be back to square one. But after hearing the frank inevitability in Skyler's tone today when he joked Deacon not being welcome at first base, I knew it was time to just man the fuck up and get over myself. And now I feel like a fucking idiot for waiting so long.

What I'm struggling with now is the realization that's just hit me with the force of a Mack truck: I'm in love with Deacon Stapleton. And it's scaring the shit out of me.

And this time it has nothing to do with attraction or gender or orientation. I've given up trying to figure out how I should identify, because it's not important to me. As far as I'm concerned, I'm Deacon-sexual and that's all there is to it.

Or all there *was* to it. Now I have this love thing to deal with. It's been a really long fucking time since I felt like this about someone. I definitely never felt it for Natalia. There were feelings there, obviously. But it wasn't like it was with Leah. And it wasn't like this.

"Here you go," he says with a gentle smile, handing me a damp, soapy washcloth.

We're standing in my wall-to-wall walk-in shower, but we're not under the spray. I guess it'd defeat the purpose of this little exercise if the water cleaned the mess away before I can.

"Thank you," I murmur, already feeling a little calmer from the mere act of wiping my cum from Deacon's abs. The fact that he knew I needed this makes my heart grow about ten times it's size.

Why does my head have to be such a fucking mess all the time?

I swallow hard as I recall his words, comparing me to arguably the greatest rock song of all time, not to mention two of the twentieth centuries most acclaimed artists. *Perfection is boring as shit, babe. You're a masterpiece.*

How the hell does he always know the exact right thing to say? And why does it have to always be him reassuring me? He's close to half my age—I should be taking care of him, not the other way around.

"Babe, are you okay?" he asks, concern clear in his features. "Is it the kissing? Tell me if that was too much. We don't have to do it again."

I give an adamant shake of my head, managing to conjure a soft smile. "No way, we're not giving up the kissing. I'm such a fucking idiot for holding back on that for so long. I've wanted to kiss you every time we've been together since…well, that first time. But I just…"

He offers a gentle smile and lifts his hands to cup my

cheeks, making me feel insanely precious. "It's okay that you wanted to be sure. I'm glad you waited for that. But does this mean I'm allowed to kiss you whenever I feel like it now? Or would you be more comfortable if I waited for you to initiate it."

"Whenever," I tell him. I've been holding out on him for way too long; I'm not going to set a new boundary now, even though I love him even more for offering the choice. "Spontaneous kisses are absolutely welcome."

His eyes light up in a way that practically makes my heart explode, and I'm suddenly not feeling as anxious about my feelings for him anymore. Why wouldn't I fall in love with this incredible man who brings me peace and comfort and laughter; who makes me feel pleasure I've never dreamed of before; who's always tried to understand me, and never judged me; and who shows so much joy at the simple thought of being able to kiss me whenever he wants to.

"Perfection's not boring," I tell him. "Perfection is you."

He grins, letting out a wry chuckle. "I think you might have some cum-colored glasses on there, babe. But I appreciate it anyway."

He leans forward to brush his lips to mine, and I let the wash cloth fall from my hands so I can run them over his body as the kiss deepens. I don't need to clean anymore anyway.

Deacon's humble nature might have prompted him to brush my comment off, but I know my words were true. Perfect isn't the same as flawless. No one is without flaws, and Deacon's certainly no exception. But there's a reason I've always felt so safe and comfortable with him, and it's because he just always seems to know what I need and when I need it, whether it's to talk, or to just chill out, or to have sex. He's never pushed me beyond where I'm comfortable, while at the same time gently encouraging me to take small steps into new territory.

I know I'm doing exactly what Dr Cho warned me about when we discussed this at my last therapy session: putting way to much pressure on a new relationship by designating it as my 'happy place', but I just don't have any other way of thinking about this. Being with Deacon *does* make me happy. I just hope I've been able to give him as much as he's given me.

Deacon breaks the searing kiss, breathing heavily as he gazes at me with heat swirling in his eyes. "So, I get to do that whenever I feel like it?"

I nod, feeling a little dazed as it suddenly occurs to me there's water falling on my skin. We must have stumbled under the shower while we were tangled up. "Uh huh."

His lips curve up at the edges. "You might want to invest in some lip balm. I have a feeling I'm going to be sucking your lips dry for the foreseeable future."

I let out a soft chuckle, nodding my agreement. "Lip balm. Breath mints. Oxygen mask…"

Deacon shifts slightly and my left hand slips from where it was resting on its torso. As it falls to my side, my fingers brush over something…his hard dick.

"Ah, yeah, sorry," he says, looking sheepish. "Should have given you a head's up."

I shake my head, unable to keep my eyes off his cock. "It's okay." And really, I should have known considering my own dick is perking up thanks to that incredible kiss.

I stare at the pulsing erection sticking straight out from between Deacon's thighs, hesitating over my next move. And then I mentally berate myself for being such an idiot and lower my right hand so I can wrap it around the thick shaft.

And what do you know? The world doesn't end.

It feels monumental, though, even though that makes no sense at all. This is the dick I've had inside my body countless times, and yet for some reason touching it with my hand felt like going too far?

I did touch it earlier tonight when I was lining it up with my entrance, but that didn't really count. With the condom on it didn't really feel like I was actually touching a guy's dick. And considering the amount of times I've ridden a dildo over the years, it was far too easy to just recall that as I was going through the motions of getting into position—something I definitely won't be divulging to Deacon.

But there's no mistaking it now. I have Deacon's hard, throbbing cock in my hand. And it feels really nice. Once again I have to berate myself for not doing this sooner. Why did I have to hold back so much?

"Are you just going to hold it?" Deacon asks. His tone is wry, but there's a tense note in his voice, and when I glance up, I see his features are tight with tension as well.

"Am I doing it wrong?" I ask, suddenly mortified. "Is this hurting you?" I thought I was holding it with the same kind of pressure I'd handle my own dick with, but maybe Deacon's more sensitive than I am?

"God no. It feels incredible. It's just…I really need you to move your hand, babe. Otherwise I'm going to shove you into that wall and just start fucking your fist myself."

My eyes widen. "Oh, right. Okay…" I start moving my hand slowly up and down his shaft, not really sure what I'm supposed to be doing. I really don't want to hurt him, so I'm keeping my grip relatively gentle.

"Harder, babe," Deacon groans. "Faster."

"But—"

"Trust me, you're not going to tear it off," he teases. "Just jerk it the same as you do for your own cock."

I nod and increase the pressure of my grip and the speed of my movements, but Jesus, it's really fucking hard to do this in reverse. "Fuck. How the hell do you do this backwards?" I grunt in frustration.

"Practice," he says with a breath of amusement, before closing his eyes and letting out a soft groan. "Don't worry, babe. You're doing great. And I'm so fucking close anyway. Just having your hand on me is going to be enough to make me explode any minute."

Close? Explode? My hand? Panic suddenly gets the better of me and I snatch my hand away, shaking my head over and over. "Sorry...I can't."

Deacon's eyes flicker open, and because it's Deacon, there's no sign of disappointment or frustration. Just concern. "What's wrong, babe? What happened?"

"I—I'm sorry...I just...you said you were close to orgasm, and you were going to explode, and my hand was right there. And I'm just still not sure...I'm sorry," I finish off, shaking my head again.

Deacon sighs. "Tanner, I've told you a million times you don't have to be sorry for not wanting to do something. And I already knew you're not comfortable getting cum on you, so that one's my fault." He let's out a heavy breath, a frown marring his features. "I like to think I could have pulled out of your grip in time, but honestly I'm not sure, so I'm really sorry about that."

"I wish you weren't constantly making compromises for me," I say with a frown. What I really mean is *I wish I could be as perfect for you as you are for me.*

"Tanner, that's what people do in re—I mean...un... when you're with someone you...want to keep being with," he says, blushing adorably at the near fumble.

I can't help letting out a soft breath of amusement at his stumbling attempt to play down what I've come to accept is indeed a relationship. I'm not ready to admit to it out loud yet, however, despite my realization earlier tonight. I'm just not ready. Another thing I'm holding back from Deacon.

"You've made plenty of compromises too," he says gently, reaching out to brush a lock of wet hair from my forehead. "Do you even realize how much of yourself you've given to me? And how much I value it? Your trust, your honesty, your time. I know you don't let a whole lot of people into your life, but you've let me in and I'm so grateful for that. And if you think a little bit of cum is more important to me than all that, you obviously haven't been paying attention."

I shake my head, offering a soft smile. "I know it's not. I just…I wish I could give you everything you want. You deserve to have everything you want."

He leans in to brush a kiss to my forehead before drawing back and gazing at me with eyes full of tender affection. "You're everything I want," he murmurs. "So as long as I have you, I'm golden."

Jesus Christ, I think we need to end this conversation before my heart actually explodes. "You're kind of a romantic, aren't you?" I say wryly, attempting to lower the intensity he's just amped up.

He grins. "Yep. And, sorry babe, but that's something I'm not going to compromise on."

I nod and lean forward to brush my lips to his. "I think I can work with that."

"Fuck, it's getting late," he says, his mouth stretching into a wide yawn. "I should take off."

As always, I really don't want him to leave. This time,

however, I actually decide to do something about it. "Stay."

Deacon's brows shoot up. "Huh?"

"Stay the night with me. Or, what's left of it, at least. I need to be heading home by around five, but…just stay," I trail off with a shrug.

He grins. "Alright then. But no more sex. You need sleep."

I let out a reluctant sigh. I'm disappointed, obviously, but I didn't ask him to stay over just so we could have sex again, and he's right—I really do need sleep. It feels like this day's lasted about a year.

I turn off the shower and we towel ourselves down before returning to the bedroom. I dig out a pair of pajama pants for Deacon, because there's no way I'll actually be able to sleep if he's lying there next to me all naked, and then I slip into some fresh ones myself.

Once we're under the covers, I switch off the light using the remote I keep on my nightstand, and then just lie there awkwardly for a moment. "What happens now?" I ask.

He lets out a soft laugh that rumbles through the darkness. "There's this thing called cuddling. I think you'll enjoy it."

And then I feel his body shift up beside me and his arms curling around me. He pulls me against his chest and I immediately sink into his hold. The physical embodiment of the waves of comfort I always feel radiating off Deacon when I'm in his presence.

No nighttime sleep ritual needed tonight; just Deacon's arms around me and his warm breath on my neck.

23

Deacon

I feel like I've been living on a cloud for days. Something changed that night Tanner asked me to stay over; between the kissing, and the cuddling, and the way he didn't even balk when I slipped and almost called what we share a "relationship"—because, let's face it, it is, even if he can't admit it yet—everything has just started to feel so much more real. And tangible.

I've slept over most nights since then, and even though he's usually gone before I wake up in the morning, it's still been amazing to be able to fall asleep at night with him in my arms.

I'm not letting myself get too far ahead of things by assuming this means he wants to actually date, or even that he's willing to tell people about us; as far as I know, Skyler and Jackson are the only ones who are aware of the current situation, and while Tanner seems fine with them knowing, I think it might be a different matter if they weren't total strangers who have nothing to do with the rest of his life.

We haven't actually spoken about his sexual identity,

which we should probably do at some stage considering he was supposed to be figuring that out. But at this point I don't feel like it's a huge deal; it's up to Tanner how he wants to identify, of course, but if he wants to be with me regardless of whether he's worked out where he fits in the rainbow alphabet then I'm more than happy to accept that. I never needed a label, just a guy who could understand his own feelings. And I'm pretty sure that's what I have now.

When I wake on Tuesday morning my phone screen reads six forty-five am, so I'm a bit surprised to hear someone moving around in the apartment. For a moment of sheer panic, I worry one of Tanner's kids might have stopped by the penthouse to grab something, or maybe hang out for some reason.

What the hell am I supposed to do in that case? Hide? Where?

I frantically scan my gaze around the bedroom, looking for hiding spots that could fit a bulky, six foot four man, when I see Tanner's phone sitting on the nightstand. And Tanner's work clothes hanging up next to the bathroom.

What the hell?

I get out of bed and creep to the bedroom door, carefully opening it just a crack so I can see out into the living slash kitchen area. There's no one in sight, though. Damn it.

"Why are you hiding behind the door?"

I jump about a foot in the air at the sound of Tanner's voice, which is coming from *right there* at the threshold of the bedroom. I swing the door wide open and narrow my eyes at him. "What the hell? Why were you standing there?"

His brows shoot up in obvious amusement. "I was coming to wake you up for breakfast. I wasn't expecting to find you lurking behind the door and spying through a crack like a creeper."

I groan, running a hand through my hair. "I heard noises and wanted to see who it was without them knowing I was here," I explain. "I thought it might be one of your kids."

"You didn't think the far likelier possibility would be the guy you shared a bed with last night?"

"Well, *now* it seems obvious. But you're always gone by the time I wake up. What are you still doing here so late?"

"Kit doesn't have class this morning, so she's getting Izzy ready for school," he explains.

Right. Kit—Izzy's nanny. I've met her a few times and I vaguely remember her telling me she attended classes at NYU. I'm pretty sure she was trying to flirt with me at the time.

"Come on, it'll get cold." He moves off toward the kitchen, gesturing for me to follow.

Did he say *breakfast?* He made me breakfast? Great, because I wasn't head over heels already.

When I get to the counter, my mouth immediately starts watering, because sitting there in front of me, all golden and fluffy and smelling delicious, are two servings of freshly made waffles.

"You know how to make *waffles?*" I ask. If he says yes I'm going to get down on one knee and ask him to marry me right now. I don't even care if we don't ever tell anyone. I just want the waffles. And the sex, obviously.

He lets out a wry chuckle, shaking his head. "Um…no. My skills in the kitchen are extremely limited. But the diner down the block does amazing waffles, so I just went and picked these up. I thought it'd be nice to have breakfast together."

I smile fondly at him. "That'd be awesome."

I climb onto a stool at the counter and Tanner slides one of the plates over to me, along with a bottle of syrup. "Or would you prefer something else? There's chocolate sauce in the pantry."

"I'm good with the syrup. That chocolate sauce could come in handy another time, though," I add with a waggle of my brows, chuckling when I see color rise in Tanner's cheeks.

I drizzle syrup on my waffle, making sure to fill every square. I feel Tanner's eyes on me, and when I glance up I find his gorgeous sapphire gaze is glimmering with amusement as he watches my fastidious syrup work.

"Got to fill every hole," I say with a shrug.

"That's what he said," Tanner quips back with a snort.

I let out a sputtering laugh, finding it difficult to believe I actually just heard those words come out of Tanner Grimsay's mouth.

The waffles are indeed amazing, and I find myself groaning around a few bites before Tanner fixes me with a pained look. "Please...you *really* need to stop doing that."

I'm confused for a moment, but then it clicks and I can't help grinning. "You're the one who brought me the incredible waffles."

"I thought it'd be a nice gesture. I didn't realize a torture session would accompany it," he grumbles.

"It is a nice gesture," I assure him. "I like eating meals with you."

This is the first "morning after" meal we've shared, but we've had dinner together before, and it's always fun.

"Does Kit know...about...um...where you go?" I ask curiously. It's something I've been wondering for a while, actually. I know Tanner only stays late on nights when Kit can stay overnight with Izzy, but he's never clarified if she knows what he gets up to when he goes out.

"She knows there's…someone," he confirms, cheeks tinting red. "But not who. I used to only go out overnight every few months, so when it started happening really regularly it was a fair guess that I was meeting up with someone in particular."

"And you're okay with her knowing…all this?" I venture.

Tanner shrugs. "It makes things a lot easier. And I don't need to tell her the specifics. She's made her assumptions and I'm fine just going with that."

I try not to wince, because I know Kit's assumption must be that Tanner is seeing a woman. But I've said I wasn't going to pressure him about this, and I meant it. What we have now is more than enough.

***

On Wednesday night, I'm making a quick dinner at home before I plan to head over to the penthouse to spend time with Tanner, when my brother stops by. At first, I'm assuming he's there to see Drew, because it turns out that they are in fact together, but once Sully's greeted his boyfriend, he makes a beeline for the kitchen, slapping a folder down on the counter in front of me.

"You want to explain what the fuck's going on with you and Tanner Grimsay?"

I just stare at my brother in open-mouthed shock. "What the hell? How did you—?"

With a dramatic flourish, he flips the folder open to reveal several pictures of Tanner and me. They're from the night we first hooked up; we're sitting at the bar, looking incredibly cozy. God, I can remember that exact moment: Tanner sliding his hand up my thigh and murmuring in my ear.

"What the fuck is this Sully?" I growl. "You've been spying on me?"

Sullivan looks at me like I'm a dumbass for suggesting such a thing. "Don't be ridiculous. Of course I haven't been spying on you. My company's investigator took these. She's been looking into Grimsay to figure out why he's been stonewalling us on this deal."

Realization hits me and my brows fly into my hairline. "Wait—*you're* the one trying to acquire Tanner's company?" He told me a little while back that one of his big sources of stress came from a relentless investor who wouldn't accept that he didn't want to sell this particular company. I had no idea he'd been talking about Sully, though. Or one of Sully's clients, I guess.

"I don't understand," Drew interrupts from beside Sullivan. "What does it matter if Deacon's dating this guy?"

"Because he only went after Deacon to get to me," he says darkly.

Ouch.

He says something else to Drew, but I don't catch it. My mind is too busy warring with the possibility that Sully could be right. Finally, I discard it as bullshit.

"You're being ridiculous," I tell him, my voice hard. "He hasn't asked me one single thing about you. I had no idea you two even knew each other."

"Well I'm sure he's just been biding his time," Sullivan growls, relentless as ever. "He's *straight*, Deacon."

Fuck, I am so done with this conversation. "Just because he's not out publicly, doesn't make him straight." I'm *so* not going into Tanner's complicated identity issues. That's not any of Sullivan's business, and I don't believe for a second that Tanner's been stringing me a long all this time, having sex, spooning, buying me breakfast…just so he can maybe, possibly, one day dig up some dirt on my brother over some business deal that Tanner doesn't even like thinking about.

"That's a fair point, babe," Drew says, backing me up. "I used to identify as straight, remember?"

"This is different," Sully says, jaw tight as he fixes me with a hard stare. "He's *married*—did he tell you that?"

I feel suddenly dizzy, like my feet are going to just give way from under me from the sheer shock of my brother's words. This can't be right. Tanner's not married. No.

Fuck, I need to get out of here. I need to get away from my brother's face, and I need to talk to Tanner. I'm only going to believe it if I hear it from his lips.

When I get to the penthouse, I'm surprised to find Tanner is already there, He flashes a bright smile when he opens the door to me, but it drops the second he registers what I'm guessing must be an incredibly tense look on my face. I definitely feel tense.

"What's wrong?" he asks, clearly concerned.

I shove past him into the apartment, but don't get too far inside before I spin around and hit him with a hard look. "You know my brother."

Tanner winces. "Shit. Yes…we don't exactly have the best business relationship."

"Yeah, I got that impression," I say with a shake of my head. "He knows about us just FYI. He thinks you're just using me to get to him."

Tanner's eyes widen in shock. "Seriously? Wait—do *you* think I'm just using you to get to him?"

I wave him off. "If you are, you're playing a long fucking game."

Tanner frowns. "How did he even—was it Skyler? He said he wouldn't…"

My head snaps up in surprise. "Skyler? What the hell does he have to do with anything?"

Tanner just shakes his head. "Never...never mind. I'm just trying to figure out how Stapleton found out."

Stapleton. It's unsettling hearing him say my own name with such disregard. I know he's not actually talking about me, but still... "He has pictures. He got a fucking PI to dig up stuff on you because of whatever the hell this deal is that you're not backing down on, and there was a picture of us from that first night at the bar."

"He did *what?*" Tanner demands. "What was he planning to do? Blackmail me or some shit?"

I shake my head. "No, he wouldn't do that. I don't know what the plan was. But I'm not here about my brother anyway..."

Tanner's brow furrows. "What do you mean? Why are you here, and why do you still look upset if you're not bothered by any of that stuff?"

"Because I need to know..." I pause for a moment to draw in a deep breath. Fuck, I don't know if I can get this question out. What if Sullivan's information is true? "He told me that you're...married."

Tanner's face turns ash white, and I know without him having to say anything that it's true.

Fuck.

I still need to hear it, though. "It's...true?" I manage to press on. "You're...m-married?"

"It's complicated," he rasps out, sounding as though talking is difficult for him right now.

"It's a yes or no question, Tanner."

He screws his eyes shut for a moment, before opening and fixing me with a level look. "Yes."

"Are you getting a divorce?" I ask, my optimistic nature unable to let go just yet.

He swallows hard, before shaking his head. "No."

And there it is. Jesus Christ, I feel like I've been stabbed in the guts and left to bleed to death. And for some reason, I can't let it be over just yet. "Were you ever going to tell me?"

"I don't know," he admits. "It's not…" he screws his eyes shut again, his breathing harsh. "It isn't…fuck." He lifts a hand to his forehead to knead at the skin there; it's a sign I've come to recognize as him struggling to focus his anxious thoughts, but right now I just can't…I can't be the understanding, empathetic Mr Nice Guy while he tries to justify his behavior.

I'm just…done.

24

Tanner

I don't think I've ever felt more pathetic as I did last night when I watched Deacon walk out my door, hurt and heartbroken, while I struggled and failed to find the words to explain my situation.

They just wouldn't fucking come. I let the panic and anxiety I was feeling over hurting Deacon and the fear of losing him from my life completely overpower me. And he just left.

So now I'm lying on the sofa in the penthouse, eating leftover waffles and watching *Pretty Woman*, because I can't seem to function enough to go to work, and I can't go home and let Izzy see me like this. Okay, maybe *this* is the most pathetic I've ever felt.

There's a knock on the penthouse door, and I pause the movie and get to my feet, stumbling a little as I make my way across to the door because it's been so fucking long since I moved from that sofa.

When I open the door, it's to find Piper at the threshold. She scans her eyes up and down my body, curling her lip in distaste. "Oh my god, Dad. You look like you've gone feral."

I glance down at myself to see the sweater I'm wearing is covered in syrup and Cheetos dust. And my pajama pants have a splash of coffee on them. Combine that with the bed hair I haven't bothered taming this morning and, yeah, I guess I probably do look pretty gross.

"What are you doing here?" I ask curiously, moving back into the living room as she trails after me.

"RJ said you didn't come in today, so I assumed you were on your death bed. Then Kit said you weren't at home and I should look here." She casts a curious glance around the place, her eyes zeroing in on the mess I've made of the couch, and on the movie I've got paused on the TV. Then she lets out a gasp, her mouth falling open in horror. "Holy shit. This is a break up."

"I have no idea what you're talking about," I grumble.

She rolls her eyes. "For fuck's sake, Dad. You haven't showered, you're binging on food. Watching *Pretty Woman?* This is break-up 101." She casts me a hesitant look. "Was it...un...that guy you told RJ about?" I can tell asking the question is making her uncomfortable as hell, but I don't know if it's because Deacon's a guy, or because talking about my love life is uncomfortable in general.

"Deacon," I confirm.

"I thought it wasn't serious between you two?"

"I lied," I say simply. "To myself as well as RJ."

"I see..."

"I love him," I admit. It's the first time I'm saying that out loud and it's ridiculous that it's to my daughter, but I need to say it to someone. "I really love him."

"Okay...um...well..."

Her discomfort is radiating off her in waves and I can't help letting out a soft chuckle. "It's okay, baby. You don't need to do anything to fix this. And I'm not going to make you sit here while I bear my soul."

"Oh, thank god," she mutters, expression full of relief.

"I just need to be sad for a while," I tell her. "It's my own fault, I totally fucked it up. And I just need some time."

Her brows draw together. "You don't mean…time like this, right?"

"I didn't sleep a wink last night," I tell her. "I really was feeling like shit today. But no, I definitely don't plan on making this a regular thing."

"Oh, thank god, because there is seriously little stink lines coming off you right now. Don't even think about hugging me goodbye."

Ah, there's nothing like the unconditional love of your first born child.

Once she's satisfied that I'm not dying, Piper makes a hasty retreat from the penthouse, and I return to the couch and flick the movie back on.

Tomorrow will be better.

Hopefully.

***

THE NEXT DAY sucks ass just as much, although to be fair I do at least put in more of an effort to connect with the world. I skip work again, but this time it's because Izzy's running a fever and I can't bring myself to ask Kit to put in even more hours when she's already done so much overtime lately.

Fortunately, Izzy's not badly ill, but caring for her does at least give me something to focus on that isn't my catastrophic fuck up of what could have been an incredible relationship with Deacon.

That is, until Jazz shows up at the house, freshly back from his trip to LA.

As usual, he strides right into the house without knocking—neither of my older kids do; this used to be their home, after all—his brows shooting up at the sight of me snuggling on the sofa with a sleeping Izzy. "You don't seem like a total wreck," he muses. "Piper made it seem like you were barely clinging to your sanity."

I wince as I recall my visit at the penthouse from Piper yesterday. "I wouldn't go that far, but yesterday wasn't a pretty sight. What are you doing home, anyway? I thought you were staying there for Thanksgiving."

He shrugs. "Piper called in an SOS." I have a feeling there's more to the story than that, but I'm not going to push him. "So…does your "friend" need any more advice?" he asks with a smirk, lifting his hands to form air quotes.

I groan, rubbing a hand over my face. I should have known as soon as any information about me and Deacon came to light Jazz would put two and two together in an instant. At the time of our last conversation, the thought of anything going public with Deacon seemed ludicrous. Now I can't believe I was ever so reluctant to get more involved with him.

"Dad, I'm not judging," Jazz assures me. "And if that's what works for you, then go for it. I'm assuming this guy was the one with all the kissing and the freaking out?"

I nod. "Yeah, but I got over that. Things were going really well."

"So what happened to fuck it up?"

I glance down at Izzy, feeling a little weird about having this conversation in her presence. She's asleep in my arms, though, and I really don't want to move her. I can keep things G rated, I'm sure. "He found out about Natalia. And when I tried to explain the situation, I just… froze. The anxiety just took over and I couldn't get the words out. And all he heard was that I'm married and I don't plan to divorce her."

"Have you tried talking to him since then?" Jazz asks.

I shake my head. "No."

"Dad, what the fuck?" Jazz exclaims. "You're supposedly really into this guy, and yet you're not even going to fight for him? You're just going to let him think you're an asshole cheater?"

"It's not that simple," I say with a sigh. "Deacon… he's…good. He's a really nice guy. He's not going to want to be with me while I'm married, no matter what the circumstances. I should have been upfront with him from the start. Now I've turned him into a cheater, and I don't think he'll be able to forgive that."

Jazz snorts. "Sounds like a fucking snoozefest if you ask me. Is he at least hot?"

I roll my eyes. "I'm not answering that."

"A non-answer always means yes, Dad. Everyone knows this."

I give an exasperated shake of my head. "I'm sorry you came all the way back here to deal with this. But I really don't think there's anything to be done about it."

Jazz looks at me for a long moment, and I can see the thoughts turning over in his eyes. Finally, he gives a decisive nod. "Yeah, we'll see about that."

25

Deacon

"He's married," I groan, just barely preventing myself from banging my head down on the table at the booth we're seated at. "How could I not have known he was married?"

"Because he didn't tell you?" Jackson suggests, one eyebrow raised.

I grunt. How could he not have told me, though? That's the real question. "I just don't get it. We talked about stuff. He told me bout all his anxiety issues, and about how his wife died."

"He made up a dead wife?" Skyler asks, brows raised.

I shake my head. "No. No, I'm sure all that was true. The woman he's with now must be his second wife."

Skyler's expression turns thoughtful for a moment. "Maybe there's an explanation for everything?"

"Like what?"

He shrugs. "I don't know. But you've never met the wife, right? So maybe she's really not in the picture anymore."

"Except that he told me she was when I confronted him about it. I asked him flat out if he was divorcing her and he said no."

Skyler winces. "Okay, yeah, that looks bad."

"Hate to point out the obvious, here, but you guys did only ever meet up at his penthouse. It was a little other womany…or other man, I guess."

Now I actually do bury my head against the table. I feel like such a dumbass. No wonder Tanner never wanted to try for anything more. He already has everything he needs at home.

But then, if that were true, why would he be out at bars looking for guys in the first place? And why would he be hooking up with me almost every night for weeks? I don't know who to feel more sorry for, myself or his wife.

"For what it's worth, I think Sullivan was way off in suggesting Tanner was only interested in you to get to him," Skyler says, sounding more irritated now than he was just before when talking about Tanner's marriage. "And he needs an ass-kicking for even thinking that would be the only reason a guy like Tanner would go after you."

"He's just being protective of me," I mumble. "And you can't kick Sully's ass, because then Drew will kick yours."

"Then I'll kick Drew's," Jackson says, smashing his fist into his other palm as though relishing the thought of kicking the ass of his buddy and business partner.

"Then Sully will kick yours," I point out, lifting my head from the table.

"Then I'll kick Sully's again," Skyler says with a far-too-eager grin. "A never ending ass-kicking circle."

"Or you could just not kick my brother's ass in the first place," I say dryly. "It's not like he just pulled that theory out of thin air to hurt me. He had no idea I even knew Tanner, while Tanner knew all about Sullivan and never mentioned anything about knowing him."

Skyler shrugs. "If you ask me, I'm pretty sure he just didn't want to get you in the middle of whatever this whole thing they have is. Those two really don't like each other."

I eye my best friend curiously. "How do you even know about all that, anyway?"

Sky's eyes light up. "Oh, well I can't go into details because confidentiality and shit, but I was in a meeting where Tanner *owned* Sully and Pax and Charlie. It was awesome."

"Why do you keep taking Tanner's side?" Jackson asks curiously. "Is it because you guys teamed up for that video game?"

Skyler shrugs, a bright smile spreading over his face. "I can't help it, I just like the guy. I'm sorry Deacon, but I'm Team Tanner. There's more to this whole thing, I'm sure of it."

I let out a weary sigh. "Skyler…"

"Deacon, he made you *breakfast,*" he presses, as though that seals the matter. "Guys don't do that for people they're just having casual sex with. Do you know how many guys I've made breakfast for before? *Zero?*"

"You make breakfast for me every Sunday," Jackson points out.

"Yeah but that's a friendy breakfast, not a sexy breakfast," Skyler clarifies.

"A friendy breakfast with whipped cream and blueberry dicks on the pancakes," Jackson says with a wry huff.

Skyler smirks. "Yeah, because then when I say I ate a dick for breakfast, you can say you did too."

Jax rolls his eyes. "Yeah, that's exactly what happens."

"This is very helpful, thank you," I deadpan.

"You're welcome," Skyler says brightly, completely missing my lack of sincerity.

I let out a heavy breath and lean my head back against the top of the booth seat. I have no idea if Skyler's "feeling" has any kind of merit at all. Surely if there were some other explanation Tanner would have told me when I asked him about it? Unless there was a reason for him not to... Maybe it's a Green card marriage and he doesn't want to risk his "wife" getting deported? Or maybe...

I shake the thoughts out of my head. I need to stop living in a fantasyland where I have a happily ever after with Tanner. He's married, he's straight, he's my brother's business rival, he's the parent of one of my students—how many more reasons do I need for it to finally sink in that this just isn't meant to be?

***

THE FOLLOWING AFTERNOON, I'm tidying up my classroom after school when I hear someone at the door.

"Are you Deacon Stapleton?"

I do my best not to let out any outward signs of annoyance or exasperation at the visitor's appearance. It's been a long as hell week and all I really want is to go home and chill and try not to think about Tanner for two seconds.

Considering the vast majority of kids in the class are dropped off and picked up by nannies, it's not exactly rare for a parent to seek me out after hours if there's something they need to discuss. But I generally insist they make an appointment first. Maybe another teacher would simply tell them to go away and come back when they've worked out a suitable time, but I've never been able to do that kind of thing. If a parent has sought me out, it's obviously something they need to tall about.

It only takes me one glance at my visitor for me to figure out he's not a parent, however. Unless he had his kid when he was about fourteen, because he looks to be a good five years younger than I am at least. There's something familiar about him, but I can't place it. I don't think I've ever met him before, so I have no idea why the fuck he's currently glaring at me like I'm the devil incarnate.

"Yeah…" I say warily. "That's me."

He nods. "Good. I have a question for you, then. What the fuck is wrong with you, asshole?"

I blink at him in utter bewilderment. "Excuse me?"

"First you end things with my dad over some stupid, fucked up bullshit that's been completely blown out of proportion. Then you don't even let him explain. And now you're just sitting around here moping like a fucking loser because you're too chicken shit to talk to him."

And now I know why he looks familiar—he has Tanner's eyes. Not the color—they're grayer that Tanner's piercing sapphire blue—but the shape is there, along with the insanely long eyelashes and the thick brows that wing out a little at the side.

"I'm not moping," I say stubbornly.

"Dude, you're a fucking wreck," he shoots back, folding his arms over his chest. "It's pathetic."

I narrow my eyes at him. "You know you're being a total asshole right now, right?"

He just shrugs. "I'm always an asshole. You're not getting special treatment." Yeah, Tanner definitely provided an accurate description, that's for sure.

I sigh and run a hand through my hair. I really don't have the energy to trade insults with this guy. And it's not something that's really in my nature, anyway. "Look, I get that you want to stick up for your dad, but you really don't know—"

"Don't know everything?" he finishes with a quirked brow. "Fuck that, I know the whole sordid story. You're the one who knows fucking shit."

I cross my arms over my chest, narrowing my eyes at him. "Fine—what don't I know? I'm not sure there's much that can top him being married this whole time."

Jazz rolls his eyes, as though I've just said something completely ridiculous. "Look, I don't know why he didn't tell you about Natalia. Maybe it's because you were only fucking for a few weeks and he wasn't ready to share every single detail about his private life."

I flinch at the sardonic tone and the way Jazz just reduced my relationship with Tanner to nothing more than casual sex.

"Or…" He sighs, his face softening for the first time since he stepped into my classroom. "Maybe you were his happy place and he didn't want to tarnish that by mentioning her. Because, trust me, that bitch is fucking poison. Even when she's not trying she's still ruining things for him."

I shake my head in confusion. "I still don't understand. He's the one who lied—"

Jazz runs a hand through his hair in obvious frustration. "Fuck, you're not getting it—she's a trigger, Deacon. And I know he told you all about that shit so don't act like you don't know what I'm talking about."

Fucking hell, I'm so confused. Clearly Tanner's marriage isn't a happy one, and I can understand why Jazz would be defending his father, but I still can't help feeling betrayed. "Yeah, I do, but I still don't—"

He fixes me with a hard glare. "Look, she is the devil. And I mean that literally. Like, the *actual* devil."

"I don't think you know what the word 'literally' means," I say dryly.

Jazz grunts in annoyance, shaking his head. "All Dad wants to do is forget she exists. Marrying her was the biggest mistake he ever made." His features arrange into a thoughtful frown and he gives a little shrug. "Well, actually, right now he'd probably say not telling you about her was his biggest mistake. But if he'd never married her to begin with he wouldn't have been keeping it from you, so…"

"But he did marry her," I say quietly, feeling my gut clench with regret. Because the reality is, even if I can forgive Tanner—and let's face it, I was pretty much there even before getting dressed down by his son—it's not as though we can ever actually be together. "She does exist. Why hasn't he just divorced her if he hates her so much? I asked him if he was planning to and he said no."

"Well if you'd given him more than two seconds to explain, you might have learned that she's holding him to ransom until the terms of their pre-nup come into effect. She's threatened to take Izzy if he tries it before they hit the ten year mark," Jazz informs me, leaving me feeling as though the ground underneath my feet has suddenly shifted.

Why the hell didn't I think of that? Tanner's kids are the most important thing in the world to him. He'd do absolutely anything for them…including staying in a marriage that made him miserable.

"Fuck," I mutter, rubbing a hand over my face and stepping back a couple of steps so I can rest against the chalkboard.

"Bet you feel pretty shitty now," Jazz says, practically crowing at the sight of my distress.

I glare at him. "Clearly you've never been heartbroken."

He lets out a snort. "Fuck no. I don't do any of that love and romance shit."

"Color me surprised," I say dryly.

"But let's just clear one thing up—you broke your own heart, dude. Dad could have explained all of this if you'd given him a chance to. You could have spent the past few days fucking instead of moping around like pathetic idiots."

I shake my head morosely, staring at the carpeted floor. I feel even more heartsick now than I did two days ago. At least then I could be angry. Now I'm just sad. I feel like I've been cheated out of something incredible. "It doesn't change anything," I mutter, letting out a heavy sigh. "It stings that he didn't tell me, but I can understand why he wasn't ready. But it doesn't change the overall situation. He's still married…"

Jazz scoffs. "On *paper,* sure. But they've been separated for years—something else he could have told you if you'd fucking asked."

I rake a hand through my hair as regret consumes me. I thought I'd given Tanner enough of an opportunity to explain himself—if an explanation had been possible—but I realize now I didn't. Not even close. I went over there feeling angry and confrontational, and when he confirmed Sullivan's revelation about him being married, I completely shut down. It's no wonder Tanner hadn't been able to find the words to explain; especially if, as Jazz said, his ex is a trigger for his anxiety.

I'm finally able to tear my gaze from the floor and look

at Jazz, offering a grateful smile. "Thank you for telling me all this."

He shrugs. "Yeah, whatever. If you want to go apologize, you should wait 'til tomorrow morning. I've got Izzy at mine tomorrow and she's going to stay the night so you'll have plenty of time to fuck."

Jesus Christ, does this guy's brain-to-mouth filter ever turn on?

"Wow, that's so sweet," I say dryly.

"Sorry…*make love,*" he drawls in a sardonic tone. He turns for the door and then glances back at me. "Just try not to give the old man a heart attack. I know he's in good shape but he's still getting on in years."

I roll my eyes. "I'll be gentle."

"Not too gentle, I hope."

"I'm really uncomfortable talking to you about this," I say, shifting my gaze to the ceiling.

"Whatever. Like I said, tomorrow morning. And you better fucking make him happy and not turn out to be a psycho or I'm seriously going to regret playing peacemaker."

I shift my gaze back to him, brows furrowed with curiosity. "Why *did* you decide to play peacemaker? No offense but you're not the most diplomatic person in the world."

"Why the fuck would that offend me?" he asks, a dismayed expression crossing his face. "I'm here because my Dad's miserable without you. And also coming back to swoop in and save the day here was a good reason to get out of LA. Certain people were starting to get clingy." I arch a curious brow at him but he just shrugs. "Guess I'll see you around, Deacon." He pauses for a moment to scan his eyes up and down my body…very slowly. Then he shakes his head, offering a wry smirk. "I was going to offer a commiseration fuck If things didn't work out after all, but given what I know about you and my dad, I have a feeling we wouldn't be a good fit."

I just blink at him. "Um…okay…"

Before I can decide whether I'm supposed to thank him for what I think amounts to consideration where Jazz is concerned, he turns out of the doorway and disappears down the hall.

26

Tanner

I love spending the weekends with my daughter, but on this occasion I'm grateful to Jazz for taking her for a fun brother-sister day and a sleepover tonight. It'll be good for them to have some time together after Jazz's time away in Los Angeles, and it leaves me free to mope about as much as I want without worrying about upsetting Izzy.

I feel completely pathetic with the way I've fallen apart since things ended with Deacon. I'm so angry with myself about not being more upfront with him; maybe it wasn't necessary at the start, but our relationship became much more than casual sex and he deserved my honesty. I don't want to make excuses for myself, but I think I grew so used to Deacon being my haven from all the stressors and triggers in my life that I didn't want to do anything to change it. But now the haven's gone and self-imploded.

About an hour after Jazz leaves with Izzy, I hear the front doorbell ringing. I let out a groan and consider just ignoring it so I can continue with my moping while I watch this five-part documentary series on the French Revolution—watching re-enactments of people getting their heads sliced off is helping to put certain things in perspective. But the bell rings again and I know I can't just sit here and pretend not to be home. It might be RJ with something important, or Piper might have forgotten her key.

I get up from the sofa and make my way through the house to the front door. When I yank it open, I'm shocked to see Deacon standing on the top step.

I stare at him in shock, unable to stop myself from drinking him in like I'm dying of thirst. He looks incredible, dressed in dark jeans, a gray t-shirt that clings to his torso, and a snug-fitting black leather jacket. All I want to do is drag him inside and strip him bare. But, of course, I manage to restrain myself.

"I guess Jazz didn't tell you I'd be coming over?" he asks tentatively. His expression is wary, and I notice lines of exhaustion on his face—I wonder if the last few nights have been as sleepless for him as they have been for me.

My brows shoot up at his words. "You met Jazz?"

"So he didn't tell you he was coming to talk to me either?" he asks, one eyebrow quirked.

I let out a breath of amusement, shaking my head. "No. But I shouldn't be surprised. That boy's always been a law unto himself."

Deacon nods knowingly. "Yep, I got that impression."

I step back and wave a hand toward the front hallway. "Do you want to come in?"

To my immense relief, he steps inside and closes the door behind him.

"He explained some things to me," Deacon says.

"What kind of things?" I ask warily. Fuck, what the hell did Jazz say to him? Knowing my son it could be anything from death threats to pick-up lines. Or maybe both.

Deacon's eyes find mine, his gaze soft and tinged with

regret. "Things I should have given you a chance to explain for yourself the other night. I'm sorry."

I'm completely blown away. Both by the fact that Jazz actually confronted Deacon in an attempt to fix things between the two of us—or at least that's how it appears right now—and that Deacon is apologizing to me. I shake my head. "You have every right to be angry with me, Deacon. I should have been more honest with you."

"I can understand why you weren't," he says, voice gentle. "It's a really complicated situation and this thing is still really new, and we're still building trust—"

I reach a hand out to close over his, cutting him off. I'm feeling a little encouraged that he's talking in the present tense, but I need to correct his assumption. "It wasn't about trust, Deacon. I do trust you—completely. It's just…" I glance away, drawing in a breath before returning my gaze to his. "I didn't want to bring all of my shit into what we have. When we're together, all I have to think about is you, and how happy I am when I'm with you. And I didn't want to lose that. So I guess you could say I was using you…as a little getaway island, I guess. But that wasn't my intention, and I'm sorry."

I'm expecting him to turn around and walk straight for the door, but instead he moves toward me. Before I can even register what's happening, he's only inches away, his hands coming up to cup my cheeks. He rests his forehead against mine, our skin searing hot as our breath mingles together.

"Deacon…"

"I'll be your getaway island," he murmurs. "I'm happy to be. Just call me St Martz."

I let out a soft laugh, my lips splitting into a grin.

"I'll be your happy place. Your haven. Your safe house. You can hide in me if you need to. But you don't have to hide *from* me. Nothing's ever going to ruin this, Tanner. If you trust me, then you know I won't let that happen. And if I know what's going on in your head—what's causing the tension you're carrying around—then I'm going to know what you need to let go of it," he says, lips spreading into a grin. "Like…do you just need a relaxing night with take-out and a movie? Or do you need a hot shower with me scrubbing your body down and swallowing your cock? Or…do you need me to fuck you so hard you can barely walk the next day?"

"Jesus, Deacon…" Unable to resist any longer, I reach for him, slipping my hands under his t-shirt and running them over his hard muscles.

He lets out a sharp breath and draws his forehead back, piercing me with an intense look. "Are you hearing what I'm saying?"

"You want to fuck me so hard I'll barely be able to walk tomorrow," I say with a smirk.

He lets out a soft chuckle. "Fucking needy bottom." He drops his hands from my face and rests them at my hips instead. "Forget about my cock, I'm trying to make a big romantic speech."

"You're the one who brought your cock into the speech," I remind him. "And I can never forget about it. It's imprinted on me like a baby duck."

He laughs, giving a wry shake of his head. Then his expression softens, his gaze gentle. "I need to know that you're hearing what I'm saying to you."

I gaze at him for a long moment, my heart swelling as I fully appreciate what he's offering me. "I hear it."

And then his lips are on mine. Fierce and hungry and hot. I sink into the kiss instantly, tugging him closer against me and groaning as our tongues clash together.

Fuck, I've missed this. I'm such an idiot for denying us

this connection for so long. I should have taken every kiss Deacon was willing to give me; I won't be making that mistake again.

Our lips finally tear apart and Deacon rests his forehead against mine again, his ragged breath hot on my face.

"Tanner…" he rasps out. "Fuck, I want you. It's just… Jazz explained, but I need to hear it from you. Before…"

I know what he's asking. He needs to make absolutely certain I'm not still involved with someone.

I lift a hand to gently stroke his hair. "If you ask the IRS, then, yes, I am married. But we've been separated for three years. I would love nothing more than to divorce her, but—"

"Jazz told me about Izzy," he murmurs. "I'm sorry."

I let out a sigh, relieved that I don't have to go into the whole saga. Deacon and Jazz must have had quite the talk. "It's not just Izzy I'm worried about though," I admit in a near-whisper. "I honestly don't think I could get through a trial. Even just the thought of it sends me spiraling."

He draws back to gaze into my eyes again. "You don't ever have to do it if you don't want to. I'm good with living in sin," he adds with a smirk. "But if you ever do decide to go through with it, I'll be there with you. And if you spiral, I'll just wind you back up again…or whatever the opposite of spiral is."

I let out a soft chuckle, leaning forward to brush my lips to his. "I love you." I feel like I've been keeping that thought to myself for a million years and now I can't stop myself from bursting out with it. "I love you." I say again. "I really love you."

"You seem a little surprised about this," he says with a chuckle.

"Not surprised to be feeling it," I tell him. "But I wasn't planning to say it."

He offers a sweet smile. "Well, I'm really glad you did."

"And now you're supposed to say…" I prod him.

"You'll have to wait your turn, babe," he tells me with a teasing smirk.

The back and forth ends when the soft kisses morph into desperate, hungry ones that make my head spin and completely steal my breath.

My hands can't get enough of Deacon's body, and soon enough his jacket and t-shirt are on the floor and I get to roam my fingers all over his heated skin and hard muscles.

Needing more of him, I tear at the front of his jeans and tug them down, my hands wrapping around his hard dick the moment it's free. Fuck, I love the way it feels pulsing in my grip; and I love the groans Deacon lets out as I stroke him. It's ridiculous to think how hesitant I used to be to touch him here. I was more than happy to have this cock fill my ass, but got forbid it touched me anywhere else. *Idiot.*

"Okay, nope. No, no," Deacon cries, grabbing my wrists and pinning them against the wall.

"What—did I hurt you?" Shit, I'm still new to the whole jerking another guy off thing—what if I've caused him permanent damage?

"Fuck no," he growls. "But if you keep your hands on me I'm going to blow before I can get inside you."

"That never seems to matter when *I'm* about to come," I point out. "Where's it written that you're allowed to tease me until I'm practically crying but I can't even touch your dick?"

His mouth curves in a wry smirk. "It's all part of the Deacon Plan—it's there in the fine print."

"Serves me right for skimming that section," I say with a soft chuckle. "What else did I miss?"

"Did you read the part about unlimited orgasms?" he

asks. "That's one of the most popular features. And you also have the option of upgrading to a lifetime subscription for no extra charge."

My lips spread into a wide grin and I lean forward for a soft kiss. "That sounds very tempting. Is it a limited time offer?"

He gives a soft shake of his head. "Nope. There's no expiration date on that one. You just need to make sure to keep your membership current with lots of kisses and cuddles and talking."

"I think I can manage that."

We kiss again and it once again turns heated and hungry in a matter of seconds.

Deacon yanks roughly at my sweater and I help him pull it off, tossing it to the ground and dragging him against me so we're skin-to-skin. The heat of his body feels incredible against my skin and all I want is to be closer.

Completely forgetting his instruction from a mere few minutes ago, I reach for his cock again, moving my hands over the hard length.

"Jesus, fuck, Tanner," he groans, panting against my cheek. He doesn't tell me to stop this time, however, instead rocking his hips forward and fucking into my grip.

His hand moves to the front of my sweats, palming my hard dick through the fabric.

"Fuck, get it out," I groan. "Touch me."

He doesn't hesitate to comply, shoving my sweats down and wrapping a large hand around my throbbing dick.

I let my head fall back against the wall, a soft moan leaving my lips. Fuck, this feels good. Maybe not as good as taking him inside me, but still pretty incredible. Being this close to Deacon, bringing him pleasure with my own hand while he does the same for me—it's a heady feeling.

I'm a little surprised when Deacon pulls my hand away

from his dick, and for a moment I think he's going to give me the same spiel about not wanting to come until he gets inside me. But then he moves even closer and I feel his bare cock slipping against mine. I barely have time to let out a gasp before he wraps a hand around both our dicks, gripping tight.

He thrusts his hips and I can't help letting out a choked groan. "Jesus Christ."

"This is called frotting," he murmurs in my ear. "You can use your safe word if you want."

"Just keep doing what you're doing," I tell him, lifting my hands to grip his shoulders as I snap my own hips forward.

It doesn't take long for us to fall into sync. Our lips crash together again in a series of desperate, frantic kisses as our cocks grind together.

I've never thought about doing this before. I have no idea why; it makes perfect sense when your partner has a dick as well. I guess it comes back to that thing of not wanting much to do with cocks unless they were in my ass. So fucking stupid. Or, at least, that's how it feels now; I have no idea whether I would have enjoyed all this stuff if I'd tried it with anyone else. What I do know is that with Deacon, I want it all. Everything.

"Deacon...fuck," I groan, feeling as though I'm about to self-combust. The feel of our throbbing cocks, slick with precum, moving against each other in Deacon's tight grip is fucking incredible. I never want it to stop. I never want him to stop kissing me. We're as close as we can get, with our bodies molded against each other, but I want to be even closer. I want to crawl inside him and never leave.

I'm alarmed at some of the thoughts swirling around in my head, but then I decide I don't care. I love him. And even though he hasn't said it yet, I know he feels the same.

Something tells me he won't mind too much that my advanced age seems to have turned me into a clingy bastard.

I feel the kindling fire of my orgasm approaching, and snap my hips faster as I chase it down. I tear my mouth from Deacon's, burying my head in his neck and letting out a harsh groan as it rips through me and I come hard. I can feel a little of the warm liquid on my abs but I'm going to presume most of it ended up on Deacon's hand. I've never been much of a squirter.

I'm still clinging tightly to Deacon, my head resting against his shoulder as I try to gather my breath when I feel him tensing up. He lets out a low groan, and then something warm and familiar is coating my chest. Jesus, that's an impressive distance.

He immediately pulls away from me and I glance up to see him wearing a horrified expression. "Shit—fuck—Tanner...I'm sorry." He can barely get the words out through panted breaths, clearly still recovering from his orgasm.

"It's fine," I assure him.

"I meant to change the angle, but it hit me so fast—"

"Deacon, it's *fine*," I say again. I glance down at the streaks of cum painting my chest. "I'm actually pretty impressed at the distance you got."

He shrugs. "It's not a PB or anything. I've shot up to my nose before."

Fucking hell.

His expression turns serious and he fixes me with a searching look. "Are you sure it's okay? Cum's always been a firm no for you."

"This isn't just cum, though," I try to explain. "It's your cum."

"It doesn't have magical properties or anything," he says wryly.

"Well I wasn't planning on using it to summon a lesser demon," I say with a breath of laughter. "I just realized that there's no need for me to be uncomfortable about something that results from the pleasure we bring each other." I run my hands over his shoulders, smiling softly. "I love that you've been so incredibly patient with me and sensitive to my needs, but I don't want you to hold back anymore. I love you, and I want everything you have to give me."

A slow grin spreads across his face and he lifts his hands to cup my cheeks in that way he does that makes me feel incredibly precious. "I love you too."

"Finally," I say with an eye roll.

He lets out a soft laugh and brushes his lips to mine. "For the record, I will happily give you everything. My heart, my body, my time, my support, my baby-sitting skills…and definitely my cum."

"You're amazing," I whisper, my heart clenching with love for him.

He offers a lazy smile. "I know." Then he runs a fore-finger through the mess he made on my chest, collecting a glob of it on the pad of his finger. He reaches toward my face and for a second I think he's going to ask me to taste it —which, I admit, I'm still a bit unsure about—but he bypasses my mouth and instead paints a stripe down my nose. "That okay?"

I offer a wry smile. "I'm never going to be able to watch Izzy finger-paint again, but yeah that's okay."

He lets out a chuckle and collects some more cum on his finger, this time reaching behind me to paint my crease.

I let out a soft gasp and my body shivers—not entirely

surprising considering how sensitive that area of my body is.

Encouraged, Deacon returns to his 'paint supply' several more times, applying more cum to my crease, around my hole, and over my ass cheeks.

By the time he's done I'm completely breathless, my cock almost fully hard again. And all I want is to know what it would feel like to have Deacon's hot cum covering my ass cheeks, or filling up my hole.

"One more, then we can go clean up," Deacon says.

I don't really want to clean up. I want to stay like this, covered in his cum until we have sex and I get even more cum on me. Then I might think about cleaning up. Maybe.

The complete one-eighty in my attitude is making me a little heady, but for once I'm not going to stress about it. I'm enjoying a new experience and there's nothing wrong with that.

I'm snapped out of my thoughts as I see Deacon's finger moving toward my face again, and this time it is going for my mouth.

"You can use the safe word," he reminds me, his forefinger pausing to hover just in front of my mouth.

The amount on the tip of his fingertip is barely larger than a chickpea, and I realize he's using his other hand, so his finger is otherwise clean. I consider using the word, because even though I've now discovered that I do actually enjoy having cum on my skin, there's a big difference between that and actually ingesting it. This is such a tiny amount, though—it seems ridiculous to be scared of it.

Wordlessly, I reach up and grip Deacon's wrist, guiding his finger closer to my mouth. I close my lips around it and collect the bead of cum with my tongue.

And what do you know? The world doesn't end.

27

Deacon

Tanner looks incredibly proud of himself, and it's adorable. I know this doesn't mean he's all of a sudden going to want to suck me off until I shoot down his throat, but I love that he's letting himself at least try these new things. It's not lost on me that my little finger-painting session really turned him on. My goal was simply to test out his comfort level; being okay with me accidentally shooting on his chest is one thing, but even with his insistence that he doesn't want me holding back anymore, I still wanted to test the waters before I let myself get all excited about the possibility of coming inside him, or on his face, or basically anywhere on his body.

To be clear, I was happy to sacrifice that aspect of sex if it was something Tanner never managed to become comfortable with. It seemed a small price to pay for the privilege of being with him. Especially if that privilege extended to a genuine, committed relationship that we can take out into the world.

But he's told me—and shown me—that I don't need to compromise anymore, and I love him even more for that.

We'll still take things slow and move at the pace he sets, but it feels like the last barrier between us has now been broken.

"You're a bit of a mess," I say with a fond smile, scanning my gaze appreciatively over his face and torso. "I think you should probably go take a shower."

"Or *we* could go take a shower?" he suggests, one eyebrow arched.

I let out a soft laugh. "I don't have that kind of self-control. You'll be all wet and sudsy and naked and I'm not going to be able to stop myself from fucking you."

"And that's bad, why?"

My brain blanks out for a moment as I try to remember why I decided getting off again so soon would be a bad idea. Then it comes back to me and I offer a soft smile. "Because for the first time ever we don't have to cram everything into a few hours. We've got all day together. And all night." I wrap my arms around his waist and pull him closer, brushing my lips to his. "For once we can actually pace ourselves, and I've got really big plans for you in the next twenty-four hours, so we need to save some energy. And you need to wash my cum off you before I completely ignore everything I just said."

"That's not exactly an incentive," he says dryly. "Neither is having your cock this close to mine." Emphasizing his words, he rocks his hips forward so our cocks bump together. Neither of us have bothered to pull our pants up yet, so it's bare, sensitive skin that touches and I can't stop the soft gasp that falls from my lips.

I somehow manage to pull myself away and tug my jeans up, covering my half-hard dick.

"Party pooper," Tanner grumbles.

I let out a soft laugh. "Go clean up. I'll find us something to eat while you're gone—you don't mind if I go through your kitchen, do you?"

He shakes his head. "No, of course not. But I'm only going to go shower on my own if you promise to be naked when I get back," he says, hitting me with a challenging look that I'm sure he must have employed many times over the years when dealing with difficult business associates. "Like you said, we've got the house to ourselves all day, so none of this crap." He gestures to my jeans with obvious disapproval.

I let out a soft chuckle. "And if I get cold?"

"I'll warm you up."

I press a soft kiss to his lips, liking the sound of that. "Deal."

Tanner shows me to the kitchen before heading upstairs to shower. I have a feeling he's going to be as fast as humanly possible, so I strip out of my jeans and toss them on one of the stools at the granite island. If he comes back down and finds me still clothed, he won't be impressed.

I thought the kitchen in the penthouse was impressive, but this one is a whole new level. All the sleek design features from the penthouse are here, just maximized in size about three-fold. Even the oven looks big enough for someone to fit in there. With the heat off, obviously.

I open what I assume to be the pantry, but instead find a two-door refrigerator. I've seen some fancy fridges in my time—Spencer has one with a touch screen that actually tells you what's inside—but this one is actually pretty normal, albeit pretty big.

I swing both doors open and am not entirely surprised to find it organized neatly and logically, with different shelves for different categories of food items, and neatly labelled containers with clearly marked expiration dates. I give a wry shake of my head and decide here and now to never let Tanner see the inside of my and Drew's fridge.

I'm not entirely sure what I'm supposed to be getting for us to eat.

Something that's not super filling—no one wants to have sex when they've just stuffed their face and are all bloated with a food baby—but something that's still going to give a bit of an energy boost. It's not just that we have the whole day and night to look forward to and I don't to want crash into a heap later; that's probably not even the main reason, if I'm being honest.

The reality is, I haven't exactly been practicing the best self-care over the past few days, and even after Jazz's reassurance yesterday, I still wasn't able to eat much this morning because I was too nervous about how things were going to go once Tanner and I started talking. I could tell the moment Tanner opened the door that the time apart has been just as hard on him, and even after we sorted things out and shared that incredible orgasm, he still looked completely wrung out. When I saw he was getting hard again, all I wanted to do was drag him off to bed and get my cock inside him. But we both need some recovery time first; not just from the sex workout, but from the past couple days.

Finding some grapes and strawberries, I decide to make a little platter that we can pick at while watching TV.

It turns out the pantry is actually a walk-in one that's almost as big as the kitchen itself, and is stocked better than most grocery stores. I find some almonds and dried apricots, and am just reaching for a box of chocolate-coated roasted chickpeas—never tried those before, but more protein options won't hurt—when I hear someone moving around in the kitchen. Grinning to myself, I grab the box and exit the pantry.

"Oh my god! What the fuck?"

I hastily shove the packages in my hands down to cover my crotch when I realize the person in the kitchen isn't Tanner, but a young woman with long, auburn hair and familiar blue eyes. She's dressed casually but her clothes are all designer and there's a Birken bag sitting on the counter. She can only be Tanner's oldest daughter, Piper.

"Oh my god, I'm never going to be able to eat apricots again," she groans, covering her face with one hand.

"You must be Piper," I say awkwardly.

"And you must be the guy Dad was a complete mess about two days ago," she shoots back, clearly unimpressed.

"We…figured things out."

"I see that…"

For all of Jazz's abrasiveness, I was confident after our encounter yesterday that he was fully on board with Tanner and me being together, provided I don't hurt him. Piper, though? To be fair, it's only been a few moments and this is an *incredibly* awkward way to meet your boyfriend's daughter, but I just can't shake the idea that she's not thrilled about this situation.

"I should put some pants on," I say awkwardly. And then, figuring she must be here to see Tanner, I add, "Your dad's just taking a shower. He should be down soon."

She cringes and shakes her head. "Yeah, I don't think I'll wait for that. I just came to grab this for RJ." She collects a file from the counter and slips it into her bag. "It was…nice to meet you, I guess," she says awkwardly. "Thanks for scarring my corneas."

Then she sets her bag in the crook of her elbow and stalks from the kitchen.

I just stare after her, a little shell-shocked. *Scarring her corneas?* I'm not that hideous am I?

28

Tanner

When I get downstairs, I'm disappointed to find that Deacon has not followed through on his promise to be waiting naked. He's sitting on the sofa in the living room, with a plate of food set in front of him on the coffee table. It's a little tasting plate with a bunch of different things that we can nibble on once we're done having sex. It's clear he's put effort into it and it's adorable.

But the jeans he's wearing are not.

"What happened to naked Deacon?" I ask with a frown.

"There was an incident," he informs me, his face flaming bright red.

I'm a little concerned by his shell-shocked expression, but as he relays the incident with Piper, the concern gives way to amusement, and as much as I try to keep it to myself, I just can't seem to stop my lips from twitching.

"It was *not* funny, Tanner! It was mortifying. Your daughter saw me naked. And really didn't like it. She said I scarred her corneas."

I give a wry shake of my head. "Piper's always had a bit of a tendency toward the dramatic. And I guess it couldn't have been the most comfortable experience to find my boyfriend naked in the kitchen of her childhood home. She's not an idiot—she would have known that if you were naked it meant we'd either recently had sex or were about to. No daughter wants to think of their dad having sex."

"That's what's so horrible—I totally traumatized her. And what if she can't look you in the eye anymore?"

I wave his concern away. "She'll be fine. She's a big girl. From now on she'll just have to knock. Or text when she's coming over." I pad over to the sofa so I can stand right in front of Deacon, in between his parted legs. "Now, about these jeans…they're a problem for me."

He lets out a breath of laughter, flashing me a wry grin. "Why don't we keep pants while we have something to eat?"

I reach down to slide a hand over my dick, which is once again rock hard thanks to the prep I did while I was upstairs. Deacon tries to avert his gaze, but his eyes keep flashing back to sneak a peek, prompting him to let out a soft curse. "I thought you loved the sight of my dick?" I tease. "But now you want me to cover it up?"

"I think it would be best," he rasps, swallowing hard.

His mouth might be saying the words, but his eyes look like he's about to tackle me and suck down on my dick at any second.

"You sure you don't want a little taste first?" I taunt, one eyebrow raised.

"*Tanner,*" he groans, closing his eyes. "Food. Eat. Energy. Please."

I sigh. *Why* did he have to say please?

"Fine, you win. I'll be back in a sec." I stride from the

living room and duck into the laundry, grabbing a pair of sweats from the clean laundry pile. I quickly tug them on and then rush back to Deacon.

"Pants," I announce, waving a hand at my lower half as though Deacon's never seen sweats before.

"Good, now come over here and eat something. And don't try to tell me you had a big breakfast," he warns me, narrowing his eyes. "I know you've been taking care of yourself about as well as I have the last couple days."

My disappointment at not jumping straight into more sex immediately vanishes as my heart swells with affection for this beautiful man. Of course he wants to make sure I'm eating right and prioritizing healthy behavior. Taking care of me and keeping me safe is what he does.

I climb onto the sofa and take up position in Deacon's lap. "I love how you take care of me," I murmur. "But it shouldn't always be you. I need to be the one looking after you sometimes as well."

"We can take care of each other," he says with a soft smile. "You want to start by feeding me some grapes? I can't reach from here."

I arch a brow at him. "Feed you grapes? How very Grecian noble of you. Should I go cut down a palm tree so I can fan you with the leaves?"

He lets out a rumbling chuckle that lights up his whole face. "Let's stick with the grapes for now. Although I wouldn't say no to you rubbing my entire body with oil later."

I sure as fuck wouldn't say no to that either.

***

. . .

"I STILL CAN'T BELIEVE Jazz tracked you down at school just to get us back together," I muse, feeling incredibly proud of and grateful to my son. "He's not exactly known for his altruism," I add with a wry laugh.

Deacon smiles. "I'm not sure "altruism" is the word I'd use. He read me the riot act, then he told me all about Natalia and seemed to take great pleasure in making me feel really guilty. Then he warned me not to give you a heart attack during make-up sex, but also not to be too gentle."

I screw my face up even as a sputter of amusement escapes my lips. "Yeah, that sounds more accurate. I'm really sorry—he's an acquired taste."

Deacon shakes his head. "Don't be. I needed to hear all that. Well, not the sex advice. but everything else. I just wish I'd given you the chance to explain it for yourself."

I reach out and brush my hands through his soft blond hair, loving the way it feels slipping through my fingers. "It's okay. I know how it all must have looked. And it's still a completely messed up situation. I'd understand if you didn't want anything to do with it."

He shakes his head. "Not a chance. But...could you maybe tell me more about it? So I can understand better?"

I sigh. "I will. I promise I'm not trying to hold anything back, I'd just really like to enjoy this weekend without any of that shit intruding."

He nods, offering a soft smile. "That's okay. Whenever you're ready is fine. I'm not going to rush you."

"How are you so perfect?" I murmur, resting my forehead against his and drawing in a deep breath of his scent.

"Only in your eyes, babe," he says wryly, still humble as ever.

"Perfect," I murmur again, before pressing my lips to his.

It doesn't take long for the kiss to grow hungry and heated. As always, his kiss is fierce and demanding, and I have to cling tightly to his shoulders to ensure I don't get completely swept away.

Before I know it, I've shifted around so I'm straddling his lap, and our hard dicks are grinding together to create delicious, heady friction.

"Fuck, fuck, fuck," Deacon groans as we rub furiously against each other. "Fuck…no, not like this. Want to be in you this time."

Hell yes. I *need* him in me. "You're the one who wanted pants," I point out. "You could be in me right now if we'd stuck with my plan."

"Babe, if we'd stuck with your plan I'd have come all over this couch two hours ago."

Fuck, that would have been hot.

I'm a little startled by the thought crossing my mind. I know I was turned on by Deacon's little finger-painting class earlier, and I've made the decision to forgo condoms on this occasion—if I hate it we can always go back, after all—but I wasn't expecting to start getting turned on by the thought of massive wet spots on my sofa.

Dashing the thought from my mind, I manage to drag myself off Deacon's lap for a moment so I can scramble out of my sweats. "Off," I tell him, pointing at his jeans.

He quirks a brow at me. "Has bossy Tanner come out to play."

I send him an unamused look. "I haven't had your dick in me for three days—chop chop, Deacon."

He cringes, but unzips and starts shimmying out of his jeans. "For the record, no one wants to hear the word "chop" when their dick is in the conversation."

I let out a soft laugh. "Fair."

Once his jeans are off and I've got my eyes on that

thick cock I love so much, I waste no time in climbing back onto Deacon's lap.

"Aren't you missing something?" he asks me, letting out a soft gasp as I start running my hands over his shaft, spreading out the drops of precum collecting at the head. My ass is plenty stretched out and slicked up so I don't think he'll be needing anything extra.

"I already took care of it upstairs," I inform him. "And before you say anything, I want to remind you that *technically* you said you didn't want to come to the penthouse and find me already lubed up."

Deacon gives an exasperated shake of his head. "Smartass. I was actually talking about a condom, though."

"I already told you we're done with that. I'm not holding you back anymore."

He smiles and runs his hands over my sides. "I really love that, babe, but I just want to make sure you're not doing this only to make me happy. I need you to want it and be comfortable with it."

"Oh, trust me, I am. I want to feel it," I tell him, my tone unwavering. I've never been more sure of anything than I am of this right now. I want to experience the sensation of having Deacon's cum in me. "I want this, Deacon," I assure him. "Not because I just want to do something that I think will make you happy. Although I do enjoy making you happy," I add as a side-note. "I love you. Every single part of you. And I want you bare inside me. And I want your cum in me."

Finally, he nods, a grin forming on his lips. "Okay. then. If it's what you really want, I'm not going to talk you out of it,"

I grin at him and lean forward to claim his lips in a soft kiss. "It's what I really want."

I shuffle up a bit to get into a better position, before taking Deacon's dick in hand and guiding it to my hole. I start sinking down slowly, and am immediately greeted by the sharp bite of pain as he pierces my outer ring, but as always, my sensitive nerves in that area start firing quickly and pleasure kicks in quickly.

What I wasn't expecting is the extreme intensity of taking a bare dick inside me. It's as though everything has been amped up and I'm being hit with so much sensation I can't even see straight.

"Jesus, fuck..." Deacon groans, and I know he's feeling the same overwhelming intensity that I am.

I sink down the rest of the way, letting out a deep groan when he's fully inside. I've taken him inside me so many times now, but this is just...different. Jesus Christ, I can actually feel his dick throbbing inside me.

I know this isn't going to last long for either of us. Deacon is trembling and panting, his fingers digging into my sides. And I'm not a hell of a lot better.

Slowly, I start to move, riding his dick just like I did the night I realized I was in love with him. This is even better, though, because there's no distance between us, so I don't need to lean over in order to crash my lips to his.

The kiss is hungry, fierce, and frenetic, and it doesn't take long for our body movements to switch tempo to match. My hands bury themselves in Deacon's hair, grabbing at the soft strands as I bounce around on his dick. Every time I push down, Deacon thrusts up, hitting me hard and deep, and causing me to lose my fucking mind.

"Jesus...fuck...*coming,*" he groans, tearing his lips from mine and tossing his head back.

I feel his body tense up and his fingers dig in harder to my sides just as warm liquid pools inside my hole.

And it feels...fucking amazing. Not only because it's the physical evidence of the pleasure I've just wrung out of the man I love, but it turns out the actual sensation of liquid pouring into my incredibly sensitive hole is really pleasurable.

Deacon lifts his head, breathing heavily as he comes down from his climax. His blissed-out expression clears a little and he arches a questioning brow at me.

I offer a grin. "How long do you think you need before you can do that again?"

He sputters a laugh and lifts a hand to rub through his hair. "Okay, I'm going to take that as a good sign."

"I'm serious, Deacon," I say in what sounds way too much like a needy whine. "I want more. What's the ETA?"

"Needy fucking bottom," he murmurs, giving a wry shake of his head. "Why don't you let me suck your dick first, and then we'll talk about coming in your ass again."

I guess that sounds like a decent compromise. I'm definitely not far off from orgasm, and coming in Deacon's mouth is always a good option.

I push up onto my knees, feeling completely empty as Deacon's cock falls from my ass. I can still feel his cum, though, so that's something.

I shuffle a little closer so Deacon only has to duck his head slightly to get his mouth around my dick. He's not going to be able to take me all the way down his throat from this angle, but that's okay. I'm not going to last long enough for that anyway.

A soft groan falls from my lips as his tongue swirls around my head before moving farther down the shaft. And then he starts sucking. And groaning. And it's game over.

"Fuck," I groan, unable to get off any more of a

warning as my orgasm rushes up quicker than expected. Deacon doesn't seem to mind though; he happily takes my load as it shoots into his mouth, swallowing every drop and then grinning up at me.

"Yum."

29

Deacon

I draw in a deep breath as we approach the apartment door.

Tanner notices my apprehension and offers me a wry smile. "Don't worry, it's going to be fine."

I screw up my face, not really sure if I can take his words to heart. "She doesn't like me."

"She just doesn't know you yet. And to be fair, your first meeting wasn't exactly under ideal circumstances."

I wince. You could say that again. Meeting Tanner's oldest daughter while I was rummaging through his pantry stark naked was definitely not "ideal," despite how amusing Tanner found the incident. But I know it's more than that. I don't want to sound like a downer, but I just can't help feeling as though Piper was set against us well before the kitchen incident. "She doesn't like that I'm a guy."

Tanner's brow creases. "I doubt that's an issue. She's never had a problem with Jazz, and he's not exactly… discreet," he says with an exasperated shake of his head.

I let out a soft chuckle. Yes, I can imagine that. But I don't think that has anything to do with how Piper feels about Tanner and me. "This is different. You're her father. You've never shown an interest in men before and now, here you are, totally gone for a guy almost half your age. I mean, if my parents suddenly announced they were poly and had fallen for a guy only a few years older than me, it'd take a fuck load of adjusting. I doubt it'd ever happen because my parents never have sex, but still." Tanner quirks a brow at me and I send him a warning look. "Don't kill the dream."

He gives a wry shake of his head and reaches for my hand, clasping it tightly in his. "I get what you're saying, but I promise it'll be fine. Even if it does take some adjusting, she'll get there eventually. And we've got plenty of time."

I smile and lean toward him, touching my lips to his for a gentle kiss.

And, of course, that's when the apartment door swings open.

"Oh, great, I *so* need to see my dad sucking face with his boy toy on my birthday," a familiar voice drawls in a tone so sardonic it almost knocks me over.

Fucking hell, this girl really has a knack for bad timing.

"Good to see you again, Piper," I say awkwardly, trying not to fidget under her fierce look of disapproval.

Either not noticing or ignoring her, Tanner offers a wide grin and steps forward to kiss her cheek. "Happy birthday, sweetheart."

She softens at the gesture, seeming unable to help herself from returning his smile. "Thanks, Dad."

"Deacon!"

I grin as I see Izzy run up to us in her adorable pink party dress. Okay, well, she doesn't quite run—her balance isn't steady enough for the same kind of movement an able-bodied five-year-old can manage—but she moves quicker than I've ever seen before, a wide grin spread over her face. When she reaches me, she hesitates, blinking up at me in confusion despite her obvious excitement to see me. "Why here?"

I crouch down so I'm at her level. I don't usually do that too often at school because it's a bitch to be always crouching down and getting up again, and because we learn in college that kids need to be given a little distance to encourage the growth of independence and shit like that. But we're not at school now, and I don't want Izzy to feel like I'm talking down to her. "I'm here for Piper's birthday," I tell her.

"Piper's birthday too," she says, pointing to herself. "My sister."

She beams up at Piper, holding up her hands. "Deacon showed me to make pictures with my fingers."

Piper's brows creep up. "You mean finger-painting?"

"Deacon's great at finger-painting," Tanner says, a teasing note in his voice that I doubt anyone but me picks up on.

Even so, I feel my face flaming bright red at the memory of using my fingers to paint cum all over Tanner's body. *Fucking hell. Please don't get hard*, I beg my cock. I don't need Piper to think I'm more of a creep than she already does.

Fortunately, Izzy comes to the rescue by speaking up again. "Made picture with fingers," Izzy says to Piper, beaming proudly. "Jazz helped. Not hanging up." She says the last part with a wary glance in my direction, as though I might disapprove of her not hanging her painting on a wire like I normally do.

I get to my feet and run a hand over her adorable pigtail braids. "That's okay. I'm sure it dried anyway."

She nods. "Jazz did it."

"Do you remember *how* we dried it?" Jazz asks, startling me a little because I hadn't noticed him enter the room.

Izzy giggles and looks up fondly at her brother. "Hair dryer!"

Jazz grins. It's an astonishing change from the guy I met a couple weeks ago, with his scowls and eye rolls and arrogant smirks. "We almost lost it, didn't we? But I saved the day with my shoes, didn't I?"

"Is that why the corner's have mud on them?" Piper asks, one brow raised.

"It's called rustic appeal," Jazz says. "Just go with it."

"Baby girl, where's my cuddle?" Tanner asks Izzy.

She beams, as though just noticing he was there. To be fair, seeing her kindergarten teacher at her sister's birthday must have been a pretty big distraction.

She rushes over to Tanner and he crouches down, pulling her into his arms. "Ah, I missed you," he says, squeezing her tight. "Did you have fun with Jazz last night?"

She nods, smiling happily. "We did piano."

Tanner looks up at his son with a warm smile, affection and pride swimming in his gaze.

I've learned a lot about all of Tanner's kids during the time we've been together, so I know Jazz is something of a musical savant. And I know he was on track to becoming a classical pianist until he broke his hand in the car accident that killed Tanner's first wife. And I also know that since then, it's been incredibly difficult for him—both physically and emotionally—to return to that instrument. So I can understand why the thought of Jazz putting that aside for Izzy's benefit would have such an effect on Tanner.

He releases Izzy and gets to his feet, his hand still petting her hair as we finally follow Piper out of the enormous entryway and through to the main part of the two-floor penthouse.

My heart twinges as I watch Tanner absently stroking his daughter's hair. It's been great to have some time to ourselves recently, with Jazz offering to take Izzy overnight on a number of occasions. But I can see how much Tanner misses her, and I don't want him to have to sacrifice time with her purely so we can have a night of sex. I love Izzy, and having her around is not going to be deal-breaker by any stretch. I guess we'll just need to play it by ear and see how we can manage. Going public is a little complicated while Tanner's still technically married, and especially while I'm still Izzy's teacher. But I'm sure we can work something out.

We reach a set of stairs, because seriously—this apartment is about as big as my entire building—and Tanner hauls Izzy into his arms so we can all follow Piper up them.

"Oh, just so you know," Piper says, pausing at the middle of the staircase and turning back with a slight smirk curving her lips that makes me quite uneasy, "Grandma's already here. And she's pretty interested to meet this one." She tosses her head in my direction and then turns back around, continuing up the stairs.

Fuuucckk. I'd been so concerned about Piper and the whole naked kitchen debacle, I totally forgot about Tanner's mother-in-law. Of course she's going to be interested to meet the *guy* her daughter's widower is now involved with.

Behind me, I hear Jazz let out a snort. "Don't worry. She's being especially bitchy today because RJ's been busy all morning and hasn't been waiting on her hand and foot. Grandma will be cool. You're super hot, so she'll like you."

"Umm...okay..." I really don't know how else to respond to that.

He steps up beside me, offering a wry smirk. "What? You think seventy-five-year-old women don't get horny?"

"I can't say I ever really thought about it…"

"Well trust me, they do. She always brings her book club into the bar on Tuesday afternoons for the five dollar wings and wine deal, and I swear those women are hornier than the twenty-somethings that come in on Friday nights."

My brows shoot up. "You do five dollar wings and wine? That's a really good deal."

He leans closer to me and holds his hand up to his mouth. "Don't tell anyone, but the wine's just what's left-over from the weekend. It's a good way to get rid of it before it goes bad."

"Huh. I didn't even realize wine went bad."

He shrugs. "Red, not so much. But no one really orders red when they're eating wings. White starts oxidizing as soon as you open it, and if you leave it too long it'll turn into vinegar."

Well there you go. I guess that's why he runs a bar and I teach five-year-olds.

It's only now I'm realizing that Jazz and I have fallen behind the rest of the group, so when we enter what I'm assuming is the living room, all eyes are on us and I feel like a laser beam is being pointed at me.

"Oh, yes, now I see it. Good choice, Tanner."

I snap my head in the direction of the speaker, finding a woman about ten years older than my mom scanning her eyes up and down my body as though cataloging every single one of my features. I almost feel like I should turn around to give her a look of the back.

She finally lifts her eyes and I see Jazz's gray ones staring back at me, a soft twinkle in them. This can only be Leah's mother, and she's definitely not what I expected. For some reason I was expecting a Hillary Clinton-type figure, all crisp and dignified. But that's not what I'm seeing at all. Not that she's a slob or anything, but she just seems…approachable. Between the spiky white hair that's shaved at the sides, the jeans casually rolled up at the ankles, and the smear of purple lipstick on her lips, I feel like I could be looking at a future version of Blair.

"Urgh, Grandma," Piper practically whines. "You were supposed to be on my side. Don't you have any problem at all with Dad dating a *guy* half his age?"

"No need to tack another five years on, Pippy" Tanner says dryly. "Forty-nine's plenty, thanks."

Piper rolls her eyes. "You know what I mean."

"Why on earth would I have a problem with your father being happy?" Leah's mother says. Shit, I can't remember her name. I'm usually awesome at that, but it's completely gone from my head.

"I just—" Piper hesitates, opening and closing her mouth a few times before giving a frustrated shake of her head.

"I thought you didn't want Dad to know you weren't comfortable with this?" Jazz says pointedly.

"That was before I saw him prancing naked around the kitchen," she shoots back, gesturing at me.

"I wasn't *prancing*," I protest.

"You saw him naked?" Beth asks, sounding impressed. *Beth!* That's her name. I try not to look to pleased with myself for having remembered something so simple.

"And she didn't even take a picture," Jazz grumbles.

"Oh, I'm sorry, I was too busy being mentally scarred," Piper says. "He's completely ruined dried apricots for me."

"What a tragedy," Jazz drawled."

"I like apricots," a little voice says, and we all turn to

look at Izzy. I'm not sure about the others, but I'd kind of forgotten she was there.

"Okay, enough," Tanner says with a weary sigh. "Piper, I think you might be blowing this incident out of proportion a little."

"Yeah, she's being a total bitch," Jazz declares.

Tanner rolls his eyes. "That's not what I said." Fixing an intent look on his daughter, he tells her, "I can understand why this might be difficult for you, but I really hope that's something you can get past, because Deacon's here to stay. I love him, and I'm happy."

"You thought you were happy last time," Piper says, her face softening into a look of genuine concern. And I can't help feeling a rush of affection, despite the way she's behaved toward me. It's not that she dislikes me. And I don't even think she has an issue with me being a guy. She's just afraid of her father being hurt again.

Tanner offers a soft smile, his eyes flicking my way for a brief, comforting moment. "Not like this."

30

Tanner

Piper's frosty attitude thaws a little once RJ arrives, thank god. I'm not sure why he's so late, but his arrival helps to put a smile on my daughter's face and distract her from Deacon, so I'm prepared to give him a promotion—not that there's much higher up for a Director to go.

I know a lot of Piper's attitude is because she's concerned for my wellbeing, and once she sees Deacon is nothing like Natalia and that I'm truly happy with him, I'm sure that fear will fade. But I also know my wellbeing isn't her only concern. Everything she's ever known about me has changed, and it will take her time to adjust.

About halfway through lunch, the staff Piper hired to cater the meal—my daughter never does anything by half-measures—start setting flutes of champagne at everyone's places. Except Izzy, obviously.

Before I can ask what we're supposed to be celebrating, RJ slides out of his chair next to Piper and drops to one knee, a ring box in hand. He barely gets the first few words of his speech out before Piper is jumping out of her chair and gushing, "Oh my god. Yes! Of course!"

RJ grins and gets to his feet, tugging my daughter into his arms.

"Oh my god, I can't believe this. This is so amazing," she rambles. "I don't even care that Dad's gay lover is here."

"Who the fuck says 'lover'?" Jazz drawls.

I roll my eyes and get to my feet, rounding the table so I can get to my daughter.

"Congratulations, baby," I say with a warm smile, reaching out to stroke her hair.

"Thanks, Daddy."

I give RJ a pat on the shoulder. "You too, buddy."

"I suppose we should probably have a toast since they gave us the good stuff," Jazz says, standing and holding up his glass.

My heart is practically bursting as I watch all the people I love come together in celebration. I want so many more moments like these.

A FEW HOURS LATER, I'm in the kitchen doing the dishes when I hear someone walk up behind me.

"You know there's a catering team just sitting on their asses right now because you've insisted on doing their job for them."

I glance behind me and offer Beth a soft smile. "I like doing them."

"I know." She steps closer so she's to my side, leaning against the stone countertop next to the sink. "I hope Piper's little hissy fit earlier didn't put you out of sorts."

"She's fine. I'd rather her be open about her feelings than bottle them up." I smile at Beth. "Thanks for being so cool about Deacon, by the way."

"Tanner, you don't have to thank me. I'm just glad you've found someone who makes you happy."

I eye her curiously. "What makes you so sure he makes me happy? The only thing you know about him is that he's hot."

She lets out a huff of laughter, grinning broadly. "Well, he is that. But I can tell by the way you look at him. I haven't seen that look on your face in a very long time, Tanner. Almost ten years…" She glances away, swallowing hard.

I just stare at her, the dishes forgotten for a moment as her words stun me. "You don't…"

Beth offers a sad smile. "No one will ever replace my daughter, Tanner. In my eyes or yours. But you can move on. You can fall in love. You can be happy."

"You make it sound like Deacon's the first relationship I've had since Leah died."

Beth purses her lips. She was never rude or unwelcoming to Natalia, but she never warmed to her either. At the time I put it down to it being difficult for Beth to see me with someone new, but now I know she's just a way better judge of character than I am. "That was never…real."

I arch my brows and return to scrubbing the pan I have soaking in the sink. "Seemed pretty real. I have the marriage certificate to prove it," I grumble.

"I meant…it never seemed *sincere,*" she clarifies. "Don't take this the wrong way, but I always got the impression that you felt as though you just needed someone—anyone —because being with someone would make everything better. And then later, when everything went balls up, it was the complete opposite—you wouldn't let anyone near you."

I set the pan in the drying rack and grab another pot

from the pile of dishes. "You might have a point," I mumble. I don't think anyone could have predicted the way things would turn out with Natalia, but I know there's a lot of truth to Beth's words: I wasn't in the right frame of mind to be jumping into a relationship back then. And I certainly wasn't in the right frame of mind to be getting married. How much pain could I have prevented if I'd just taken time to think things through the way I usually do?

But then I wouldn't have Izzy, and there's no alternate reality in which that outcome is better.

"That wasn't meant as a criticism," she says gently. "I was just clarifying why I think Deacon's so different."

"He is different," I agree, unable to keep a soft smile from forming on my lips.

"And I'm glad. But that's not really why I came in here."

I arch a brow at her. "It's not?"

She fixes me with a level look. "I've been talking to Jazz. And RJ."

I groan. "I didn't mean to give Jazz so many specifics. I told him I was asking for a friend."

She blinks at me. "I literally have no idea what you're talking about. He just mentioned that you're still struggling with your anxiety."

I sigh. "It's not really something that goes away. But I manage it. I wouldn't say I struggle."

"And RJ told me about the offer for MesiTec," she continues, as though I haven't interrupted.

"Don't worry, I'm not selling," I assure her.

"I think you should."

My head snaps up and I gape at her. "What?"

She shrugs. "He said it could save Grimco Media from bankruptcy. Sounds like a no-brainer to me."

"He's being dramatic. We're not that far in the red."

"But there *are* issues?" she presses.

"It's nothing we haven't got through before. I'm not selling Leah's company," I say firmly.

"It's not Leah's company anymore, Tanner. It hasn't been for nearly a decade." I flinch from the sting of her words and she reaches out to place a gentle hand on my arm. "I know you want to hold onto every piece of her that you can, and trust me, I understand it. But you know as well as I do, she'd kick your ass for dragging your feet on this. If this MesiTec deal can save Grimco, and give you fifty fewer things to stress about, Leah would do it in a heartbeat."

I finally pull my hands from the water and tear off the rubber gloves I was wearing. Spinning around, I lean back against the sink, letting out a heavy sigh as I rub a hand over my forehead. "They're going to tear it apart," I murmur. "Nothing of Leah's vision will be left."

"There's that risk," Beth agrees. "But is clinging onto it going to help? Do you have the resources to turn it into the company she dreamed about?"

No one's ever put it to me like that; not even RJ in some of his more passionate spiels. I consider the question for a long moment, but finally I have to admit the truth. "No, we don't. Not unless we can fill our coffers some other way."

"Is that likely?"

Of course it's not. If there was another way I would have found it by now.

Beth gives me a reassuring pat on the arm. "You do what's best for your business. And for yourself. I just wanted you to know that if you decide to sell, you don't need to worry about upsetting me."

I manage a small smile at the gesture. "Thanks, Beth."

. . .

***

"YOU'VE BEEN QUIET," Deacon comments later on as I'm driving him home. "I figured you'd be over the moon right now, father of the bride and all that." He reaches across the console to run his fingers through the hair at my nape. "You're way hotter than Steve Martin, if that's what you're worried about."

"What?"

"Steve Martin—*Father of the Bride.*"

I roll my eyes. Deacon and his movie references. "That's not what I'm worried about," I say wryly. "And I am over the moon. Although I think I'll be taking the hands-off approach to wedding planning. Best to steer clear of Hurricane Piper."

Deacon snorts in amusement. "She's that bad?"

"She won't become a bridezilla or anything," I assure him. "She just likes things done in the exact way she wants them and doesn't have patience for people messing up."

He nods, his fingers continuing to brush through my hair. It's so soothing and comforting, I just want to pull over and crawl into his arms. Obviously that's not a possibility; not only because we're driving through Lower Manhattan, but because Izzy is asleep in the back of the car. I glance in the rearview to check on her, and see that she is indeed still snoozing.

"So what's up then?" Deacon asks, concern in his voice.

"Beth thinks I should sell MesiTec," I tell him.

He shifts in his seat to stare at me, brows raised. "The company my brother's trying to buy?"

"Well, it's your brother's client, but yeah."

"But that's Leah's company," Deacon says, and my

heart swells at the way he says her name, as though he also knew and loved her.

I nod. "Yeah. But Beth pointed something out to me that I hadn't really considered before—that I'm not really saving it by not selling, I'm just clinging onto it because I can't bring myself to let go."

"That's a completely valid reason," he says gently. "If you're not ready to sell, that's okay."

I offer a wry smile. "You're not a businessman, Deacon, and I love that about you. But I can't keep holding onto an asset for purely sentimental reasons. Not when its sale can breathe life back into the entire corporation."

"From everything you've told me about Leah, I think she would have been happy to have given you that lifeline," Deacon says gently.

Lifeline. I've never thought of the MesiTec offer that way. But I have to admit, it takes a lot of the sting out of selling to think of it as Leah reaching he hand out to save me from drowning. Or something sappy like that.

I nod, my throat tightening. "Yeah. You're probably right."

"And if you are going to sell, this might be a good week to do it—I think Sully could really use a win right about now."

I wince at the reminder of the garbage article that some online tabloid printed about Stapleton last week. I've never really liked the guy—although I guess now I'm going to have to make an effort, aren't I?—but I wouldn't wish something like that on my worst enemy. Add in the fact that it completely screwed with the guy's relationship and I'm left in the very odd situation of feeling sorry for Sullivan Stapleton.

I offer Deacon a warm smile. "Alright. I'll put Leona

onto it tomorrow. And I guess once your brother and I are no longer business rivals we can all sit down for a nice dinner together. And then I can kick his ass for having me tracked by a PI."

Deacon's lips twitch in obvious amusement. "I agree with the sentiment, babe. But why don't you let *me* kick his ass?" He waggles his eyebrows at me. "And then after dinner I can lick yours."

31

Deacon

"Friendsgiving?" Tanner asks curiously. "That's an actual thing?"

I nod. "Yep. At least that's what most of us call it. Skyler calls it "Spanksgiving" but I'm sure that's just because he likes to be punny. There isn't any spanking. At least, not at Spencer's place...well, not at Spencer's place while everyone's there." I give a shake of my head. "I really need to stop talking."

Tanner flashes an affectionate smile, amusement dancing in his eyes. "You're adorable."

I let out a soft chuckle. "Mmmhmm...I bet you think that when I've got your cock down my throat as well."

He arches a brow at me. "Adorable? That's not exactly the word that comes to mind for that particular situation."

I shift in closer on the sofa, putting me practically in his lap, which is where I belong as far as I'm concerned. We've both totally forgotten about the documentary playing on the TV; it's one about the Space Race that Tanner chose, and I'm sure it's fascinating...just not as fascinating as my boyfriend. "So, are you interested?" I ask him.

"In you going down on me?" His brows shoot up in question. "Always."

I flash a broad grin. "I like where your mind's at, but I was actually talking about Friendsgiving. It would be a good opportunity to do that whole dinner-mending fences thing with Sully we talked about. But, of course, if you've already got plans with your family that's totally fine." He hasn't mentioned anything, but after Piper's less than enthusiastic reception at her birthday lunch a couple days ago I wouldn't blame him if he wanted to keep Thanksgiving drama-free.

"*Our* family," he corrects me, causing my insides to turn to goo. "And, no, actually. Piper's with RJ's family and Jazz will be at the bar because, and I quote "Thanksgiving isn't just about turkey and pumpkin pie. Plenty of people want to commemorate the thieving of native lands by drinking whiskey and singing along to better-performed versions of nineties songs.""

"I'm really worried about his self-esteem issues," I say with a shake of my head. "If only he had more confidence in himself."

Tanner sputters a laugh. "If only."

"So you're in, then?" I press, perhaps a little too eagerly. It's not just that I'm keen to celebrate our first important holiday together as a couple; I want Tanner to get to know all my friends and for them to know him. He's met some of them already, of course, but in a completely different environment. They need to all hang out on a level field where everyone can just be themselves.

He smiles at me. "Alright. If it's something you want to do. And if Izzy's allowed to come along—Kit will be away for the weekend."

"She'll be more than welcome," I assure him. "There

might be other kids there too. I can't remember if Aaron and Kylie decided to go away for the weekend or not."

Tanner smiles and leans in to kiss my lips. "Sounds perfect."

I kiss him back, and it's not long before I really am in his lap.

"So...maybe now you want to give me that blow job?" he gasps out after we've been making out long enough to get well and truly worked up.

I grin. "*Now* who's got their bossy pants on?"

"It wasn't an order, merely a polite request."

I quirk a brow at him as I scramble off him and take up position on my knees in front of the couch. "I don't remember hearing "please"."

Not that it matters; I'm never going to turn down an opportunity to get my mouth around this beautiful dick, and he damn well knows it.

***

I CAN'T HELP SMIRKING at the way Tanner is fidgeting nervously as we ride the elevator up to Spencer's penthouse on Thursday. Social situations aren't usually too much of an issue for him, but he's clearly nervous about this particular engagement if the way he's been fingering the hem of his cashmere sweater and smoothing out the non-existent flaw in his cow-lick. There haven't been any forehead rubs yet, however, so I know this is only nerves and not genuine stress or anxiety.

"You're going to ruin that sweater," I say wryly. "Which would be a shame, because you look freakin' hot in it."

"Take sweater off, Daddy," Izzy says, peering up at us

curiously with those bright blue eyes framed by the adorable rainbow glasses. "If too hot."

"I'm not too hot, baby girl. I'm just fine," Tanner says, beaming down at Izzy. He leaves his sweater alone, though, and instead threads his hands through Izzy's hair, which is free of its usual pigtail braids today because Kit is out of town and apparently she's the only one Izzy will let braid her hair.

"You didn't tell me why you do this whole Friends-giving thing," Tanner murmurs as we get off the elevator at the top floor and head down the hall toward the sole apartment door. "We got...um...distracted the other day."

My lips curve into a wry smirk at the memory of the way I blew Tanner and then came all over him on Tuesday night. It was a good thing we were at the penthouse, because there are cumstains all over that couch now, which would have been awkward to explain in the brownstone. Mental note—be more careful with couch sex.

"Spence and his sister, Emily, have been doing this for years. I think it started because Em used to live in England, and she tried to bring the whole traditional English Christmas thing home with her but it didn't really go over that well. And then the next year Spence and Em and Pax and a couple of the guys were trying to work out vacay plans for Thanksgiving but couldn't get any of their sched-ules to line up. So Emily decided to shift her idea for a big festive lunch to Thanksgiving instead."

Tanner offers a wry smirk. "If only someone else had thought of doing something like that decades ago."

I let out a snort, and then manage to sober up a little. "Yeah, it's a bit crazy, the round-about way it came to be, but I guess you'd understand if you knew about Spence and Emily's upbringing. Let's just say it wasn't a Thanks-giving dinner-type family."

The door to the penthouse swings open and I'm greeted by a beaming Will. "Deacon! It's so good to see you, man," he gushes, as though we didn't just catch up after the rugby tournament a couple weeks ago. His gaze shifts to Tanner and his lips quirk into a knowing smirk. "And I'm guessing this is Tanner? Sky's told me all about you."

"*All?*" I ask warily. Knowing Skyler, he really could have dished anything. I really have no idea how he's going to manage to keep his client's confidentiality once he starts to practice.

"Just that your new guy is a sexy silver fox who looks like stepped off the cover of *GQ.*" He casts his eyes up Tanner's body, then down again, then back up again. "Yep, I can definitely see it." Turning to me, he gives a sly wink. "Nice work, Deac."

"Umm…thanks?"

"This is Izzy," Tanner says, holding his daughter protectively against him. She's huddled against his leg at the sight of the newcomer, looking up at Will with curious eyes.

Will offers Izzy a bright smile. "Hi Izzy, I'm Will. Do you like cookies?"

Slowly, Izzy pries her grip free of Tanner's leg and fixes her attention on Will, nodding at his question. "I like chocolate chip. And peanut butter. And oatmeal."

Tanner's lips form into a wry smile, his hand brushing through Izzy's hair again. "She's not fussy when it comes to cookies."

"Would you like to come with me?" Will asks, holding out his hand. "There's a nice lady in the kitchen who has lots of cookies."

I arch a brow. "You realize you just did a step by step

demonstration from the *What Creeps Do to Lure Kids Away From Parks* handbook, right?"

Will snatches his hand back, his jaw falling open in horror. "Oh my god! I'm a predator!"

"It's fine," Tanner says with a wry shake of his head, before suggesting, "Why don't we all go get a cookie?" He holds his hand out for Izzy and she happily accepts, then we all follow Will inside the apartment.

"When did Brad Pitt and Charlize Theron have a kid?" Tanner murmurs to me as we trail after Will.

I let out a soft laugh. Yeah, there's no doubt about it, Will is definitely movie star hot. Not that he ever acts like it.

"Wow," Tanner says, clearly impressed when we reach the vast, immaculately designed kitchen. And given how amazing his *two* kitchens are, that's definitely saying something.

The "nice woman" Will mentioned turns out to be his mom, Claire, and I can verify that she is indeed very nice. Her face lights up when she sees Izzy, and she immediately reaches for a tray of fresh-baked cookies for Izzy to choose from. They haven't been decorated yet, but they appear to be turkeys, pumpkins, and little people with pointy heads that I'm guessing are going to become pilgrims. Or maybe witches…?

"Just one," Tanner says firmly. "You can have some more later."

She pouts in disappointment, but ultimately picks one of the circular blobs that I'm assuming are going to become pumpkins once they're decorated.

"You know what, Izzy?" Claire says, bending down so she's closer to Izzy's level. "I could really use a helper to finish decorating these cookies. Would you like to help me?"

Izzy looks confused for a moment, and then Tanner explains. "To paint the cookies and make them pretty."

Izzy's face lights up and she holds her hands out to Claire. "With fingers!"

"She's a champion finger-painter," I explain.

Claire straightens back up, grinning. "Perfect. Just as long as you don't lick your fingers to clean them."

"Lick?" Izzy's face screws up, as though she thinks Claire couldn't sound more absurd for suggesting such a thing. "We use water bowl." She wiggles her fingers to mime washing them off in a water bowl, the way she does when she's finger-painting at school.

Claire chuckles. "Perfect."

We leave Izzy in Claire's hands and venture farther into the sprawling penthouse. Will has disappeared somewhere—no doubt to continue with his hosting duties—so I guide Tanner along myself.

When we reach the living room, where the party seems to be happening, we're greeted by an incredibly enthusiastic Skyler.

"Tanner!" he cries, flashing a mile-wide smile. "So good to see you. And you too, obviously, Deacon," he says to me, casting a dismissive wave.

"I'm touched," I deadpan.

"Thank god you guys are here. Jackson abandoned me and I got trapped in a conversation with Bryce and Emme about P in V sex. It was so gross." His face screws up in distaste as though he's just seen a video of some guy who returned from a tropical vacation with fly larvae germinating in his cheek.

"They're trying to conceive," I clarify for Tanner's benefit. "They've been very…open, and…graphic about the experience."

"I see," Tanner says with a nod.

At that moment, Jackson appears, handing Skyler a beer.

"Oh, thank god. I really need this," Skyler says, gratefully taking the beer and downing several large gulps.

"I thought you said Jackson abandoned you?":

Jackson rolls his eyes. "Drama queen. I went to get drinks."

"At the worst moment in the history of moments," Skyler whines. "Jax, I had to listen to...*vagina* shit. And stuff about..." He gives a full body shiver and I brace myself for what could possibly be worse in Skyler's mind that "vagina shit." Finally, he spits it out like there's a bad taste in his mouth. "*Ovulation.*"

Jackson, Tanner, and I all stare at him, completely bewildered.

"Why is *that* so traumatizing for you?" I can't help asking.

Skyler's expression makes him look like he's swallowed an entire lemon. "Because it's weird and gross. I don't want to know what goes on with all that. Or what day it's happening on. Or what happens...when it happens."

"You need more women in your life, buddy," Tanner says with a wry grin. "I think you should definitely go work for Leona."

"Oh my god, Tanner just called me 'buddy'," Skyler stage whispers to Jackson, looking star-struck.

Jackson rolls his eyes and grabs Skyler by the elbow, pulling him away.

"I'm pretty sure he's, like, half in love with you," I say with a chuckle.

"He's not really my type," Tanner says, gazing at me with affection in his eyes.

I quirk a brow at him. "He would have been not that long ago. Think of all the trouble you'd have saved yourself if you'd gone home with Skyler that night instead of me."

Tanner just shakes his head. "I can only think about what I would have missed."

I smile and step closer so I can brush my lips to his.

"Oh, great. So this is actually happening," a grumbling voice says from behind us. Looks like my brother's arrived.

32

Tanner

I reluctantly unlatch my lips from Deacon's at the sound of his brother's voice and turn to face a glowering Sullivan Stapleton, who's holding hands with a guy I can only assume is the boyfriend he recently reconciled with—Deacon's roommate, Drew. I have to admit, the guy is not at all what I was expecting; I haven't had a chance to meet him yet—no doubt because he's been too busy rolling around with Sullivan—but I wouldn't have picked a scruffy, tattooed mechanic as Stapleton's type at all. I guess you just never know people.

I ignore the scowl directed my way and hold my hand out to Drew. "Hey, you must be Drew. It's good to finally meet you," I say with a smile. "Deacon and the others have told me a lot about you."

His brows shoot up in question. "The others?"

I feel an arm being casually slung over my shoulders and it doesn't take much guesswork to know Skyler's returned from wherever Jackson dragged him off to.

"Tanner's taken over your spot for video game night, since you were busy doing...you know." He gestures between Drew and Sullivan, as though we needed further clarification. "We teamed up for NBA and kicked *aassss!*"

"Skyler, it was *one* game," Deacon says with an eye roll.

"Grimsay, I had no idea you were so into sport," Sullivan says with a smirk. "Maybe you should join us for rugby next year."

"Hell no," Deacon growls. "He's not playing rugby. He's too pretty to get hurt."

"Whoa—and I'm not?" Skyler demands. "Tanner, tell him I'm pretty."

"Skyler, stop flirting with Tanner before I make you very *un*-pretty."

Skyler cranes his head around me to send Deacon a startled look. "Did you just threaten me with a TLC song?"

Deacon offers a wry smirk. "Not intentionally. But if you don't get your hands off my boyfriend your new nickname will be 'Left Eye'."

No doubt unable to resist teasing Deacon, Skyler gives me a kiss on the cheek before finally stepping away.

"Ew. No. Just no, no, no," Sullivan rants, shaking his head. "*He* is not a boyfriend. He's an old man."

"Something to aspire to, I'd say," Skyler murmurs.

"Watch who you're calling old, Sully," I hear a familiar voice say. "He's only a couple years older than I am."

I turn to see Paxton Greenwood striding across the living room towards our little group. For a moment I'm startled to see him here, but then I remember he's the Cox siblings' step-brother. Fortunately, we've already cleared the air after that strange meeting a couple weeks ago, so there's no awkwardness today. Now that he's been a hundred per cent reassured that there won't be any changes to his show, he's been happy to step back and let us get on with things; I can tell he's still a bit uneasy about changes at the network, but I don't think there's too much risk of him making a big fuss about it once the ball gets rolling.

"Yeah, well you're not sleeping with my brother," Sullivan grumbles to Pax.

Paxton turns his attention on Deacon, raking his gaze up and down my boyfriend's incredible body. "Well, I wouldn't have said no had the offer ever been put out there."

"Watch it, Greenwood," I practically snarl. "There are plenty of ways for me to make your life hell."

He lets out a loud chuckle. "Chill, boss. It was a theoretical musing. I know he's all yours."

All mine. I love how that sounds.

"Urgh, I think I'm going to vomit," Sullivan grumbles.

"Sully, you're being a fucking dick," Deacon says, folding his arms across his chest and staring his brother down. "Tanner and I are together. We love each other. Get used to it."

Sullivan sighs, running a hand over his face in obvious agitation. "Deacon, come on—you can't trust this guy."

"Why? Because he's still legally married to a woman he hasn't seen for three years?" Deacon demands. "Because he *was* your business rival? Because he didn't tell me some things after only a couple weeks of being together?"

Sullivan's jaw tenses and he turns to Drew. "Babe, help me out here."

Drew's brows shoot up. "Why would you expect me to help you. I'm with Deac—you're being a dick."

Sullivan's mouth falls open in shock. "Wha—only the other day you told me you love me," he reminds his boyfriend, almost accusingly. "When you love someone you stand by them no matter what."

Drew rolls his eyes. "No, when you love someone you

have to tell them when they're being a dick. Which is why I'm telling you right now—Sullivan, you're being a dick."

Sullivan just stares at Drew for a long moment, a strange expression on his face.

"Sully? Are you even listening right now?" Drew asks, brow creased in concern.

Sullivan blinks rapidly, as though coming out of a stupor. His cheeks flush and his lips curve into a bashful smile. "Sorry. I just heard you say 'dick' about a thousand times and kind of lost focus. And then you did that thing with your tongue and your lip ring…:"

"Ah, okay, are we done here? Is the air clear?" Deacon asks, clearly uncomfortable as he tries not to look too closely at the way Sullivan and Drew are now staring at each other. "I'd like to get out of here before they start going at it."

Sullivan lets out a grunt of annoyance and tears his eyes from Drew, turning on me with an intense look. "Did you give up MesiTec because you were trying to get back into my brother's good books?"

I share a curious glance with Deacon. I hadn't even considered how it might look that way to Sullivan.

"Because I don't want him dating some asshole who's just going to buy his way—"

"Jeez, calm down," Deacon drawls. "We were well and truly back together by then."

"Then what was with the change of heart?" Sullivan asks, clearly baffled.

I let out a sigh. I guess there's no need to keep this from him now. "MesiTec was my wife's company."

His brows draw together. "The one you're apparently desperate to divorce?"

"The one who died ten years ago," I clarify.

"Oh."

I give him the broad strokes of what Leah's plans for the company had been and how I'd hoped to protect her legacy, and then about my conversations with Beth and Deacon that ultimately led to the sale.

"I'm surprised that PI of yours didn't dig all this up," I muse.

Sullivan shrugs. "She might have. I sort of forgot about everything else when I saw the pictures of you two."

"I still can't believe you sicced a PI on him," Deacon growls.

"Well, I needed to do something," Sullivan protests. "He was completely stonewalling us and I wanted to know why. At that point he wasn't even taking meetings any more."

I narrow my eyes at him. "What the fuck are you talking about? I had a meeting with you and Steele the day that photo of Deacon and me was taken. Half the reason I was even in that bar was because…" I trail off, shaking my head. "Never mind."

"Wait." Deacon holds up a hand. "Sully, when did you set this shit up?"

Sullivan shrugs. "I don't know. It was before…no, wait —" His eyes light up with memory and he turns to Drew, flashing a cocky smile. "It was the day you came to my office to yell at me and we made out in my bathroom."

Drew's cheeks redden and he lifts a hand to fidget with one of his earrings, but he otherwise doesn't respond.

"After the wedding?" Deacon asks. "So how the fuck did you get a picture of us from two weeks before that?"

Sullivan drags his gaze back to Deacon, looking puzzled. "I…don't know. Dani had them. I didn't think to question it."

"So either she was hired by someone else as well, or she sourced them from someone else who's been investigating you…" Deacon muses, eyes full of concern as they land on me.

I don't need to think too hard to come up with the most likely culprit. "Natalia." I murmur, giving a weary shake of my head. "It's exactly the kind of thing she'd do."

I try to put any further thoughts of Natalia and what she might do with photos of me picking up a guy at a gay bar out of my mind as we all gather to eat.

Based on Deacon's description earlier, I was expecting a very traditional Thanksgiving dinner, with an immaculately laid table with a twenty pound roasted turkey as the centerpiece. But that's definitely not the kind of meal that's served up, and I guess with the roughly forty people now packed into the penthouse, a huge sit-down feast would have been a little impractical.

Instead, the food is served in a mix of buffet and cocktail style. At the buffet, there's an array of things like shellfish, salads, vegetables, sliced turkey meat and stuffing, along with a bunch of different sauces and dressings. You'd think that spread would be enough on its own, but evidently Emily Cox went to the same event-hosting school as my daughter, where the "more is more" principle applies. So there are also catering staff walking around presenting the guests with trays of Thanksgiving-themed finger food, like bite-sized turkey meatballs, pumpkin pies small enough to hold between a thumb and forefinger, and bacon-wrapped sprouts.

"Ah fuck!" I hear someone exclaim from right behind where Deacon and I are standing chatting with Will and Spencer.

I glance back to find a guy Deacon introduced me to earlier as Bryce staring daggers at the empty toothpick in his fingers. "There was a fucking Brussels sprout hidden in that bacon."

Deacon lets out a soft chuckle. "Yeah, man. Pretty sure that's why they call them bacon-wrapped sprouts."

Bryce just continues to glower at his toothpick. "How am I ever supposed to trust bacon again?"

"If it helps, I hear sprouts are great for fertility."

His eyes light up. "Seriously?"

I nod. "They call it a superfood for a reason, right?"

He grins and rushes off, calling out to his girlfriend as he strides across the room.

"Is that true?" Will asks me, and I turn back to find his brows climbing in curiosity.

I have to press my lips together to keep them from twitching. "Um, well, it is…but I'm pretty sure it's only for female fertility," I confess, recalling Natalia's strict dietary and exercise regimen when we were trying to get pregnant with Izzy. I manage to shake the thought away, however; if there's anything that fucks up my head more than trying to deal with the bitter, unfeeling woman my ex has become, it's remembering the time before that when she was happy and caring, and desperately wanted to be a mother.

At my admission, Spencer tosses his head back and lets out a loud burst of laughter. "Oh god, please don't anyone tell him. He'll be choking down sprouts for months until he finally knocks her up."

A stab of guilt hits me about the way I've so clumsily messed around in what is probably a very stressful time for Bryce and Emme. "Shit, I kind of feel bad for misleading him," I say with a wince. "Have they been having a lot of trouble?"

Deacon gives my arm a reassuring squeeze. "Don't worry, babe, it's only been a few months."

"Yeah, but then there was the six months before that when they were *planning* to try," Spencer says with an eye roll. "We all really enjoyed that part."

I let out a huff of laughter. I've never had a friendship group as tight knit as this, so it's an interesting experience being in on all the teasing and banter. It actually reminds me of the way Jazz and Piper often snipe at each other, while simultaneously offering unwavering loyalty and support. Not just an amateur sports team. A family; it's no wonder they all want to spend Thanksgiving together.

"I'm really glad you brought me here today," I murmur to Deacon when we find ourselves alone for a few minutes. "I mean, I'm definitely looking forward to meeting your parents and sisters, but I'm glad I'm getting to know this family." I hold out my hand to gesture at all the people milling around the room.

Deacon smiles at me. "And I'm glad they're getting to know you. Even if my brother's still being a bit of a dick," he adds with a weary sigh.

"He seems less scowly since I explained all that stuff," I point out. "I'm sure he'll come around eventually. And if you can deal with Piper, I can deal with Sullivan." The words aren't mere platitudes to reassure Deacon; I've genuinely noticed a softening in Sullivan's attitude toward me, and I've even glimpsed a hint of that warm and fuzzy side I could have sworn people were just bullshitting me about. He hasn't directed any of that my way, of course, but I saw him with Izzy earlier and he was making an effort to really engage with her, which I greatly appreciated.

As though our words have summoned him, Sullivan himself approaches Deacon and me, with Charlie Campbell at his side.

"Sully says your wife is stalking you?" Charlie asks, looking utterly baffled as he swings his gaze between Deacon and me, no doubt registering our close proximity and the way Deacon has his finger hooked in one of my belt loops.

"Ex-wife," I clarify. "We've been separated for three years. And I don't know if "stalking" is the right word. We just know someone took a picture of Deacon and me at a bar about six weeks ago and somehow Sullivan's PI ended up with it."

"We don't know for sure it was Natalia," Deacon says. "She just seems like the most likely suspect."

"It has to be her," I say adamantly. "Sullivan says it wasn't him, and there's no one else who's that interested in digging into my life."

"I can't possibly be the only person you've pissed off enough to want to get answers in an unconventional way," Sullivan says with a huff.

"Believe it or not, I'm actually pretty well-liked," I say with a shrug. "It's been a really long time since I've had any dealings as…acrimonious as things became with you and Steele. And you know my reasons for that."

"Okay, let's say it is the wife," Charlie says, cutting off Sullivan's attempt at a retort. "Why did you drag me over here? What do you expect me to do about it?"

"Give him legal advice, obviously."

"He already has a lawyer," Charlie points out. "Talk to Leona about it."

"Just do it, Charlie," Sullivan says. "He's here to stay, apparently. That means he gets all the perks."

I blink in surprise, feeling oddly touched. Does this mean Sullivan has actually accepted me as Deacon's boyfriend? That would make things a hell of a lot easier.

Charlie sighs. "Okay, fine. But a) I really don't see what help I'm going to be, and b) I'm not going to be the one dealing with Leona bitching about me moving in on her client. That's all on you, buddy," he tells me.

I shake my head. "I really don't think this is nec—"

"Shh, he might be able to help," Deacon says, squeezing my arm.

I sigh. Leona and her team have been over every possible legal option for removing Natalia from my life. If there was a legal loophole I could use to put an end to this situation, I would have found it by now. "Fine," I say, motioning for Charlie to go ahead.

"This woman...you're still married to her, but you're separated I'm guessing? Is that why you think she's been investigating you—to gather leverage for settlement negotiations?"

I let out a harsh scoff. "Dude, I can't even get her to the negotiation part. She won't agree to the divorce because our pre-nup won't hold until we hit the ten-year mark. The one offer I made, which was a couple years ago now, included everything the pre-nup would have given her *except* the allocated stake in Grimco. And it wasn't enough." I rub my fingers into my forehead to ease some of the growing anxiety this conversation is causing, but it doesn't ease at all until I feel Deacon's hand rubbing soothing circles over my back. Letting out a sigh, I glance back up to find both Charlie and Sullivan wearing frowns of concern. Fuck, I hope I can get through this without completely losing it.

Thankfully, Deacon swoops in to explain the current situation and what I've been dealing with over the past few years. He keeps things broad, and I appreciate him not going into all the gory details, but his explanation is enough to give the two men a decent picture of my current relationship with Natalia.

"So you're thinking she could use this photo to blackmail you if you decided to file and go to court anyway?" Charlie asks. "Or use as evidence against you?"

I nod. "Seems most likely. A month or so ago, a move like that might have worked. Now it feels like a pretty insignificant threat," I say with a soft smile in Deacon's direction. "But she's also pretty money hungry, so there's also the possibility of her selling it to make some cash. I think it probably would have been splashed all over the media by now if she'd done that, though."

I see Sullivan cringe, no doubt recalling his recent experience with tabloid journalism.

"Okay, not going to lie, it sounds like a really shit situation all around," Charlie says, stating the obvious. "Have you tried for a no signature divorce?"

"What's that?" Deacon asks.

"In New York a divorce can be granted without the second party's approval if—"

"They fail to respond to the summons," I finish for him. "Yeah, I know. Trust me, I've tried. She might be a bitch, but she's not an idiot. She won't ignore a summons. There's too much at stake for her."

Deacon's expression turns thoughtful. "How does someone respond to a divorce summons? Can they just call a number and be like, "Got the summons, don't want a divorce.'?"

Charlie lets out a soft chuckle. "It's a bit more involved than that. There are whole bunch of forms that need to be lodged and notarized and stamped. It takes a bit of time to get it all done. "

"And you need to do it in person?" Deacon asks curiously. "In New York?"

Charlie nods. "Yep."

Deacon turns to me, suddenly looking hopeful. "How easy would it be for her to get back here from Bermuda in time to do all that?" he asks me, before his expression wavers a little. "Or do they have, like, a year to do it?"

"Thirty days if she's not in New York when the notice is served," Charlie says.

My mind starts whirring with possibilities I hadn't considered before. The last time I tried filing was before she left the country. With only twenty days to get herself organized to contest the notice, I thought the likeliest scenario would be that she'd simply agree to the terms and accept the settlement and that would be that. But I vastly underestimated her, and with her threats of a custody battle hanging over my head after that I didn't have much choice other than to withdraw the filing and accept the possibility that there may not be a way out.

But now…

"Her guard is down," I murmur, thinking out loud. "And if she wasn't able to easily access money, getting back here wouldn't be that easy. She could manage it, I'm sure, but it wouldn't be easy. And it's not like her lawyers would be willing to work pro bono…" The thought of cutting off her cash supply and leaving her stranded on a ridiculously expensive Caribbean island makes me a little queasy, but if it could get me out of this mess…

"Do you know if she's been saving any of it?" Deacon asks. "Rainy day money?"

I shrug. "I'd have to get it looked into. But she's never been the most fiscally responsible type so I tend to doubt it."

The edges of Deacon's mouth curve up. "Well…I guess it's something at least."

I offer a soft smile in return. "It's something." Leaning closer, I brush a far-too-chaste kiss to his lips, acutely aware that his brother is still standing close by.

There's a good chance this won't pan out. I could be opening myself up to a world of hell if I go through with this and Natalia manages to contest the divorce and follow through on all her threats. But for the first time, the fear of that possibility isn't crippling enough to force me to back down.

I want a life with Deacon. A future. And I'm not going to let fear and anxiety stop me from doing whatever I can to secure it.

Epilogue
DEACON

My brows crease in concern as I watch Tanner pace back and forth across the carpet of the plush waiting area in Leona Fisher's offices. It's not an entirely surprising sight; today was always going to be a rough day for him, but that doesn't make me feel any less helpless right now.

He finally pauses for a moment, but it's only so he can rub at his forehead and draw in several deep breaths. Not a good sign.

"Babe, come here," I tell him, holding out my hand. "Talk to me. Tell me what's going on in your head."

He turns to me, those sparkling sapphire eyes now dull with dread. "You don't want to know what's going on in my head."

"I always want to know what's in that head, Tanner," I assure him. "Now, come here. Talk to me."

He sighs and comes over to join me on the couch. I reach behind him and run gentle circles over his back, glad when I feel some of his tension ease. I know that one simple act won't be enough, but it's something.

"Talk to me, babe," I say again.

He shakes his head. "What if this was a mistake? What if she goes back on her word and decides to fight me after all? She's done it before, Deacon. She could waltz in here with a team of lawyers and make all kinds of threats, and I'll be right back where I started. Or she could just skip past the threats and go straight to filing for custody."

After months of being with Tanner, his tendency to catastrophize isn't exactly foreign to me. He works really hard with all his behavioral techniques to keep these kinds of thoughts under control, but considering his history with Natalia, it's understandable that his worst fears would all be bubbling to the surface today.

"Babe, we have the papers. It's all taken care of," I reminds him. "After today, it'll all be over."

He shakes his head. "I don't know. I just feel like a trap's about to spring. Maybe I shouldn't have offered her the settlement."

After our talk with Charlie at Thanksgiving about six months ago, Tanner did some investigating and learned Natalia's sole income stream was indeed the money he provided her, and that she hadn't set up any kind of savings account in case of an emergency. So he was able to cut her off and serve the divorce papers, knowing it would make it incredibly difficult for her to contest it again.

But as desperate as the situation had become, this wasn't something Tanner was thrilled about doing. He felt sneaky and underhanded, and despite everything she's put him through, he was also really unsettled by the thought of Natalia being stranded outside the country, suddenly cut off from all sources of cash.

So when she inevitably called to bitch him out, he told her she could either try to contest the divorce again, but if she couldn't get it done within thirty days she'd walk away with nothing; or she could agree and accept a generous settlement. Needless to say, we were all insanely relieved when the papers came back with her agreement and signature.

But there's still this one last step of confirming the settlement. It's something the lawyers could have wrapped up on their own, but Natalia insisted on being here so Tanner has to be as well. And I wasn't about to let him come alone.

"You offered her the settlement because you're generous, and caring, and you never would have been comfortable leaving her with nothing even though she probably deserves it."

I kiss his lips and he hesitates for a moment before kissing me back, the tension slowly leaking out of his body.

"Ahh, sorry to interrupt," I hear a familiar voice say from behind us.

Jolting in surprise, I break away from Tanner to find Skyler standing in the doorway of the waiting room, a wry grin on his face. "Just wanted to let you know that they're here. But I can tell them to wait if you guys want to keep going…"

I roll my eyes. "Thanks, Skyler."

I rise from the sofa and grab Tanner's hand as he follows me to his feet. "One meeting," I tell him. "It's just one little meeting, and then this will all be over. And afterwards I'll give you a BJ that makes your head spin around *Exorcist* baby-style."

He lets out a breath of laughter. "Because a boner's exactly what I need right now."

I grin and kiss his cheek, then we follow Skyler through the hallways of the law offices and into a meeting room.

There are four people already there: Leona, and a guy named Greg, who is the firm's divorce specialist and has been handling the settlement deal. They sit on one side of the table, and opposite them is a woman in her mid-thirties and a crisp-looking guy in an expensive suit who I can only assume is her lawyer.

So this is Natalia.

Tanner and I take seats on the same side of the table as his lawyers, and I try my best to be discreet as I examine the woman who's been making my boyfriend's life miserable for years.

I'm not sure what I was expecting; devil horns, maybe? Or maybe a total diva who'd be flashing bling with every movement and making demands for more and more money? I thought there'd at least be some resting bitch face...

But she seems completely normal. Her mousy brown hair is up in a simple ponytail; her make up is natural and understated, and she's wearing a simple green and white dress.

She doesn't look at Tanner at all as his lawyer reiterates the details of the settlement, her eyes fixed on the shiny surface of the meeting table. I can't help thinking that she seems sad, and tired, and despite myself I can't help feeling kind of sorry for her. I know she doesn't deserve any sympathy after the way she's behaved, but I've learned enough over the past few months to know the situation's not completely black and white.

"So, we're all agreed?" Greg asks once he's finished going over everything.

Natalia nods wordlessly.

"Agreed," her lawyer says.

Once the formalities have been taken care of, the lawyers start to file out. I know there's something else Tanner needs from Natalia, though, so I'm not surprised when he doesn't rush to get out of there.

But I am a little surprised to see Natalia lingering back

as well. She finally manages to look at Tanner as she speaks for the first time since we entered the room. "Can I talk to you for a moment?"

Tanner nods curtly, and when her eyes flick to me, he cuts off any request for me to leave at the pass. "Deacon stays."

She nods and averts her gaze again, clearly struggling to look at Tanner. "I just…I wanted you to know that I'm seeing someone. A therapist, I mean. I'm not trying to make excuses or anything, but I just wanted you to know that I'm trying." She shakes her head, her features tightening in regret. "I really don't want to be that vindictive, destructive bitch. I don't even know how I got there…I just…"

"I hope the therapy helps," Tanner says gently. "I'm glad you told me."

She nods, her features seeming to relax a little now that she's got that out there.

"I need you to sign something else for me," Tanner says, reaching inside his suit jacket and retrieving a folded document.

He hands it over to Natalia, who takes it warily.

She carefully unfolds the document, biting her lip as she sees what it is. "Forfeit of parental rights?" She flicks her gaze up to Tanner. "This is a condition of the settlement?"

He shakes his head. "No. You'll get what we agreed on regardless. But I'm asking for this as well. This is something I need."

She's quiet for a long time before finally nodding. "Okay."

I let out a breath of relief as she signs the document. Despite her declaration of wanting to change, you can never have too many guarantees.

"Thank you," Tanner murmurs as Natalia hands the document back.

"What about…when she's older?" Natalia asks. "If she wants to see me?"

"It'll be her choice," Tanner says.

"Can you…can you send me updates about her? Every now and then…photos or whatever."

Tanner nods. "If you want. But that'd be the extent of your involvement. Like a birth mother in an adoption."

I can sense Tanner's relief coming off him in waves. Not only because the document has been signed, but because I know he's been feeling uneasy about permanently cutting ties between Izzy and her mother. This sounds like the ideal compromise.

Natalia doesn't stick around for much longer, and once Tanner and I are alone in the room together, I pull him into a tight hug, breathing in his delicious scent as he sinks into my hold.

"I told you everything would be sorted out today," I murmur.

"Mmm…can I have that blow job now?"

I let out a loud chuckle and pull away from him. "Why don't we head home first? I don't want Skyler walking in on us and complimenting your dick."

He grins at me. "Have I mentioned how much I love that we have the same home now?"

"Maybe once or twice," I say wryly. It's a relatively new thing, since the school year ended and Izzy was no longer one of my students. That conveniently coincided with Natalia finally agreeing to a divorce, so when Tanner and I went public with our relationship there wasn't a whole lot of fuss about it.

And, obviously, I love that we have the same home now as well. Not just because it means I get to hold him in my arms every night, and we have way more time together, but because of how much time I get with his family as well. Helping out with Izzy is awesome, and although I still feel like I'm on a bit of a learning curve, I love every moment I get to spend with her.

Jazz and Piper are regular visitors at the house, of course, and I'm glad to say Piper has finally warmed up to me. The other day she even asked for my opinion on a wedding dress she was looking at. I'm not sure my answer of, "Um, it's…nice" was in any way helpful, but I'm taking the win anyway.

I grab Tanner's hand and start moving toward the meeting room door. "Come on, let's go home."

He smirks at me. "Yeah, home's good. Then I can cum on your face."

The End

What to read next

Want more of Jazz? *Whiskey Tango Foxtrot* is now available as a Patreon-exclusive serial. With several chapters released monthly, available for all tier levels. The first eight chapters are now available to read for free!

Want more *Suits & Sevens*? *Mr Big Shot* (Spencer's book), and *Mr Right Now* (Sullivan's book) are available now. *Mr Blue Sky* (Jackson & Skyler's book) is coming soon!

Want more age gap by Isla? Check out *Virtually Screwed*, *Crazy Little Fling*, *The King and Jai*, and *Legend (with Willow Thomas)*

Want more single dad by Isla? Check out *Hopeless Romantics*, *Two Men and a Baby*, and *Legend (with Willow Thomas)*

For more book info check out www.islaolsen.com

Isla & Her Books

Isla is a cocktail-loving, history-obsessed Aussie who writes low-angst queer romantic comedy full of spice, shenanigans and swoon-worthy men. She's best known for the *Love & Luck* series, and *P.S. I Loathe You*

Her favorite tropes include:
Queer-awakening
Friends to Lovers
Enemies to Lovers
Secret Fling
Age Gap
Sibling's/Best Friend's Ex
and many more…

Check out her website islaolsen.com for everything you need to know, including how to get in touch via social media and where you can get her books on ebook, paperback, and audio.

Printed in Great Britain
by Amazon